SHERLOCK HOLMES™ VOL. 1
OMNIBUS

SHERLOCK HOLMES™ OMNIBUS VOL. 1

YEAR ONE

Written by:
SCOTT BEATTY

Illustrated by:
DANIEL INDRO

Colored by:
TONY AVIÑA

Lettered by:
SIMON BOWLAND

Dedicated to:
SIR ARTHUR CONAN DOYLE

Special thanks to:
LESLIE KLINGER
Editor of The Sherlock Holmes Reference Library

THE TRIAL OF SHERLOCK HOLMES

Written by:
LEAH MOORE &
JOHN REPPION

Illustrated by:
AARON CAMPBELL

Colored by:
TONY AVIÑA

Lettered by:
SIMON BOWLAND

Dedicated to:
SIR ARTHUR CONAN DOYLE

LIVERPOOL DEMON

Written by:
LEAH MOORE &
JOHN REPPION

Illustrated by:
MATT TRIANO

Colored by:
BRENNAN WAGNER

Lettered by:
SIMON BOWLAND

Dedicated to:
SIR ARTHUR CONAN DOYLE

Omnibus Collection Design by:
GEOFF HARKINS

DYNAMITE®

Nick Barrucci, CEO / Publisher
Juan Collado, President / COO
Joe Rybandt, Executive Editor
Matt Idelson, Senior Editor
Rachel Pinnelas, Associate Editor
Anthony Marques, Assistant Editor
Kevin Ketner, Editorial Assistant
Jason Ullmeyer, Art Director
Geoff Harkins, Senior Graphic Designer
Cathleen Heard, Graphic Designer
Alexis Persson, Production Artist
Chris Caniano, Digital Associate
Rachel Kilbury, Digital Assistant
Brandon Dante Primavera, V.P. of IT and Operations
Rich Young, Director of Business Development
Alan Payne, V.P. of Sales and Marketing
Keith Davidsen, Marketing Director
Pat O'Connell, Sales Manager

On Visit us online at **www.DYNAMITE.com**
On Twitter **@dynamitecomics**
Instagram **/Dynamitecomics**
On Facebook **/Dynamitecomics**
On Tumblr **Dynamitecomics.Tumblr.com**
On YouTube **/Dynamitecomics**

ISBN-13: 978-1-5241-0119-0
First Printing 10 9 8 7 6 5 4 3 2 1

SHERLOCK HOLMES VOLUME 1 OMNIBUS First printing. Contains materials originally published in Sherlock Holmes Issues1-6(Year One), The Trial of Sherlock Holmes Issues 1-5, and Sherlock Holmes: Liverpool Demon Issues 1-5. Published by Dynamite Entertainment. 113 Gaither Dr., STE 205, Mt. Laurel, NJ 08054. **Printed in China**.

For media rights, foreign rights, promotions, licensing, and advertising:
marketing@dynamite.com

"He has few friends. He has even less relations – a brother in the government; no other family to speak of. And from the vantage of a detached observer, he is as much a cipher as the inscrutable clues he spies so readily in plain sight. I watch this detective, and I watch him some more.
And yet, in spite of my admitted aversion to mysteries, I find my mind unable or perhaps unwilling to dismiss the enigma dogging my every waking thought: Who is this Sherlock Holmes?"

-Dr. John Watson

Year One
issue 1

Year One Issue 1 Cover by Francesco Francavilla

SHERLOCK HOLMES YEAR ONE
THE BUTLERS DID IT
I hate mysteries.

And I need no second opinion as a diagnostician to pronounce that this boy before us is consumed by conundrums.
NASTY BUMP THERE, LAD--
LUCKY FOR YOU THAT THE CONSTABULARY RETAINS A PHYSICIAN...
My name is John Hamish Watson, doctor by profession, lately disposed to the needs of London's guardians...
WATSON!
A MOMENT OF YOUR TIME?
As well as those the guardians guard over, be they highborn or low.
YOU'RE A PHYSICIAN...
CAN'T YOU GIVE LADY SOMERSET SOMETHING TO EASE HER DISCOMFITURE?
BEG PARDON, LORD SOMERSET--
With no horses or carriages to convey them home, London's pampered princes and princesses will simply have to walk it off...
BUT ALL OF YOUR ILLS SEEM TO BE A RESULT OF TOO MUCH MEDICINE.
That is an expert opinion that requires no guesswork.
DOES THIS HURT?
EXCEEDINGLY.
LIKELY MORE SO IF MY CHEEKBONE WERE BROKEN, THOUGH IF YOU PRESS ON YOU'LL SEE THAT IT IS NOT.

DILATION OF THE PUPILS...
HAD A NIP AT THE SAME BOTTLE AS THESE HAPLESS GUESTS?
WRIT LARGE ON MY BLOODSHOT EYES, IS IT?
I EXPECTED TRIAGE ON THE LAD, DOCTOR WATSON--
YOU NEEDN'T ASSESS HIS BLOODY MEDICAL HISTORY.
UH.
OH, SORRY THERE. SHOT IN THE LAST AFGHAN CAMPAIGN, WOT?
ONCE IN THE SHOULDER AND ANOTHER THROUGH THE THIGH.
"BATTLE OF MAIWAND, INSPECTOR FELLOWES.
"NOT THE ROYAL HORSE ARTILLERY'S FINEST HOUR..."

"THE WOGS HAD US IN FULL RETREAT...
"WHAT BETTER VANTAGE FOR A SHOT IN THE BACK?
"A JEZAIL BULLET ADDING INSULT TO INJURY BY NICKING MY SUBCLAVIAN ARTERY AFTER SHATTERING THE SHOULDER BONE.
"I BEGAN MY COMMISSION AS ASSISTANT SURGEON OF THE ARMY MEDICAL DEPARTMENT, 66TH FOOT IN THE SECOND AFGHAN WAR...
"BUT I ENDED MY MILITARY CAREER AS A SIMPLE SOLDIER DOING HIS LEVEL BEST TO STAY ALIVE."

I'M LESS A SURGEON AND MORE A *GENERAL PRACTITIONER* AS A RESULT--
WITH YOUR GIFT FOR DESCRIPTION AND NARRATIVE, I WOULD HAVE PEGGED YOU AS AN *ASPIRING AUTHOR.*
NOW, IF YOU DON'T MIND THE INTERJECTION.
I WAS INFORMING THE GOOD INSPECTOR ABOUT A CERTAIN CLASS OF--
CRIMINAL.
I LOOK LIKE THE VILLAIN IN A *PENNY DREADFUL.*
CHIN UP, CHUM--
IT IS A *COSTUME BALL,* AFTER ALL...
ALL THE HELP WEARS RESPECTABLE *BLACK.*

AND NO ONE OUTSHINES THE DUKES AND DUCHESSES AND DAMES IN THEIR FEATHERS AND FRILLIES.
YOU CAN USE THE EXTRA COIN AS MUCH AS I.
SURELY YOU CAN'T AFFORD TUITION AND HALF A FLAT WITH JUST THE ALLOWANCE YOUR BROTHER POSTS EACH MONTH?
TAKE THIS, BOY.
AND DON'T DAWDLE.
THE MASTERS AND MISTRESSES HAVE RICH APPETITES THIS NIGHT...
AN UNDERSTATEMENT TO BE SURE...
JEEVES...
THASH YOUR NAME, RIGHT?
I MEAN TO COMPAIN ABOUT THE SERVISH...
THE SOUP...
TOO MUSH SALT...

IAIN, A WORD...
THERE IS *EVIL* AFOOT HERE.
OH, PISH-POSH...
NOW ISN'T THE TIME NOR PLACE TO REGALE ME WITH YOUR THOUGHTS ON THE SOCIAL DIV--
SHUT UP AND COUNT THE BOTTLES OF WINE UPON THE TABLE.
IN VINO VERITAS.
NOT NEARLY ENOUGH OF *ANY* VINTAGE POURED IN THEIR GLASSES TO STUPEFY THESE MEN AND WOMEN SO.
HOLMES, WHAT ARE YOU GETTING AT?
AWAY FROM THE KITCHEN, IAIN.
I NEED YOU TO SLIP OUT AS SURREPTITIOUSLY AS YOU CAN--
AND FETCH THE CONSTABULARY.
ASK FOR INSPECTOR BRATTON.
HE'LL BLANCH WHEN HE HEARS MY NAME, BUT HE'LL COME WITH ALL SPEED.

AS THE BROTH THICKENS, SO DOES THIS PLOT...
CUMIN.
CELERY.
POTATO LONG PAST RIPE.
AND SALT OF COURSE...
NOT ADDED TO FLAVOR, BUT TO *HIDE* A MORE BITTER TASTE.
I TOLD MISSUS DIGBY IT WAS A *MISTAKE* TO HIRE ON ADDITIONAL HELP LIKE ALL THE OTHER HOITY-TOITY PARTIES...
BUT WE HAD TO KEEP UP *APPEARANCES* FOR THE MASTERS, EH?

WHERE'S YOUR FRIEND?
IF HE MAINTAINS CONSTANT PACE--NO DOUBT FUELED BY A HEALTHY RUSH OF FEAR--THEN HE'S LIKELY HALFWAY TO THE BOBBIES.
AND I CAN ONLY SURMISE THAT THEY WILL REMEMBER TO LOAD *THEIR* PISTOLS.
WHAT ARE YOU *BLATHERING* ABOUT, BOY?!
THIS IS THE LORD'S OWN DUELING PISTOL, STRAIGHT FROM--
HIH!
LAUDANUM

EATS LIKE A PRETTY PIG, SHE DOES...
BUT WE CAN'T HAVE THE DUCHESS DROWNING IN HER SOUP.
IT'S UNSEEMLY.
AND MURDER'S NOT ON THE MENU IF WE PLAN TO GET OFF WITH THESE PLANS.
THE KITCHEN!
THERE'S A ROW!
WE'RE FOUND OUT!
BARTITSU, CHAP. A MARTIAL SKILL.
THOUGH I'M MUCH MORE ADEPT IN ITS PRACTICE WITH A CANE THAN A SPOON.
GET HIM!
TAKE OFF HIS MASK!
YES, PLEASE...
LEST I BE MISTAKEN FOR YOUR LOT OF CHEAP THUGGERY--
ENOUGH!
DO WE NOT HAVE A SCHEDULE TO KEEP, MAIDS AND MANSERVANTS?
YES, MISSUS DIGBY.

BUT I WON'T HAVE YOU RABBLE LEAVING MY MISTRESS'S KITCHEN IN SUCH A STATE...
EVEN IF I INTEND TO ROB THE SOW BLIND AND LEAVE HER TO UNCINCH HER OWN BLOODY WHALEBONE CORSET.
I COMMEND YOUR AMBITION.
IT IS ONE MATTER TO ASPIRE BEYOND ONE'S STATION.
BUT TO MAKE COMPLICIT THE STAFFS OF EACH HOUSE REPRESENTED HERE DEMANDS TRUST.
WE ALL HAVE OUR OWN COMPLAINTS, YOUNG MAN...
WHAT BETTER CURE FOR WHAT AILS US THAN A BIT OF LAUDANUM?
A SIP CAN CERTAINLY CALM MY NERVES--
AND LOOK WHAT IT DID FOR THOSE PREENING PEACOCKS IN THE GRAND DINING HALL WHEN ADDED TO THEIR SOUP?

BEST NOT TO FIGHT...
IN THE END YOU WON'T FEEL A THING...
BUT I FEEL *EVERYTHING*...
LET THE SACKING BEGIN!

THOUGHT WE ALL AGREED NO ONE WOULD DIE...
THIS ONE KNOWS TOO MUCH--
QUITE A LOT ACTUALLY...
MORE THAN YOU'LL EVER KNOW...
HE'LL MAKE A BETTER SCAPEGOAT THAN HE DID A SERVER...
WHAT'S THIS THEN?
ARE YOU HOLDING OUT ON US, LAD?
HAVE YOU HAD YOUR HAND IN THE HOUSE'S SILVER ALREADY?
IT'S MINE...
UNTIL I LOST HER...
PITY YOU THEN.
THIS ONE MUST HAVE HURT.

TOSS HIM OVER THE PARAPET AND LET'S BE OFF...
CAN'T HAVE MISSUS DIGBY AND THE OTHERS KEEPING ALL THE SPOILS *THEMSELVES,* WOT?
YOU *HEARD* HIM, BOY--
THERE'S NO *HONOR* AMONG THIEVES.
BEG YOUR PARDON...
I MUST BE SICK...
WHAT?
HURK
I WARNED YOU--
I CAN ONLY STOMACH SO MUCH ROT!

Which accounts for the young man's present state, sodden from head to foot with the muck and murk of the castle keep's brackish moat...
His mind swimming from a near overdose of Laudanum and the devilish details of this most sinister scheme...

CRIMINALITY ALMOST ALWAYS LEADS TO DESPERATE ACTS...
AND DESPERATION TO DEATH, NO MATTER WHAT INVISIBLE LINE THE CRIMINALS SWEAR NEVER TO CROSS.
BLIGHTER BROKE HIS NECK.
UPON BREAKING MY FALL.
And he is as unmoved by the demise of his foe as he is his own brush with the Grim Reaper...
AND YOUR FRIEND CAN CORROBORATE THIS WILD TALE?
LIKELY NOT.
IAIN MISSED THE MOST EXCITING PARTS.
AND HE'S NOT VERY BRIGHT.
SAYS THE AMATEUR SLEUTH WHO DIDN'T FIGURE OUT THIS EMPRISE UNTIL HE WAS UP TO HIS ARCHED EYEBROW IN THE MUCK OF IT!
HOW ARE WE TO NAB THE LOT NOW WHEN THEY'VE GOTTEN AWAY WITH IT SCOT-FREE?
ELEMENTARY, MY DEAR INSPECTOR.
YOU SEE, THE CRIME YET COMMENCES...

"I TOLD YOU THAT THIS CONSORTIUM OF CRIMINAL MAIDS AND MANSERVANTS WAS *AMBITIOUS.*
"THEIR AIM WAS NOT MERELY TO PILFER THE RICHES FROM JUST *ONE* OF THEIR MASTERS--
"BUT *ALL* OF THEM.
"AND WITH THE LORDS AND LADIES DRUGGED INTO A SOPORIFIC STUPOR AT THIS CASTLE KEEP, *TIME* WOULD NO LONGER BE A FACTOR IN THE SUCCESSFUL COMMISSION OF THEIR CAPER."

"WHAT BITTER IRONY THAT A PROFESSION THAT PRIDES ITSELF ON PUNCTUALITY OF SERVICE MIGHT BE UNDONE BY IGNORING THE INEXORABLE TICKS OF A CLOCK?
"THE RICH DO NOT TRIFLE OVER THE HOUR.
"THE *NOUVEAU RICHE* CARE EVEN LESS SO."
AND NEED I MENTION ALSO THAT ONE MUST BE MINDFUL OF THE TIMES OF THE TIDE WHEN SETTING SAIL TO NEW LANDS?
THAT'S JUST POOR PLANNING.
ONE MUST CLIMB THE SOCIAL LADDER ONE RUNG AT A TIME.
ROUND THEM UP!

And in the end, life mirrored art. That vagary of the Penny Dreadful was proved quite real by the boy who fell in the moat...
The butlers did do it.
THIS ISN'T THE *FIRST* TIME HE'S HELPED THE POLICE, IS IT?
NO. AND IT BLOODY WELL SHOULD BE THE *LAST* IF I HAVE ANY SAY IN THE MATTER.
THE FOOL IS GOING TO GET HIMSELF KILLED.
OR SOMEONE ELSE FOOLISH ENOUGH TO FOLLOW HIM.
THIS THE BAUBLE IN QUESTION?
THE VERY ONE.
AND YOU CAN VERIFY THE CONTENTS?
A WOMAN OF UNCOMMON BEAUTY.
TO GAZE INTO HER EYES IS TO LOSE ALL REASON.
ONE COULD DROWN...
ALRIGHT THEN--
SPARE THE SWEET NOTHINGS FOR THE LADIES-IN-WAITING, MASTER SHAKESPEARE...
And who can argue that the bard was not inspired by the mysteries of the human heart?

In this life, mysteries abound...
JUST ANSWER THE QUESTION. AS IF YOUR LIFE DEPENDED ON IT.
IS EVIL NATURAL--
OR IS IT NURTURED?
I DON'T BELIEVE IN ORIGINAL SIN.
EVIL IS A LEARNED BEHAVIOR.
CRIMES OF PASSION?
CRIMES OF OPPORTUNITY?
THERE IS PROFIT IN EITHER.
AND AN APPRECIATION OF GAIN OR DESIRE FOR IT SPRINGS FROM AN INTELLIGENT MIND, NOT ONE PREDETERMINED TO MALIFICENCE.
AND YOU WOULD STAKE YOUR LIFE ON THIS DEDUCTION?
THE LOGIC IS SOUND, PROFESSOR--

DING DING DING DING
SHALL WE CONTINUE THIS DUEL NEXT SESSION?
WHY NOT?
YOU'RE THE FIRST WORTHY OPPONENT I'VE HAD IN *AGES*--
EVEN IF YOU CHOOSE TO *AUDIT* THE SEMINAR ON ETHICS RATHER THAN ATTEND AS A PROPER STUDENT.
He has few friends...
He has even less relations. A brother in the government. No other family to speak of...
And from the vantage of a detached observer, he is as much a cipher as the inscrutable clues he seems so able to spy so readily in plain sight...
JOVERS
I watch this detective, and I watch him some more...

Year One Issue 2 Cover by Francesco Francavilla

SHERLOCK HOLMES
YEAR ONE
WHY THIS IS VIOLENCE
Murder is everywhere.

And lately it is my bread and butter...
WELL THEN, WATSON...
HAVE AT IT.
Had fate taken a different path, my career as a physician would have found me working to extend the lives of my charges...
But the injury to my shoulder during my military service rendered a career as a surgeon quite suspect...
Thus, all of my present patients are good and–
DEAD.
AND YOU CALL YOURSELVES DETECTIVES...
EARN YOUR KEEP, DOCTOR.
WHAT KILLED HIM?
LOSS OF BLOOD.
A CATASTROPHIC HEMORRHAGE HASTENED BY THESE VERY NUMEROUS PUNCTURE WOUNDS.
TWENTY-THREE, I'D SAY.

ASSUMING, OF COURSE, THE CHAP WASN'T STABBED IN THE BACK FOR GOOD MEASURE...
HAVE YOU A CLUE TO THIS MAN'S IDENTITY?
HE'S BLOODY BRYAN RAFFERTY, ENEMY OF THE CROWN!
PERHAPS YOU'VE HEARD OF THE LITTLE CRIMINAL FIEFDOM HE'S CARVED OUT OF LONDON'S UNDER--
INSPECTOR BRATTON!
WHAT'S THIS THEN?
IS THIS TROLLOP YOUR PRIME SUSPECT, OFFICER LESTRADE?
GO AHEAD, SIOBHAN...
TELL THE INSPECTOR WHAT YOU TOLD ME.
'ELLO, GENTS.
ROBBIE.
LONG TIME, WOT?
SPARE THE PLEASANTRIES, SIOBHAN.
THE INSPECTOR'S TIME IS IMPORTANT--
SHOW HIM THE BIT OF PAPER...
HE... HE SAID TO GIVE YOU THIS.
THE FIRST BOBBIES TO FIND HIS BODY.
S-SAID HE'D CUT ME LIKE BLOODY BRYAN THERE IF I D-DIDN'T...

GIVE IT TO ME THEN!
AM I THE ONLY GENTLEMAN AMONG YOU?
OR WOULD YOU CONSTABLES RATHER YOUR KEY WITNESS EXPIRE IN THIS DREADFUL CHILL?
BEG PARDON, DOCTOR WATSON...
THE BROTHEL IS JUST AROUND THE--
BALDERDASH!
YOU KILLED HIM, DIDN'T YOU?
BLOODY BRYAN'S AS FAMOUS FOR HIS APPETITES AS HE IS HIS CRIME AND CALUMNY!
WAS THE BASTARD DRUNK? DID HE HURT YOU ONE TOO MANY TIMES?
NO, IT'S NOT LIKE THAT!
BRYAN WAS ALWAYS SWEET TO ME!

THEN WHAT WAS IT, GIRL?
A RIVAL FOR YOUR AFFECTIONS?
OR WAS IT ONE OF BLOODY BRYAN'S COMPETITORS?
WERE YOU PAID TO GUT HIM AFTER OTHER "SERVICES" RENDERED?
TELL ME!
WHAP
Ista quidem vis est!
WHY, THIS IS VIOLENCE!
YOU'RE BLOODY RIGHT, IT IS!
WHEN NEWS OF BRYAN RAFFERTY'S MURDER SPREADS THROUGHOUT THE UNDERBELLY, HIS WON'T BE THE ONLY BLOOD SPILLED!
I NEED DISSECTION, NOT COMMENTARY ON THE OBVIOUS!
I WAS MERELY TRANSLATING THE LATIN UPON THE SLIP OF PAPER, INSPECTOR...
AND I CAN ONLY OFFER CONJECTURES ON THE CAUSE OF RAFFERTY'S UNTIMELY DEATH.
IF YOU REQUIRE DEDUCTIONS UPON MOTIVE, THEN PERHAPS WE SHOULD ALERT THE CONSTABULARY'S OTHER CONSULTANT--

HOLMES!
OUT, I'D WAGER...
COMING AND GOING AT ALL HOURS, HE DOES.
LIKELY END UP LIKE THAT OTHER POOR LAD.
BEST YOU CALL AGAIN, DOCTOR...
THANK YOU, MA'AM...
But in the months since our last meeting, I have often found my idle thoughts meandering back to this most tantalizing mystery...
Sherlock Holmes himself.
And just when I confidently peel back one layer...

I find another layer as undecipherable as the first...
And another.
And another.
And another.
And another.
IF I FAIL ANOTHER EXAMINATION, I'LL GET A SOUND THRASHING FROM FATHER FOR SURE!
HAVE YOU CONSIDERED THE MILITARY? I'M TOLD IT BUILDS ONE'S CHARACTER AND CONSTITUTION...
By the landlady's account, Holmes lives alone, but not always...

The space a fellow lodger would occupy is marked not by dust, but rather a curious patina of fine powder...
Upon it, one's fingerprints are laid bare, like fossilized tracks preserved in relief within some ancient and untouched sedimentary rock...
As for Holmes' own trails...
Suffice it to say that the young sleuth's eclectic belongings are as random as any theories I have formulated to gain even a rudimentary understanding of him.
The edge of a blade...
Occam's razor. Lex Parsimoniae. More Latin...
A WORLD of WONDERS REVEALED THE MICROSCOPE
The Law of Succintness...

The simplest explanation is invariably the correct one.
AND WHO MIGHT YOU BE, OLD CHAP?
ZENO, OF COURSE--
GOOD HEAVENS!
FATHER OF STOICISM!
YOU GAVE ME QUITE A FRIGHT, MISS--
PIPPA. PHILLIPA ACTUALLY.
BUT THERE'S ANOTHER UNFORTUNATELY NAMED GIRL IN MY DORMITORY, SO I'M LEFT WITH MY FATHER'S SILLY PET NAME TO AVOID CONFUSION.
I IMAGINE YOU'RE THE ELUSIVE MYCROFT?
COME AGAIN?
MYCROFT HOLMES.
SHERLOCK SPEAKS QUITE HIGHLY OF YOU.
I'M A BIT LESS WORSHIPFUL OF MY OWN ELDER--

OH, BOTHER!
MISS...
PIPPA?
I KEEP TELLING SHERLOCK TO PUT UP A RESPECTABLE SHELF.
OR A WARDROBE.
HE DOESN'T KNOW YOU'RE HERE, DOES HE?
WELL, I WAS HOPING TO... UH... SURPRISE BABY BROTHER.
I SUPPOSE MY SIBLING IS IN SOME CLASSROOM AT THIS HOUR?
OH, NOT ON THURSDAYS...
YOU KNOW YOUR BROTHER...
ON THURSDAYS HE DABBLES IN ONE OF HIS SILLY HOBBIES.

HAJIME!
KRANG
IS THAT YOUR BEST?

HERH!
HAI!
YOU FORGET BALANCE, MISTER HOLMES.
WHAT?
MUST KEEP BALANCE, EVEN WHEN ATTACK.
WHEN OFF-BALANCE--

YOU FALL!
I KNEW THAT...
NOW YOU REMEMBER IT.
NEXT TIME LESSON HURT MORE--
STOP THERE!
TRUST THAT I'M A CRACK SHOT.

AND I AM AWARE THAT WE ARE WELL BELOW THE *WATERLINE.*
A SHOT THROUGH THE *HULL* COULD BE JUST AS DAMAGING AS ONE THROUGH YOUR *SKULL*--
OH, WATSON--
DO *BEHAVE.*
THANK YOU, KADO...
AND THANK *YOU,* MASTER SAITO...
I WILL ENDEAVOR TO LEARN FROM MY *MISSTEPS.*
OH, OF COURSE...
IT'S ALL THERE.

TIME TO TAKE OUR LEAVE, DOCTOR WATSON.
I EXPECTED TO FIND YOU IN SOME ILLICIT OPIUM DEN, HOLMES...
IT APPEARS MY SUSPICIONS HEWED CLOSE TO TRUE.
THE TRADE HERE ISN'T IN OPIUM--
No, something far sweeter and no less addictive to some...
Penny candy, the perfect currency for someone whose life more and more resembles the plot of a penny dreadful...
HOW DID YOU FIND ME?
A LITTLE BIRD WHISPERED A SECRET.
PIPPA? OR WAS IT MARTHA? SURELY NOT ELIZABETH...
HOLMES, I'VE NO INTEREST IN YOUR DALLIANCES.
I HAD A MOST DIFFICULT TIME ALREADY CONVINCING INSPECTOR BRATTON OF YOUR USEFULNESS, DESPITE WHAT I'M TOLD YOU DID TO SORT OUT THAT MUSGRAVE BUSINESS...
YES, WELL...THAT CASE WAS--
THERE'S BEEN A MURDER.
WATSON, HAVEN'T YOU READ THE PAPERS--
MURDER IS EVERYWHERE.

ACCORDING TO HIS VIRTUE LET US USE HIM, WITH ALL RESPECT AND RITES OF BURIAL...
WITHIN MY TENT HIS BONES TO-NIGHT SHALL LIE, MOST LIKE A SOLDIER, ORDER'D HONOURABLY...
SO CALL THE FIELD TO REST; AND LET'S AWAY, TO PART THE GLORIES OF THIS HAPPY DAY!
BRILLIANT!
SHALL WE CALL IT A DAY, GENTLEMEN?
DYING IS SO TIRESOME...
BUT YOU, LAD--
REAL PASSION AND A COMMAND OF THE STAGE...
YOU'RE OVERSHADOWING JULIUS CAESAR IN MORE WAYS THAN ONE.
AND YOU'RE TOO KIND, REGINALD.
LIKE OCTAVIAN, I CAN ONLY HOPE TO SUCCEED MIGHTY CAESAR, NOT REPLACE HIM.

NOT EVEN ONE ALE?
THE PUB AWAITS!
THE OLD VIC
I'M A BIT KNACKERED...
HOIST ONE IN MY NAME?
REALLY...
GO ON WITHOUT ME, LADS.
A DRINK WOULD JUST PUT ME UNDER THE--
GURK!
OCTAVIUS. OCTAVIAN. CAESAR AUGUSTUS...
YOUR NAMESAKE LIVED TO THE RIPE OLD AGE OF SEVENTY-SIX.
GUH!
FOR A TRULY ACCURATE PORTRAYAL, YOUR EXIT WILL BE AS UNEVENTFUL AS HIS...
THOUGH NO LESS HONOURABLE AMONG CAESARS...

BLOODY BRYAN...
"BLOODLESS BRYAN" WOULD BE MORE APPROPOS CONSIDERING HIS CURRENT STATE.
THE UNDERBELLY MUST BE IN QUITE A STATE WITH ITS KING LAID OUT LIKE A FILLETED CARP...
HEAVY IS THE HEAD THAT WEARS THE CROWN, WATSON.
I DON'T SUPPOSE THE CONSTABLES DISCOVERED THE WEAPON THAT RENDERED THESE WOUNDS?
HOLMES, YOU SHOULD WEAR GLOVES...
OR USE INSTRUMENTS TO TOUCH THE CORPUS.
DECAY BRINGS DISEASE.
DOCTOR, THERE'S AN INSTRUMENT IN MY COAT POCKET THAT I REQUIRE...
WOULD YOU MIND?

A RULE?
AND WHY WOULD THE MEASURE OF EACH CUT BE IMPORTANT?
THE SHEER NUMBER OF WOUNDS KILLED BLOODY BRYAN, NOT THE SIZE OF ONE OR ALL.
MY DEAR WATSON...
EVERY KNIFE MAKES ITS OWN CUT.
A CLEAVER WOULD POINT TO A BUTCHER.
A BONING KNIFE TO A FISHMONGER.
AND A SHIV IN THE HAND OF THE THUG WHO UNDOUBTEDLY TURNED ON HIS CRIMINAL OVERLORD.
BRATTON WANTS US TO CONSIDER MOTIVE, NOT MEANS--
I'LL GIVE YOU LADS MOTIVATION!
BLOODY BRYAN HAD ENEMIES FROM THE WHARFS TO BUCKINGHAM PALACE.
A COUNTRY CAN'T HAVE TWO KINGS, EH?

WHAT ARE YOU MEN DOING?
THIS MAN IS THE VERY CENTER OF A CRIMINAL INVESTIGATION!
AND WHAT ARE YOU BRIGHT LADS GOING TO DO ABOUT IT?
YOU PRESUME THAT THE DOCTOR AND I WOULD NOT ENGAGE IN SOME FORM OF VIOLENCE TO THWART YOUR EFFORTS.
DESPITE APPEARANCES, I AM ADEPT.
THOUGH I'M STILL LEARNING.
OFFICER LESTRADE, THANK GOD!
ARREST THESE MEN!
I'M SORRY, DOCTOR--
BUT THEY ARE WITHIN THEIR RIGHTS...
AS REPRESENTATIVES OF BLOODY BRYAN'S GRIEVING WIDOW, THEY'VE COME TO BEAR HIS BODY TO THE MORTUARY FOR FUNERAL ARRANGEMENTS.
BUGGER ALL!
THE CONSTABULARY IS ALLOWING LONDON'S CRIMINAL ELEMENT TO WALTZ AWAY WITH THE MOST CRUCIAL PIECE OF EVIDENCE--
THE DECEDENT'S OWN BODY!
WE'RE ALL AWARE OF THAT, DOCTOR WATSON--
BUT THERE'S BEEN ANOTHER KILLING...

AND THIS ONE ALSO LEFT A NOTE.
THAT YOUNG PROSTITUTE GETS AROUND...
I'LL BROACH NO INSOLENCE FROM YOU, DOCTOR WATSON...
WHAT DOES IT SAY, HOLMES?
Have I played the part well? Then applaud as I exit!
HOLMES?

Year One Issue 3 Cover by Francesco Francavilla

SHERLOCK HOLMES YEAR ONE
THE TWELVE CAESARS
In ancient Rome, the Gemonian Stairs gained infamy as a place of execution...

There, the condemned were throttled to death, ligature strangulation to be precise, hanged without gallows...
Once dead, or merely at the edge of death, unconscious from oxygen deprivation, their bodies were bound...
And cast down the stairs as if consigned to mythic Hades...
A plummet from grace suffered by pauper or prefect, a dishonarable death regardless of one's station within the Eternal City...
The end no less Hellish...

The dead remained for days at the foot of the steps, food for the carrion beasts...
When the smell of decay was too great, or perhaps another victim was fated for the fall, the corpus was consigned to the river Tiber...
Tristissimus hominum
No coins upon eyes to pay Charon...
Tristissimus hominum
For the river Tiber runs dark and deep with the souls of the criminals submerged in it...
Tristissimus hominum

Tristissimus hominum
THE GLOOMIEST OF MEN.
DO YOU BLAME HIM?
I VENTURE I'D BE GLOOMY TOO AFTER STUMBLING DOWN STAIRS AND BREAKING MY BLOODY NECK.
ANOTHER VICTIM, ANOTHER CRYPTIC NOTE IN LATIN.
PERHAPS IT WASN'T THE FALL THAT KILLED HIM, LESTRADE...
PERHAPS YOUNG HOLMES MIGHT HAVE AN IDEA WHAT IT MEANS.
BEYOND THE LITERAL, OF COURSE.
WHERE IS THE INTREPID DETECTIVE?
AND WHY AREN'T THERE MORE CONSTABLES ABOUT, LESTRADE?
SOME SLEUTH YOU ARE, WATSON...
HAVEN'T YOU NOTICED MY SPECIAL STATUS?
THE POLICE ARE SPREAD THIN AND INSPECTOR BRATTON HAS US MAKING ROUNDS IN PLAINCLOTHES OFF HOURS--
WHAT WITH ALL THE OTHER MURDEROUS NUTTERS RECITING LATIN...
AMOS! AMAS! AMAT!

AMAMUS! AMATIS! AMANT!

ABOMINO! ABOMINAS! ABOMINAT!
COME ON, LADS! PILE ON!
HE'S TOO STRONG!

ABOMINAMUS! ABOMINATIS! ABOMINANT!

I LOVE HER!
AND I HATE HER!
THAT'S WHY I CUT HER UGLY THROAT!
WHAT'S THIS THEN?!
BUT I SAVED HER PRETTY--
FACIES, LADS!
THAT'S THE MAGIC--
KLOD
I'D SAY YOU USED THE WRONG BLOODY END, LESTRADE!
EVERY MAN DESERVES HIS DAY IN COURT, INSPECTOR BRATTON--
EVEN THE DRUNKEN GITS WHO CONFESS THEIR SINS TO A HOUSE FULL OF CONSTABLES...

TROUBLE IS, THAT BIG BLOKE ISN'T EVEN THE FIRST...
I MEMORIZED MY LATIN DECLINATIONS IN SCHOOL ALSO, BUT THAT DOESN'T GIVE ME BLOODY LICENSE TO GET KNACKERED AND COMMIT MURDER AND MAYHEM.
FEAR BRINGS OUT THE WORST IN US ALL, LESTRADE...
THE DRINK JUST LUBRICATES THE GEARS OF ALL THE INFERNAL ENGINES.
SEE? THE FALL MERELY FINISHED THE JOB...
THIS MAN WAS STRANGLED. GARROTED BY THE LOOKS OF THESE DEEP CUTS.
EACH END DIFFERENT FROM THE LAST.
PERHAPS OUR KILLER--OR KILLERS--IS MURDERING BY DISSIMILAR MEANS TO THROW THE POLICE OFF HIS TRACKS.
OF COURSE, BECAUSE STABBING OR SHOOTING JUST BORES THE DEVIL TO DEATH.
AH, RIGHT ON SCHEDULE--

THE VICTIM'S *CHARIOT* AWAITS...
I THOUGHT A DEAD MAN ONLY NEEDED *TWO* COINS FOR THE JOURNEY ACROSS THE RIVER STYX.
THE FERRYMAN'S RATES HAVE *RISEN,* WATSON.
I'LL TELL YOU WHO PROFITS IN MURDER...
EVERYONE BUT *US* GOOD, GODFEARING GENTLEMAN, WOT?
NOW DON'T JUST STAND THERE, MAN--
HOIST A HOOK OR HE'LL BE STUCK FAST TO THE GROUND UNTIL SPRING THAW!
I'D MUCH RATHER HOIST A *PINT*...

BUT IT'S BARELY NOON...
AH, WELL...
WHEN IN ROME.
NO TRUER WORDS, DOCTOR.
WHAT SAY WE SPARE YOU THE GUESSWORK AND ORDER SECOND ROUNDS NOW, BESS?
FAIR ENOUGH, CONSTABLE.
LONG AS YOUR TIP'S THE SAME.
YOU APPEAR TO HAVE SOME REACH HERE, CONSTABLE.
HMM...
KINGS AREN'T THE ONLY AUTHORITIES WITH LONG ARMS.
SOMETHING ON YOUR MIND, JOHN?
HOW DID YOU COME TO KNOW SHERLOCK HOLMES?
GLORIA SCOTT.
A GIRL?
A SHIP.

"A *PRISON SHIP,* TO BE PRECISE...
"BERTHED IN FALMOUTH AND BOUND FOR AUSTRALIA."
I NEVER HEARD OF IT *EITHER.*
"FIVE AND TWENTY YEARS AGO IT EXPLODED AND SANK SOMEWHERE PAST AFRICA'S CAPE OF GOOD HOPE.
"GUNPOWDER IN THE HOLD IGNITED BY SOME CAPRICE..."
OR *CALUMNY?*
WERE THERE ANY SURVIVORS?
"NONE IN THE OFFICIAL RECORDS...
"AND I *CHECKED.*"

SO AM I TO DEDUCE THAT HOLMES LOST SOMEONE IN THIS MARITIME DISASTER?
THANK YOU, LUV.
NOT HOLMES AND NOT LOST...
HOLMES *FOUND* SOMEONE.
HIS FRIEND AND FLATMATE'S FATHER.
BUT HERE'S THE THING. FOLLOWING THE WHOLE SORDID AFFAIR, A BIT OF BLACKMAIL AND REVENGE FOR GOOD MEASURE--
"HE *LOST* HIS FLATMATE..."
VICTOR TREVOR.

VIC'S NOT BEEN AROUND IN QUITE A WHILE.
BUT YOU KEEP INQUIRIN' ANYWAYS, DONCHA LAD?
THINK HE MIGHT 'AVE FOUND THIS TART A BIT MORE INTOXICATIN' THAN A HOOKAH?
OR IS SHE YOUR GIRL, LAD?
PERHAPS YOU'LL JUST LET ME LOOK FOR MY--
RUN ALONG, BOY...
YOU LOOK LIKE A CLEAR-HEADED SORT.
DON'T WANT YOUR BRAINS ADDLED BY THE PIPE--
OR A FEW THUMPS TO THE HEAD, EH?
I SUPPOSE YOU'RE RIGHT.
OPIUM NEVER RAISED MY CONSCIOUSNESS--

NOT LIKE THE RUSH OF ADNENALIN!
GAH!
UNH!
SHITE!
HE'S BROKE MY BLOODY--
NUH!
YOU'LL NEED ALL THE OPIUM YOU CAN SMOKE AFTER I'VE TORN YOUR DANDY HEAD--
KRAK
UNF!

WATSON, LOOK SMART!
EH?
SPLAF
MOVE ALONG, YOU WEE DELINQUENTS!
GET BACK TO YOUR STUDIES!
DON'T TELL ME THERE'S BEEN *ANOTHER* MURDER, CONSTABLE...
NOT THIS TIME...
IT WOULD SEEM YOUR COHORT HOLMES HAS BROKEN THE CASE.
OR AT LEAST HE *WILL*--
ONCE WE'VE SPRUNG HIM FROM JAIL!

I SEE...
AND THE STUMBLE?
A *FEINT* IS WHUT.
LOWERS THE GUARD--
THEY THINK THEY'RE HELPIN' YOU WHEN YOU'RE HELPIN' *YOURSELF!*
HOLMES!
INSPECTOR BRATTON IS WAITING!
COMING RIGHT ALONG, CONSTABLE--
WOOPS!
STEADY THERE, HOLMES!
YOU LOOK AS IF YOU HAVEN'T SLEPT IN--
IS THAT MY *WATCH?*
DAFT BOY!
WHUT GOOD IS PICKIN' A POCKET IF YOU DON'T KEEP WHUT YOU PILFER!

ONCE IS HAPPENSTANCE.
TWICE IS COINCIDENCE.
THRICE ESTABLISHES A PATTERN.
WHAT SORT OF PATTERN?
SPARE ME THE RIDDLES AND GET TO THE POINT, HOLMES--
OR I SWEAR I'LL TOSS YOU BACK IN THAT CELL AND LOSE THE KEY DOWN A DRAINPIPE!
LATIN IS THE PATTERN, ISN'T IT?
THE MURDERER'S FINAL BON MOTS ON THE BITS OF PARCHMENT.
I'M SPEAKING OF A PATTERN OF INTENT, DOCTOR WATSON.
LATIN IS THE LANGUAGE OF THE CAESARS, WHOSE DEATHS THIS ENTERPRISING CRIMINAL IS TRYING QUITE HARD TO REENACT.
AND NOW THAT I KNOW HOW THE FIRST THREE VICTIMS DIED--
I CAN PREDICT WITH SOME CERTAINTY HOW THE NEXT SHALL FALL.

CALIGVLA
"HE WILL BE A MAN OF SOME ILL-REPUTE--
"BUT A KING WITHIN HIS CHOSEN ARENA.
"HIS VICES WILL BE MANY.
"AND HIS END WILL COME AT THE HANDS OF SOMEONE HE MIGHT OTHERWISE HAVE NO REASON NOT TO TRUST.
"HE WILL DIE IN A TUNNEL. A CORRIDOR UNDER THE STREETS PERHAPS.
"AND LIKE THE ELDER JULIUS CAESAR, HIS DEMISE WILL FOLLOW THIRTY STABBINGS.

CLAVDIVS
"BUT STABBING IS NOT THE PATTERN.
"DEATH IS THE PATTERN, THE END NOT THE MEANS.
"THE FIFTH CAESAR'S DEMISE WAS NOT A VIOLENT END.
"LIKE HIS PREDECESSORS, CLAUDIUS'S MURDER WAS CONSPIRED BY SOMEONE WHO TOOK ADVANTAGE OF HIS LOVE OF FOOD AND DRINK.
"MUSHROOMS, IN PARTICULAR...
ARSENIC
"SOMETIMES POISONOUS IF NOT PICKED WITH CARE.

NERO
"NEXT WILL COME A FIDDLER.
"UNDOUBTEDLY, A VIOLINIST PEERLESS OF SKILL.
"HIS DEATH WILL BE MADE TO LOOK LIKE A SUICIDE.
"PERHAPS INDUCED BY SHAME OR A MORE PALPABLE FEAR.
"BY SOME ACCOUNTS, NERO HAD HELP MAKING THE FINAL CUT.
HARK, NOW STRIKES ON MY EAR THE TRAMPLING OF SWIFT-FOOTED COURSERS...
"AND I WOULD WAGER THAT HIS MURDERER WOULD FIND AN APPROPOS TIME TO INVOKE HOMER'S *ILIAD* AS NERO DID IN HIS FINAL MOMENTS."

Year One Issue 4 Cover by Francesco Francavilla

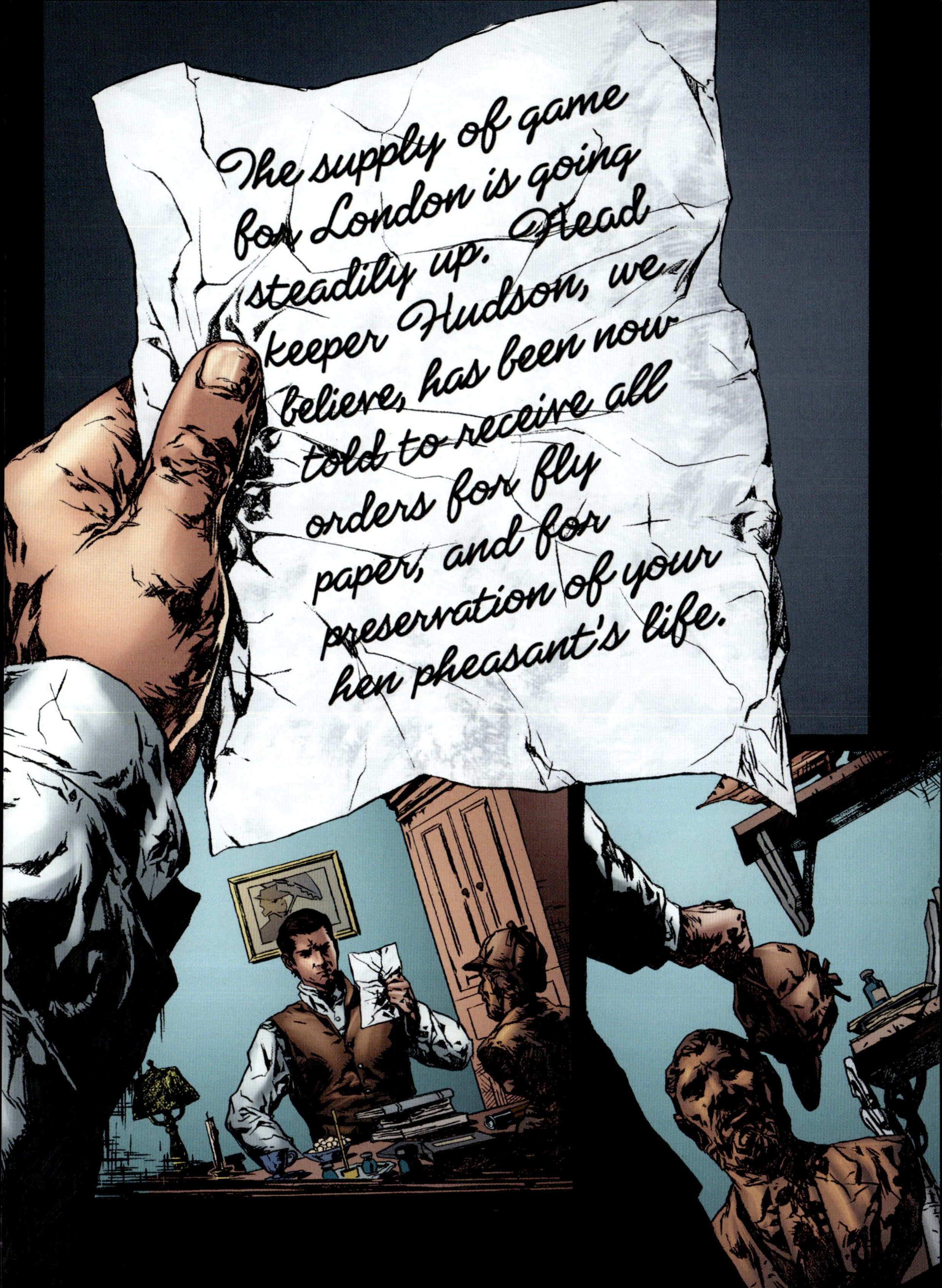

SHERLOCK HOLMES YEAR ONE

SHIPS ARE SAFE IN HARBOUR

YOU SHOULD BE BOLTING THAT.
HAVE YOU NOT HEARD THAT THERE ARE VILLAINS ABOUT?
MY DOOR IS NEVER LOCKED, DOCTOR WATSON.
KNOWLEDGE IS MY ONLY TREASURE, AND I CARRY IT WITH ME AT ALL TIMES.
WELL PUT.
PERHAPS YOU WOULD SHARE A TRIFLING PORTION OF THAT TROVE WITH ME.
I HAD HOPED THAT WE MIGHT FURTHER DISCUSS YOUR THEORIES ON THE TWELVE CAESARS KILLER.
I...
I'M AFRAID I MUST GO AND IDENTIFY A BODY JUST NOW.
GOOD LORD, NOT ANOTHER MURDER SO SOON?
IF ONLY...

HOLMES?
HOLMES!
WUXTRY! WUXTRY!
LAST NEWS OF THE DAY, BUT FIRST IN THE EVENING STAR!
READ IT BEFORE THE INK'S ALL BUT DRY!
The EVENING STAR
SIX 'CAESARS' FALLEN, SIX AWAIT THEIR END!
WHO'S NEXT?
ACCORDING TO THE CENSUS, THERE'S 3,816,483 OF US LONDONERS!
AND THE SEVENTH CAESAR MIGHT WELL BE ONE OF YOU!

I'VE NO MORE TO SAY ON THE MATTER!
NOW WILL THE LOT OF YOU DECAMP FROM MY DIVISION AND LET US DO THE JOB OF *CATCHING* THIS BLOODY MADMAN?!
HAVE YOU ANY CLUES TO THE KILLER'S IDENTITY?
WHAT MAKES YOU THINK THE SCOUNDREL WILL STOP AT TWELVE?
IS IT TRUE THAT YOUNG SLEUTH SHERLOCK HOLMES IS NOW FULLY IN THE EMPLOY OF THE CONSTABULARY?
DOES THE MURDERER REALLY MAKE KIPPERS FROM HIS VICTIM'S--
HE'S A ROYAL, ISN'T HE?
CHIEF INSPECTOR BRATTON!
THERE'S SOMETHING YOU SHOULD *SEE*--
WATCH OUT THERE!
OOF!
NO NO!

GOD DAMN IT ALL!
WHERE'S THE *REST* OF HIM?!
LESTRADE?!
MOSTLY JUST HIS HEAD, SIR.
AND HIS *TRUNK.*
IT'S ALL A BLOODY *CIRCUS!*
GET OUT HERE, ALL OF YOU!
AND SOMEONE GATHER UP THAT HEAD BEFORE THESE NEWSPAPER HEATHENS USE IT FOR A SODDING *FOOTBALL!*
Strike, if it be for The Good Of The Romans!

SO IF YOUR THEORY BEARS OUT, THEN THE NEXT CAESAR TO FALL WILL BE *GALBA*...
SERVIUS SULPICIUS GALBA. EMPEROR OF ROME FOR JUST SEVEN MONTHS BEFORE HIS ASSASSINATION.
BEHEADED.
HIS HEAD AND TRUNK BURIED BY A LOYAL STEWARD ALONG THE AURELIAN--
OH, I'M SO SORRY!
MIND WHERE YER GOIN'!
WHERE I'M ***GOING?***
TRUTH BE TOLD, I'VE NO IDEA WHERE I PRESENTLY *AM*...

HOLMES, WHERE *ARE* YOU?
OH... IS THAT THE CORPUS YOU MENTIONED?
WELL, HE AIN'T A PAYIN' BOARDER ANY MORES!
AND HE MAKES FOR A PISS POOR *CHANDELIER*, WOT?

MONEY IS THE LEAST OF THIS MAN'S WORRIES.
THIS SHOULD COVER HIS RENT TO DATE PLUS AN HOUR MORE IN THIS FILTHY STY.
ALONE.
EXCEPT FOR THE PHYSICIAN AND MYSELF.
I have kept company with Sherlock Holmes for many weeks now.
STAY THE NIGHT IF YOU LIKE--
TOSSERS.
My theories abound as to the roots of his numerous peculiarities.
But what happened in this room and Holmes' complicity, if any, is his tale alone to tell...
And in my most limited experience, he is not one to embellish.
HIS NAME IS VICTOR TREVOR.
AND HE WAS MY FRIEND...
BLEHH!

ARE YOU REALLY THAT UNFLAPPABLE--
LODGERS WANTED
HOLMES, WAIT!
I'VE BEEN MEANING TO PROPERLY APOLOGIZE FOR MY DOG'S BAD BEHAVIOUR.
HOW'S YOUR LEG?
A BULL-TERRIER HAS A STRONG BITE WHEN IT FREEZES UPON ONE'S ANKLE. I MAY HAVE TO TAKE UP A CANE.
I'LL PAY FOR ANY MEDICAL EXPENSES YOU'VE SUFFERED, OF COURSE.
WANT ME TO TAKE A LOOK? I'VE BEEN MEANING TO PUT TO PRACTICE WHAT I LEARNED IN THE ANATOMY SEMINAR WE SHARED LAST QUARTER.
I RECALL YOUR PECULIAR THEORIES ON FINGERPRINTS. "NO TWO EVER ALIKE, PROFESSOR"--
AND I RECALL YOU DOZING MOST LECTURES, MISTER TREVOR.
VICTOR, IF YOU PLEASE.
AND YOU COULD DO WORSE THAN SHARING A LODGING WITH ME.
ONLY IF THAT DEVILISH HOUND IS QUARTERED ELSEWHERE. SWEAR IT.
ON MY FATHER'S GOOD NAME!
SHERLOCK HOLMES.
VICTOR TREVOR...

MY FORMER FLATMATE.
HOLD STEADY WHILE I CUT HIS BODY DOWN, DOCTOR WATSON--
I WON'T HAVE HIM SUFFER *FURTHER* INDIGNITY AS FOOD FOR THE WHARF RATS INFESTING THIS SQUALID--
I COULD STEP OUT IF YOU WANTED A MOMENT ALONE--
WHAT I WANT IS FOR YOU TO EXAMINE THE CORPSE FOR SIGNS OF *FOUL PLAY*...
INDICATORS OF *MURDER* OR OTHER *MALFEASANCE* COMMITTED UPON HIM.
AND NOT AN ANSWER SO SIMPLE AS *SUICIDE!*

SUICIDE IS THE COURSE OF LAST RESORT FOR THE *CURSED* OR *CONDEMNED.*
NOT FOR SOMEONE WITH SO MUCH TO LIVE FOR...
SLEEP WHEN YOU'RE *DEAD,* VICTOR!
WUZZAT?
GO WAY...
FWAP
CLEAN YOURSELF UP, MASTER TREVOR.
IF WE'RE LATE, SHE'LL *KILL* US.
YOU'LL SLEEP THE ETERNAL SLUMBER, AND OUR TIGHT CIRCLE OF FRIENDS WILL BE SUBTRACTED ONE CARELESS POINT ON THE COMPASS.

I'VE HEARD BETTER...
QUIET!
DON'T BLINK!
LET HER GO, HOLMES!
OR SHE'LL BE LATE TO HER NEXT PERFORMANCE!
SHERLOCK HOLMES...
MY FATHER, JUSTICE OF THE PEACE TREVOR.
THE PLEASURE IS MINE, SIR.
VICTOR HOLDS YOU IN NOTHING BUT THE HIGHEST ESTEEM.
COME LADS...
SHAKE OFF THE DUST OF TOWN AND ENJOY THE BOUNTY OF DONNITHORPE!

A DEAD SHOT, HOLMES!
THAT'S IT, LAD!
DRAW HIM IN!
WE'LL HAVE FRESH FISH TONIGHT!
HOLMES!
JOIN US FOR A GLASS OF PORT ON THE LAWN!
SO, SHERLOCK...
MY SON TELLS ME OF YOUR REMARKABLE GIFTS OF EXAMINATION.
I'M AN EXCELLENT SUBJECT. WHAT CAN YOU DEDUCE FROM ME?

I FEAR THAT THERE ISN'T MUCH.
I MIGHT SUGGEST THAT YOU HAVE CAUSE TO FEAR PERSONAL ATTACK WITHIN THE LAST TWELVE MONTHS.
YOUR HANDSOME WALKING STICK BEARS AN INSCRIPTION THAT INDICATES YOU HAVE NOT HAD IT MORE THAN A YEAR.
WHILE THE BORINGS IN THE HEAD AND YOUR PAINS TO WEIGHT IT WITH LEAD MAKE IT MORE A CUDGEL THAN A CANE.
SUCH PRECAUTIONS WOULD SEEM DRIVEN BY FEAR OF SOME IMPENDING DANGER.
ANYTHING ELSE, LAD?
YOU DISSECT ME AS ONE PEELS BACK THE SKINS OF AN ONION!
YOU'VE DONE A GOOD DEAL OF DIGGING JUDGING BY THE CALLOSITIES UPON YOUR HANDS.
MADE ALL MY MONEY IN THE GOLD FIELDS.
THE COLLECTION OF TRIBAL ART IN YOUR LIBRARY REVEALS THAT YOU HAVE BEEN IN NEW ZEALAND.
AND YOU FOUGHT A GREAT DEAL IN YOUR YOUTH. A BOXER, NOT A BRAWLER.
IS MY NOSE KNOCKED A LITTLE BIT OUT OF TRUE?
A MASHED NOSE MARKS A MAN PRACTICED IN FISTICUFFS. CERTAINLY NOT ALWAYS THE VICTOR...
BUT YOUR FLATTENED EARS BELONG TO A BOXING MAN.
ANYTHING ELSE?
I AM TRULY A CAPTIVE AUDIENCE.

YOU HAVE BEEN MOST INTIMATELY ASSOCIATED WITH SOMEONE WHOSE INITIALS WERE J.A.--
AND WHOM YOU AFTERWARDS WERE EAGER TO ENTIRELY FORGET.
I...
I...
FATHER?
JUSTICE TREVOR?
FATHER!

GASP
I HOPE I'VE SAID NOTHING TO *PAIN* YOU, SIR.
WELL, YOU CERTAINLY TOUCHED UPON RATHER A TENDER POINT. HOW DID YOU--?
I SPIED YOUR BARE ARM WHEN YOU REACHED TO DRAW THAT RATHER LARGE CARP INTO THE BOAT YESTERDAY.
THE LETTERS TATTOOED IN THE BEND OF YOUR ELBOW, STILL LEGIBLE DESPITE SOME EFFORTS TO *OBLITERATE* THEM.
WHAT AN *EYE* HE HAS, VICTOR!
LIKE A SURGEON'S SCALPEL!
PERHAPS *THAT'S* WHAT I SHOULD HAVE TAKEN TO THESE DAMNABLE LETTERS...
BUT WE WON'T TALK OF IT...
OF ALL GHOSTS, THE GHOSTS OF OUR OLD LOVES ARE THE *WORST*...

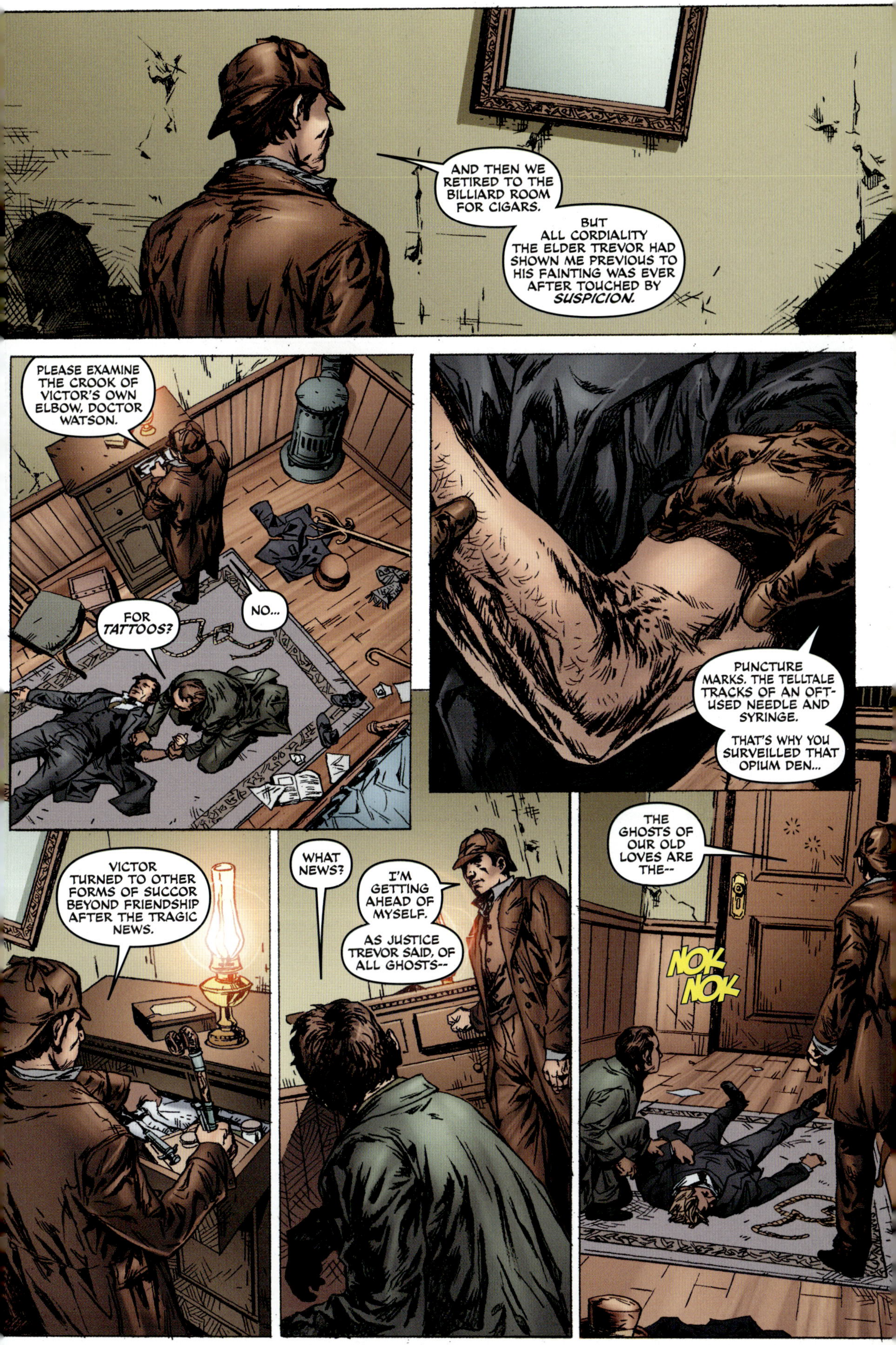
AND THEN WE RETIRED TO THE BILLIARD ROOM FOR CIGARS.
BUT ALL CORDIALITY THE ELDER TREVOR HAD SHOWN ME PREVIOUS TO HIS FAINTING WAS EVER AFTER TOUCHED BY *SUSPICION.*
PLEASE EXAMINE THE CROOK OF VICTOR'S OWN ELBOW, DOCTOR WATSON.
FOR *TATTOOS?*
NO...
PUNCTURE MARKS. THE TELLTALE TRACKS OF AN OFT-USED NEEDLE AND SYRINGE.
THAT'S WHY YOU SURVEILLED THAT OPIUM DEN...
VICTOR TURNED TO OTHER FORMS OF SUCCOR BEYOND FRIENDSHIP AFTER THE TRAGIC NEWS.
WHAT NEWS?
I'M GETTING AHEAD OF MYSELF.
AS JUSTICE TREVOR SAID, OF ALL GHOSTS--
THE GHOSTS OF OUR OLD LOVES ARE THE--
NOK NOK

CHIEF INSPECTOR?
IT'S THATCHER, SIR!
WHAT IS IT, THATCHER?
YOU DON'T MEAN--
ANOTHER ONE SIR...
THE EIGHTH CAESAR!
OTHO
"STABBED WITH A KNIFE HE KEPT UNDER HIS PILLOW FOR PROTECTION."
A PROFESSOR AT UNIVERSITY. PHILOSOPHY, SAID HIS WIDOW.
IT ALL HAD THE LOOK OF SUICIDE, BUT SHE WOULDN'T HEAR OF IT.
GO ON AHEAD TO HEADQUARTERS.
I JUST NEED TO FETCH MY COAT AND HAT...
AND MY BLOODY UNDERCLOTHES TOO.
I MAY AS WELL SLEEP AT 14 WHITEHALL UNTIL THIS MADMAN IS--

STOPPED?
WITH BUT FOUR CAESARS LEFT?
WHO'S THERE?!
GUH!
UHHH...
THERE IS AN IMPORTANT LESSON TO BE LEARNED HERE, CHIEF INSPECTOR BRATTON--
CLUD
OR MAY I CALL YOU VITELLIUS?
SURELY, YOU'RE NOT SURPRISED THE REAPER WOULD KNOCK FOR YOU?

I SHOULD HAVE SUSPECTED...
THAT I'D COME?
YOU SHOULD HAVE KNOWN IT WITH ALL CERTAINTY, SHERLOCK HOLMES.
I...I AM AT A LOSS...
PERHAPS AN INTRODUCTION IS IN ORDER, HOLMES.
WOULD THIS BE ONE MORE OF YOUR YOUNG FEMALE ACQUAINTENCES?
MY NAME IS IRENE ADLER, GOOD SIR--
AND I AM THIS MAN'S BETROTHED.

FWAP
FWAP
LET GO OF MY WRIST!
ONCE IS HAPPENSTANCE, IRENE.
TWICE IS COINCIDENCE.
THRICE IS A PATTERN OF ILL INTENT.

Year One Issue 5 Cover by Francesco Francavilla

Indesputably, the 9th Caesar was personal…
SPLUT
WUZZAT?
WHERE THE BLOODY HELL AM I?!

LIKE *VITELLIUS,* NINTH CAESAR OF ROME, YOU ARE AMONG YOUR SUBJECTS--
THE VILLAINS OF LONDON, ALL OF WHOM YOU HAVE LORDED OVER AS THE ARBITER OF THEIR CRIMINAL CONDUCT AND SINS UNCOUNTED!
QUITE SIMPLY, AND PARDON THE VULGARITY, INSPECTOR BRATTON--
YOU'RE IN THE *SHITE* OF IT.
IS THAT WHY YOU INVITED US HERE?
TO DO YOUR DIRTY WORK?
HARDLY, MISTER NORFOLK...
MY INFAMY GROWS WITH EVERY CAESAR BROUGHT LOW AND DELIVERED TO HIS DEATH.
WHILE YOU HAVE YOURSELF *CAPITALIZED* ON MY CRIMES TO TAKE OVER BLOODY BRYAN'S ENTERPRISES THROUGHOUT THE UNDERBELLY.
AND JUST *WHO* IN CHRIST'S NAME ARE YOU, MADMAN?!

HAVEN'T I LEFT SUFFICIENT CLUES?
I AM THE NEXT KING OF ENGLAND!
SHERLOCK HOLMES YEAR ONE
CUI BONO?

Who profits in death?
All ends are personal, and the outcomes leave nothing but bankruptcy of heart and spirit.
IS THAT--?
VICTOR.
WELL?
WELL WHAT?

I CAN UNDERSTAND MASTER HOLMES' LACK OF MANNERS GIVEN HIS UNCONVENTIONAL UPBRINGING.
BUT YOU HAVE ALL THE BEARING OF A RETIRED SOLDIER AND GENTLE--
OH, SOD IT!
MISS ADLER...
IRENE...
WHAT POINT IS THERE IN TIDYING?
MOREOVER, YOU RISK DISJARRING AND TRODDING OVER ANY CLUES WE MIGHT--
STUFF YOUR CLUES, SHERLOCK HOLMES!
VICTOR WAS YOUR BEST--
YOUR ONLY FRIEND!
AND HE DESERVES AT LEAST ONE DIGNITY IN DEATH--
ESPECIALLY AFTER THE SHAME HE SUFFERED FOLLOWING YOUR CLEVER DEDUCTIONS!
MISS ADLER, WE MEANT NO DISGRACE...
I AM A PHYSICIAN AND WAS CONDUCTING A POST-MORTEM EXAMINATION OF MISTER--
OF VICTOR.
AN AUTOPSY?
TO WHAT END?
HASN'T HE SUFFICIENTLY BEEN DRAGGED THROUGH THE MUCK?

PLEASE...
ENOUGH...
VITELLIUS WAS PELTED WITH ANIMAL EXCREMENT BEFORE HIS DEATH.
SHAME BEFORE REDEMPTION.
WHY?!
WHAT *PURPOSE* IS THERE TO THESE MURDERS?!
CONSIDER IT A TEACHING EXERCISE, INSPECTOR...
AN OBJECT LESSON IN *MORALITY*--
THE TRUE NATURE OF *EVIL.*
AIEEEEEEEEE!
POKPOKPOKPOKPOKPOKPOKPOKPOKPOK

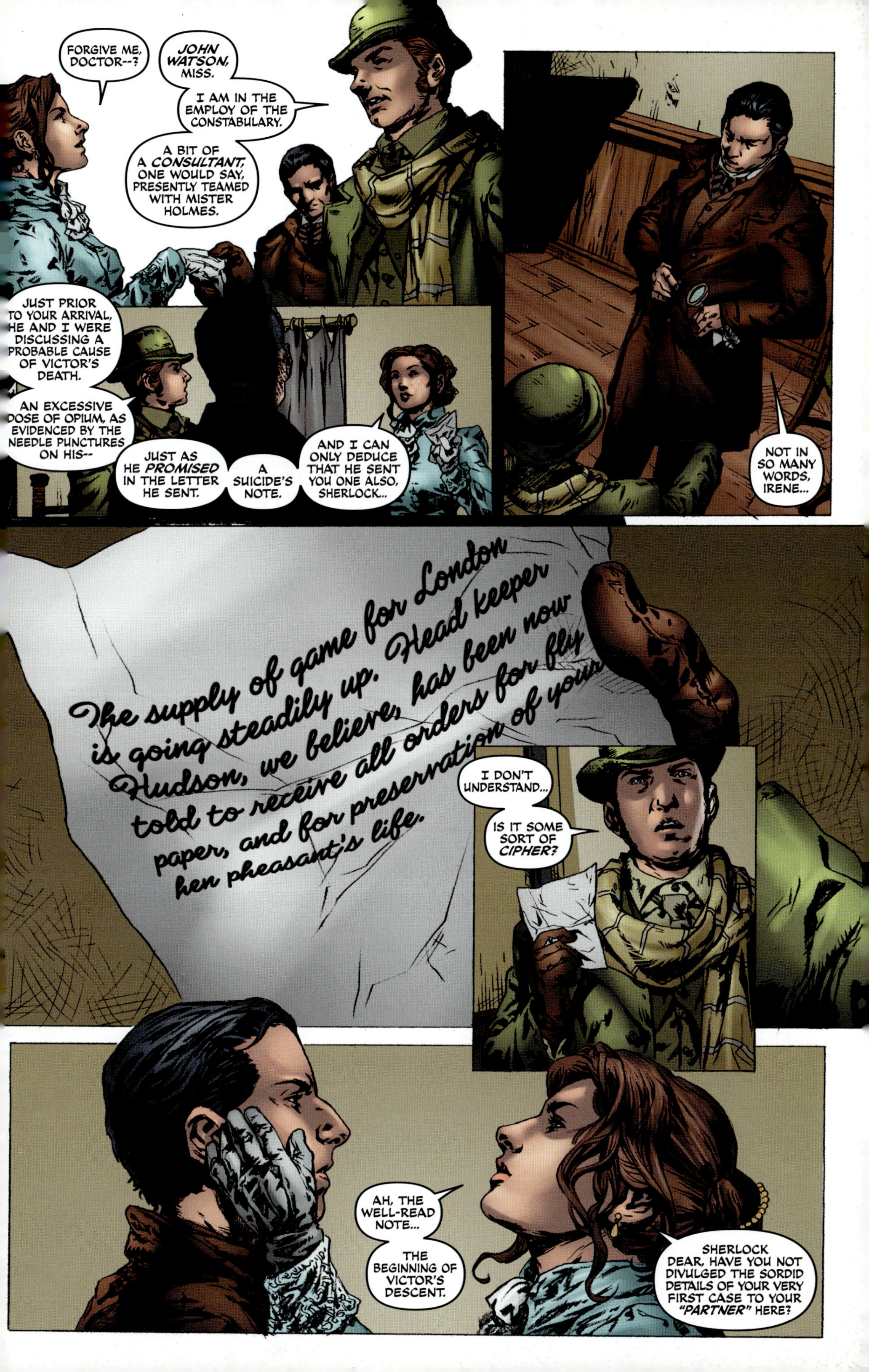
FORGIVE ME, DOCTOR--?
JOHN WATSON, MISS.
I AM IN THE EMPLOY OF THE CONSTABULARY.
A BIT OF A CONSULTANT, ONE WOULD SAY, PRESENTLY TEAMED WITH MISTER HOLMES.
JUST PRIOR TO YOUR ARRIVAL, HE AND I WERE DISCUSSING A PROBABLE CAUSE OF VICTOR'S DEATH.
AN EXCESSIVE DOSE OF OPIUM, AS EVIDENCED BY THE NEEDLE PUNCTURES ON HIS--
JUST AS HE PROMISED IN THE LETTER HE SENT.
A SUICIDE'S NOTE.
AND I CAN ONLY DEDUCE THAT HE SENT YOU ONE ALSO, SHERLOCK...
NOT IN SO MANY WORDS, IRENE...
The supply of game for London is going steadily up. Head keeper Hudson, we believe, has been now told to receive all orders for fly paper, and for preservation of your hen pheasant's life.
I DON'T UNDERSTAND...
IS IT SOME SORT OF CIPHER?
AH, THE WELL-READ NOTE...
THE BEGINNING OF VICTOR'S DESCENT.
SHERLOCK DEAR, HAVE YOU NOT DIVULGED THE SORDID DETAILS OF YOUR VERY FIRST CASE TO YOUR "PARTNER" HERE?

I SUPPOSE IT MAKES NO DIFFERENCE NOW.
THE STORY ENDS THE SAME WAY REGARDLESS.
BUT IT BEGINS WITH THE *GLORIA SCOTT,* DOES IT NOT?
MISS ADLER, WOULD YOU CARE TO SIT?
I WOULD GUESS THAT THIS TALE IS *COMPLICATED* TO BE SURE...
I SEE YOU'VE ENGAGED IN A BIT OF *VIVISECTION,* DOCTOR WATSON.
MY PAST LIFE LAID BARE BY...*CONSTABLE LESTRADE,* WAS IT?
YOU'LL BE A *DETECTIVE* YET.
VICTOR'S STORY DID INDEED BEGIN WITH THE *GLORIA SCOTT,* A PRISON SHIP OUT OF FALMOUTH AND BOUND FOR AUSTRALIA...

"BUT THAT WAS IN THE YEAR OF OUR LORD 1855, LONG BEFORE VICTOR'S BIRTH. AND THE SHIP *NEVER* REACHED ITS DESTINATION.
"TREVOR'S FATHER WAS AMONG A RABBLE WHO OVERTOOK THE GLORIA SCOTT IN A BID FOR FREEDOM. BUT IN THAT DAY HE WAS KNOWN BY HIS BIRTH NAME, *JAMES ARMITAGE.*
"TO HIS CREDIT, ARMITAGE AND A PITIFUL FEW REFUSED TO MURDER THE CREW IN COLD BLOOD AND OPTED TO TAKE THEIR CHANCES ON THE HIGH SEAS IN A SMALL DINGHY.
"LITTLE DID ANY OF THEM REALIZE THAT THIS SMALL VIRTUE, AT LEAST ON THE SUBJECT OF HOMICIDE, WOULD ULTIMATELY SPARE THEIR OWN LIVES.
"THEY SAY THAT SHIPS ARE ONLY SAFE IN HARBOR...

THOUGH, IT WAS UNCONVENTIONAL TO HAVE THE BUTLER TAKE HIS DINNER WITH HIS EMPLOYER AT THE DINING TABLE.
CLEARLY, JUSTICE TREVOR *FEARED* HUDSON. BUT IN LIFE HE REFUSED TO DIVULGE SUCH CONCERNS TO HIS ONLY SON VICTOR.
UNTIL THE ARRIVAL OF THIS CRYPTIC NOTE, I WOULD IMAGINE.
INDEED, DOCTOR...
"EVENTUALLY, HUDSON TOOK HIS LEAVE, HAVING HAD--IN HIS WORDS--'*HIS FILL OF NORFOLK.*' NEITHER OF THE *GLORIA SCOTT'S* SURVIVORS LABORED TO CONCEAL THEIR ACRIMONY BETWEEN ONE ANOTHER, OR VICTOR HIMSELF, WHO HAD PUT HANDS UPON THE OLD MAN AFTER AN INSOLENT REMARK MADE TO THE JUSTICE."
TRAVEL WELL, HUDSON.
YOU'RE NOT GOING AWAY IN AN UNKIND SPIRIT, HUDSON, I HOPE?
I'VE NOT HAD MY *'POLOGY.*
YOU'VE HAD THE PLEASURE OF MY COMPANY JUST *TWICE* IN THIS OR ANY OTHER LIFE.
YOU'D PAY WELL TO SEE ME A *THIRD* TIME, WOT?
"I LEFT THE TREVOR ESTATE NOT LONG AFTER TO ATTEND TO MY OWN AFFAIRS. I SAW THE CLUES NEVERTHELESS. DOOM WAS IN THE AIR...

"THAT WELL-READ NOTE ARRIVED IN THE POST FROM A *MISTER BEDDOES,* ANOTHER OF THE SMALL AND SECRET FRATERNITY OF *GLORIA SCOTT* REFUGEES.
"THE WORDS UPON THE PARCHMENT UNRAVELED JUSTICE TREVOR."
FATHER, WHAT'S THE MATTER?
NO NO NO NO NO NO NO NO
FATHER!
"EVEN *WORDS* CAN KILL, WATSON.
"THE JUSTICE SUFFERED A STROKE AND RECOVERED CONSCIOUSNESS BUT ONCE...

"TRAGICALLY, VICTOR HAD LEFT HIS FATHER'S BEDSIDE IN THAT FINAL MOMENT. A DOCTOR FORDHAM RELAYED THE JUSTICE'S DEATHBED REVELATION...
"HE HAD CONFESSED ALL TO VICTOR IN HIS OWN LETTER CONCEALED AMONG PAPERS IN A JAPANESE CABINET.
"WORDS CAN KILL."
PLEASE, SHERLOCK...
USE THAT FINELY TUNED INTELLECT OF YOURS AND TELL ME WHAT *HIDDEN* MEANING LURKS IN THIS POISON LETTER!
"I READ AND I RE-READ. I EXAMINED WORDS FOR MEANINGS BOTH LITERAL AND SYMBOLIC. ETYMOLOGY. SYNONYMS AND HOMONYMS. PREARRANGED SIGNIFICANCE OF PHRASING. BUT AT THE HEART OF IT, THE REFERENCE TO HUDSON PROVIDED THE KEY TO BREAKING THE MOST SIMPLE OF CODES..."
YOU'D PAY WELL TO SEE ME A *THIRD* TIME, WOT?

ONCE IS HAPPENSTANCE.
TWICE IS COINCIDENCE.
THRICE IS A PATTERN OF ILL INTENT.
"HUDSON DID INDEED CALL UPON BEDDOES, LIKELY TO RECRUIT HIS FELLOW SURVIVOR IN A SCHEME TO BLACKMAIL JUSTICE TREVOR FOR HAVING THE TEMERITY TO PROSPER IN THE YEARS SINCE THE GLORIA SCOTT EXPLODED AND SANK BENEATH THE SOUTH PACIFIC WAVES.
"BUT BEDDOES WAS AMONG THE SMALL RETINUE THAT LEFT THE SHIP RATHER THAN MURDER THE CAPTURED CREW. DESPITE THE WELL-WORN MAXIM, PERHAPS THERE IS HONOR AMONG THIEVES.
he supply of game for London is going steadily up. Head keeper Hudson, we believe, has been now told to receive all orders for fl paper, and for preservation of hen pheasant's life.
"AND I WOULD DEDUCE THAT PRIOR TO HUDSON'S ARRIVAL ON THAT DINGHY, THOSE FEW TRULY HONORABLE MEN MADE THEIR OWN PACT. PERHAPS THEY ESTABLISHED THEIR OWN CODE WITH WHICH TO RECOGNIZE THEIR NUMBER..."

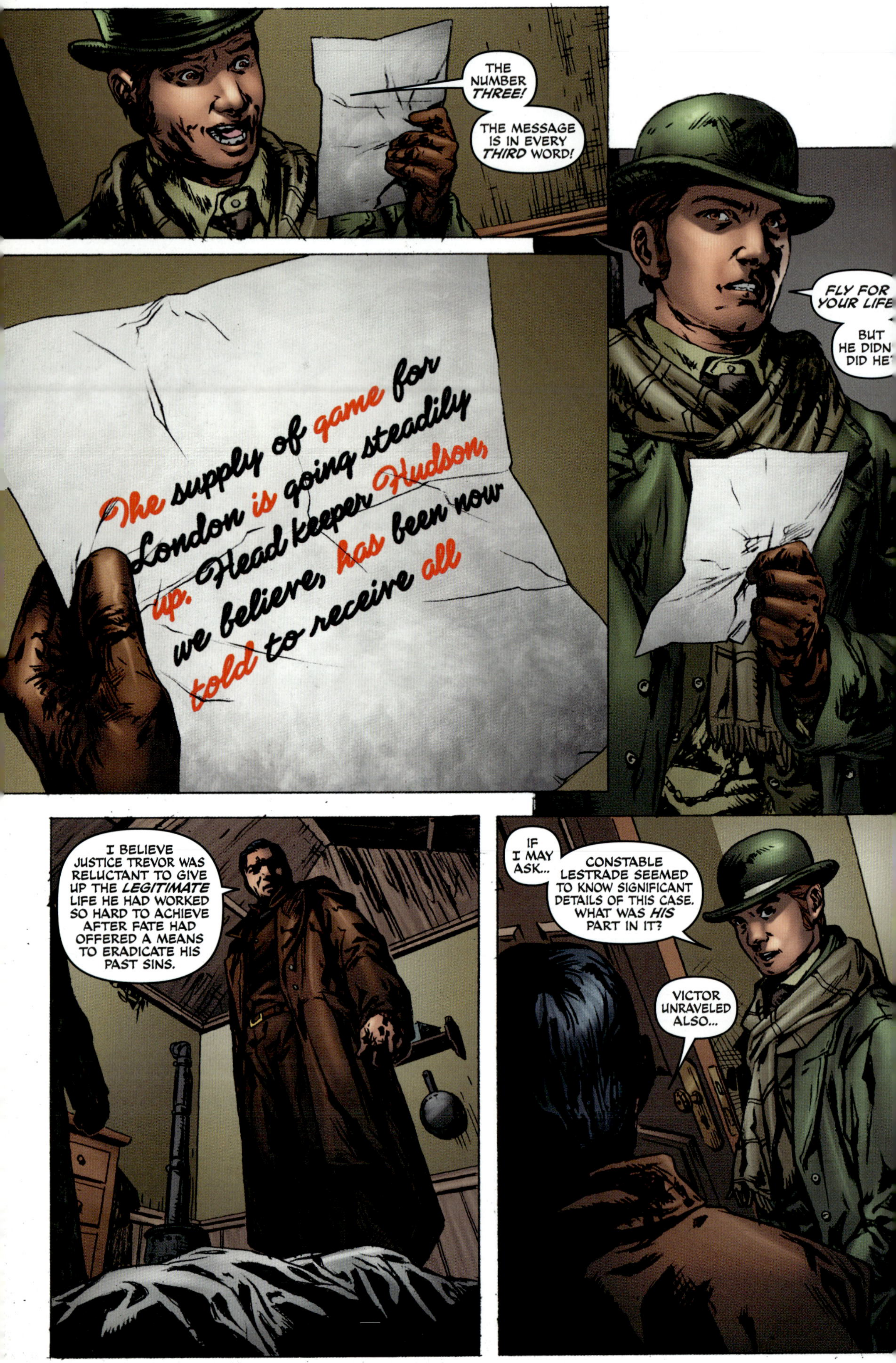
THE NUMBER *THREE!*
THE MESSAGE IS IN EVERY *THIRD* WORD!
The supply of game for London is going steadily up. Head keeper Hudson, we believe, has been now told to receive all
FLY FOR YOUR LIFE
BUT HE DIDN DID HE
I BELIEVE JUSTICE TREVOR WAS RELUCTANT TO GIVE UP THE *LEGITIMATE* LIFE HE HAD WORKED SO HARD TO ACHIEVE AFTER FATE HAD OFFERED A MEANS TO ERADICATE HIS PAST SINS.
IF I MAY ASK...
CONSTABLE LESTRADE SEEMED TO KNOW SIGNIFICANT DETAILS OF THIS CASE. WHAT WAS *HIS* PART IN IT?
VICTOR UNRAVELED ALSO...

"NOT SIMPLY GRIEF...
"JUSTICE TREVOR WAS NOT THE MAN VICTOR KNEW HIM TO BE. AND IN TURN, VICTOR CEASED TO BELIEVE IN HIMSELF."
HUDSON, ARE YOU HERE AMONG THESE DREGS?!
"HE TURNED TO OPIUM TO EASE HIS PAIN, AND HIS THOUGHTS RAN TO REVENGE ON HUDSON, IF ONLY HE COULD FIND HIM. BUT BOTH BEDDOES AND HUDSON DISAPPEARED AS ENTIRELY AS THEY DID FROM THE RECORD OF THE ILL-FATED GLORIA SCOTT."
"FOR MY FRIEND'S PART, I TURNED TO HIGHER AUTHORITIES IN ORDER TO POLICE HIM.
ANSWER ME!
"CONSTABLE LESTRADE PROVED TO BE A DISCREET ALLY, RESPECTED ON BOTH SIDES OF THE LAW."
MY THANKS, CONSTABLE...
IF I'M TO HELP, THEN I EXPECT A FULL ACCOUNTING OF YOUNG MISTER TREVOR'S TROUBLES.
A FAIR TRADE.
WE DID OUR BEST--
DIDN'T WE, IRENE?
BUT THE AFFAIR OF THE GLORIA SCOTT BROKE SOMETHING WITHIN VICTOR THAT COULD NOT BE PUT TO RIGHTS.
WORDS CAN KILL.
I CAN NOW INFORM LESTRADE THAT THIS CASE IS OFFICALLY CLOSED.
A PRINCE HAS FALLEN...

"NOW ALL THAT REMAIN ARE THE CAESARS..."
'EY, BOBBIE!
LOOK SHARP!
HAWKES JEWELLER
GOOD LORD...
INSPECTOR BRATTON!
STAY AWAKE! YOU MUST TELL ME--
WHO DID THIS TO YOU?!
NO ONE...
NOBODY SPECIAL...
A TEACHER

AT UNIVERSITY...
I FELT LIKE A STUDENT IN THE THROES OF RESEARCHING A GHASTLY DISSERTATION.
UNDOUBTEDLY, THE TWELVE CAESARS KILLER HAS READ SEUTONIUS ALSO.
THE MURDERS ECHO EACH CAESAR'S END.
THE PATTERN SOLVED, JUST NOT THE PLANNER.
I'LL ASSUME THAT THE DOOR IS LEFT UNLATCHED AS ALWAYS, SHERLOCK.
HOLMES? A WORD?
YOU HAVE MY SINCEREST CONDOLENCES FOR THE LOSS OF YOUR FRIEND.
BUT I REALLY DO THINK WE MUST PRESS ON WITH OUR DISCUSSIONS OF THE MOTIVES BEHIND THE MADMAN TERRORIZING LONDON.
YOUR PROFESSOR, THE MAN WHO LOANED ME THIS TOME, SEEMED KEEN ON YOUR ABILITIES TO ROOT OUT THE KILLER'S--
MY PROFESSOR?
AIEEEEEEEEE
THE NINTH CAESAR
VITELLIUS
Cui Bono?

IRENE!
TOOK YOU LONG ENOUGH, SHERLOCK...
SO MUCH FOR YOUR VAUNTED DEDUCTIVE PROWESS.
IN THE END, AND IN ALL PRACTICALITY, I HAD TO LEAVE THE MOST *TELLING* CLUE RIGHT AT YOUR DOORSTEP.
I WAS...
I'VE BEEN...
DISTRACTED.
CLUD
THAT'S QUITE ENOUGH!
CEASE THIS VIOLENCE OR I'LL PARSE MY OWN!
AND I ASSURE YOU THAT I'M QUITE THE CRACK SHOT.
ALLOW ME TO CALL YOUR *BLUFF,* DOCTOR WATSON.
PHILOSOPHY IS NOT MY PRIMARY DISCIPLINE.
I FIRST LETTERED IN *MATHEMATICS.*
BUT IT DOESN'T TAKE A SCHOLAR TO SEE THAT YOU AND YOUR SIX-CHAMBERED PISTOL ARE CLEARLY *OUTNUMBERED.*
YOU...
PROFESSOR MORIARTY!

NOW THAT WE'VE DISPENSED WITH INTRODUCTIONS, SHALL WE BEGIN THE DISCOURSE?
ROME'S FAILURE WAS *INEVITABLE.*
THE CAESARS WERE FOOLS AND THE ROMAN MASSES MORESO FOR BLINDLY FOLLOWING THEIR INBRED LOT.
BRITTANIA FACES THE SAME END IF ITS CITIZENRY PERSIST IN SWEARING FEALTY TO ROYAL DUNCES AND THEIR PARLIAMENTARY PAWNS OVER THOSE *MOST* FIT TO RULE...
WHY DO WE FOLLOW THE MOST *POWERFUL* RATHER THAN THE MOST *EDUCATED?*
AND ARE THE TWO MUTUALLY EXCLUSIVE?
HOLMES, WAKE UP--
IT'S IMPOLITE TO NOD OFF DURING A LECTURE.
GIVE ME YOUR FULL ATTENTION--
GOOD V. EVIL
YOU MIGHT LEARN *SOMETHING...*

Year One Issue 6 Cover by Francesco Francavilla

And we have come to the end of a most troubling one at that.

My name is John Hamish Watson, doctor by profession, lately partnered in sleuthing with the young man at far right: Sherlock Holmes. The fair lady betwixt us is Miss Irene Adler, Holmes' fianceé.

As to the identity of the man we now face?

BUT THAT'S NOT THE *END* YOU'VE PLANNED, NOW IS IT?
THE TWELVE CAESARS WAS PRECURSOR TO SOME *GRANDER* STRATEGEM.
PITY THAT YOU *DIDN'T*--
HOLD THAT THOUGHT, MASTER HOLMES...
MISTER HEGGS, MAY I HAVE YOUR ASSISTANCE?
AYE, PROFESSOR.
YOUNG SHERLOCK HOLMES BELIEVES THAT EVIL IS A *LEARNED* BEHAVIOR. AN ACCUMULATION OF SINS LEADING TO A MIXTURE OF MALFEASANCE.
I, ON THE OTHER HAND, HOLD THAT EVIL IS *INHERENT.*
REDUCED TO OUR BASEST ESSENCE, LIKE THIS MOST SLIPPERY OF CHEMICAL ELEMENTS, WE ARE WHO WE ARE FROM *BIRTH.*
DRINK IT.
W-WHY?
TO PROVE A POINT. *ORIGINAL SIN,* AS IT WERE...
I WASN'T *ALWAYS* A BAD MAN, PROFESSOR...

THEN WOULD YOU SAY THAT YOU *LEARNED* TO BE BAD, HEGGS?
W-WELL, IT'S NOT AS IF SOME BLOKE PUT A GUN TO MY--
CLIK CLIK CLIK CLIK CLIK CLIK CLIK CLIK CLIK
THIS IS MADNESS!
SIR, YOU *DON'T* HAVE TO DRINK THAT VILE CONCOCTION!
ACTUALLY, I *DO*...
DRUTHER TAKE MY CHANCES WITH ONE QUICK DRINK THAN MORE BULLETS THAN I CAN COUNT, CHAP.
WE'VE SWORN LOYALTY TO OUR CAESAR.
And the quickest of all...
Quicksilver...

Mercury, one of the rarest elements...
SKISH
Conversely it has been abundantly prescribed in the domain of healers as a cure-all for a panoply of maladies...
Despite its great toxicity...
NOW, WE'LL COME BACK TO HEGGS IN A BIT...
I BELIEVE YOU WERE FORMULATING A *QUESTION*, HOLMES?
I WAS ABOUT TO INQUIRE AS TO YOUR RATIONALE FOR STOPPING AT--
RAISE YOUR HAND, BOY!
SMAK
OH!
GOOD V EVIL

I WOULD, PROFESSOR...
BUT YOU KNOW FULL WELL THAT PRESENT CIRCUMSTANCES PRECLUDE ME FROM HONORING YOUR USUAL CLASSROOM DECORUM...
AH, YES...
I SUPPOSE THIS LESSON WILL FOLLOW A LESS CONVENTIONAL METHOD.
TIME IS SHORT, ESPECIALLY FOR MISTER HEGGS.
MORIARTY, I COULD HELP THAT MAN!
YOU'VE MADE YOUR POINT!
WE'LL ALL CONCEDE THAT YOU ARE THE SMARTEST MAN IN THIS ROOM!
YOU KNOW NOTHING OF ME, DOCTOR WATSON...
WHAT I WANT...
WHAT IS OWED TO ME.

ONE CANNOT PROFESS PHILOSOPHY AS I DID TO SOME SMALL SUCCESS WITHOUT BEING A STUDENT--
NAY, *SCHOLAR* OF HISTORY.
THE TRUE FATE OF DOMITIAN'S ONE AND ONLY SON IS NOT IN SUETONIUS HERE...
"WHAT IF THAT CHILD HAD NOT PERISHED?
"SON OF DOMITIAN, LAST OF THE FLAVIAN CAESARS...
"SLAIN BY A DESCENDANT OF THE VERY FIRST, THE CIRCLE COMPLETE...

"BUT THAT'S THE THING ABOUT *CONSPIRACY THEORIES*...
"RARELY IS THERE ANY END RESEMBLING WHAT ONE MIGHT CONSIDER *CLOSURE*...
"HISTORY REPORTS THAT THE FLAVIAN TYRANTS WERE FOLLOWED BY THE SO-CALLED *'FIVE GOOD EMPERORS'*...
"AND NOT ONE OF THEM FIT TO BE A KING...
"NOT SO THE SON OF DOMITIAN...
"OR HIS SON'S SON AND THEREAFTER, EVER VIGILANT, EVER PATIENT...

"KNOWING FULL WELL WHAT AWAITS THE HEIRS TO THE TWELVE CAESARS..."
MORITURI
MORITURI.
MORITURI
FROM THE LATIN...
FOR THOSE ABOUT TO DIE.
MORITURI
MORIARTY.
FORGOTTEN HEIR TO DOMITIA AND DOMITIAN, SOON TO DOMINATE A NEW ROMAN DYNASTY...
STARTING WITH THIS MOST NORTHERN LAND OF THE ONCE GREAT EMPIRE...
LONDINIUM.
MORITURI

SO THEN IT IS AS YOU BELIEVE...
EVIL *IS* BORN TO IT.
BUT YOU *WON'T* GET AWAY WITH IT.
AND WHY *NOT,* HOLMES?
BECAUSE LIKE ALL YOUR LECTURES--
YOU'RE TOO DAMN LONG-WINDED AND YOU SAY NOTHING OF CONSEQUENCE!

YOU INSOLENT WHELP!
MY BIRTHRIGHT WILL NOT BE DENIED!
PROFESSOR!
MIGHTY CAESAR!
WHAT WILL YOU 'AVE US DO?!
I HAVE GRIPPED LONDON IN FEAR, BOY!
MY ARMY WILL BURN THE CITY TO ITS FOUNDATIONS!
AND THEN I'LL HAVE ANYTHING I DESIRE!
ROME HAD ITS DAY, PROFESSOR.
AND ANY TRULY FORWARD-THINKING DYNASTIC SCHOLAR WOULD ACCEPT THAT THE NEXT GREAT EMPIRE--
IS RISING IN THE FAR EAST!

THE FIRE!
PLAY WITH IT AND YOU GET *BURNED*, YOU TOSSER...
DOCTOR WATSON! WE'RE HELPLESS!
NOT SO MUCH AS YOU MIGHT THINK, MISS ADLER.
I'VE PRACTICED MEDICINE UNDER FULL ARTILLERY.
ANY FORWARD-THINKING SURGEON ALWAYS CARRIES A *BLADE* ON HIS PERSON, OFTEN IN PLACES LEAST SUSPECTED...
SOMEONE SHOOT THE BLOODY LAD!
GOOD v EVIL
SMASH

IT'S NOT THAT BAD...
BUT YOUR BURNS WILL BE CONSIDERABLY WORSE IF WE DON'T DECAMP FROM THESE PREMISES!
NOW, SHERLOCK!
THOSE HELLISH GREEN FLAMES ARE BETWEEN US AND THE ONLY EXIT, HOLMES!
THE ONLY CONVENTIONAL EXIT, DOCTOR...
BUT AS THE PROFESSOR HAS TAUGHT US--
PRESENT CIRCUMSTANCES REQUIRE LESS CONVENTIONAL METHODS IF WE ARE TO ESCAPE!
KRASH
TAKE OUR BONDS. TIE THEM TOGETHER AND LOWER YOURSELVES TO SAFETY.
WARN LESTRADE ABOUT THE GREEK FIRE. THE FLAMES MUST BE SMOTHERED, NOT DOUSED WITH WATER.
AND ONE MORE THING--

MAKE SURE SHE'S SAFE, MISTER WATSON.
THAT GOES WITHOUT SAYING, MISTER HOLMES.
In the heat of battle, I have found minutes stretched into interminable hours...
Time burns the candle at both ends...
For we are all about to die...

Some sooner than others...
GIVE ME THE DAGGER.
IT'S AN HEIRLOOM, YOU UNDERSTAND...
COME AND GET IT.
ANOTHER DAY, DETECTIVE...
ANOTHER DAY!
KRISH
He has few friends, this determined detective...
But perhaps he could use one more.
YOU HEARD HIM, HOLMES.
ANOTHER DAY.

I have watched this detective, and I have watched him some more…
And I must concede that perhaps Sherlock Holmes himself is the most insoluble of mysteries.
221B BAKER STREET
221B BAKER STREET
But I have found new purpose in putting to rest my self-admitted enmity for such enigmas. An "immersion therapy," if you will, designed to face my demons straightaway…
221B
I SAY, WATSON…
I REALLY CAN'T BELIEVE THAT WE'RE MUTUAL ACQUAINTANCES.
I IMAGINE YOU AND YOUR NEW FLAT MATE WILL BURN THE MIDNIGHT OIL WITH ALL SORTS OF SPIRITED DEBATES…
MUST YOU LEAVE SO SOON?
YOU HAVE *YOUR* PROFESSION, SHERLOCK--
AND I HAVE *MINE*.
EVENTUALLY, WE'LL SORT IT OUT.

HOLMES!
WHEN ARE YOU GOING TO BEHAVE AS A PROPER GENTLEMAN AND MARRY THAT GIRL?
I HAVEN'T A *CLUE*, STAMFORD...
AND I HAD NO IDEA THAT WE ALL KNEW ONE ANOTHER!
PERHAPS I SHOULD JOIN YOU IN YOUR LODGINGS AND MAKE IT A TRIO!
THE DOCTOR AND I HAVE FACED *LIFE* AND *DEATH* TOGETHER--
LET'S NOT MAKE IT A *HABIT*, SHALL WE?
I HAVE CERTAIN *STIPULATIONS*, BEGINNING WITH EQUAL CONSIDERATION--
HOLMES!
WATSON!
INSPECTOR LESTRADE.
ENJOYING THE BADGE OF OFFICE SO SOON...
THERE'S BEEN A *MURDER*...

MARK MY WORDS.
WHEN THIS THING IS SOLVED, I'LL WAGER A MONTH'S SALARY THAT A WOMAN NAMED RACHEL WILL BE INVOLVED.
HMM...
POISON?
WITHOUT A DOUBT.
THERE'S NO WOUND UPON THE BODY, YET SPLASHES OF BLOOD ALL ABOUT...
LIVIDITY OF THE CORPSE WOULD INDICATE A MOST RECENT DEMISE. MERE HOURS AGO...
INSPECTOR GREGSON FOUND A WOMAN'S WEDDING RING IN THE FOLDS OF HIS CLOTHES. THIS COMPLICATES MATTERS EVEN MORE...
PERHAPS RATHER IT WILL SIMPLIFY THEM...

In this strange case, (not) the first he solved in my presence (nor the last), Sherlock Holmes performed one of the greatest feats of deduction that henceforth would be known as…

A STUDY IN SCARLET

The Trial of
Sherlock Holmes
issue 1

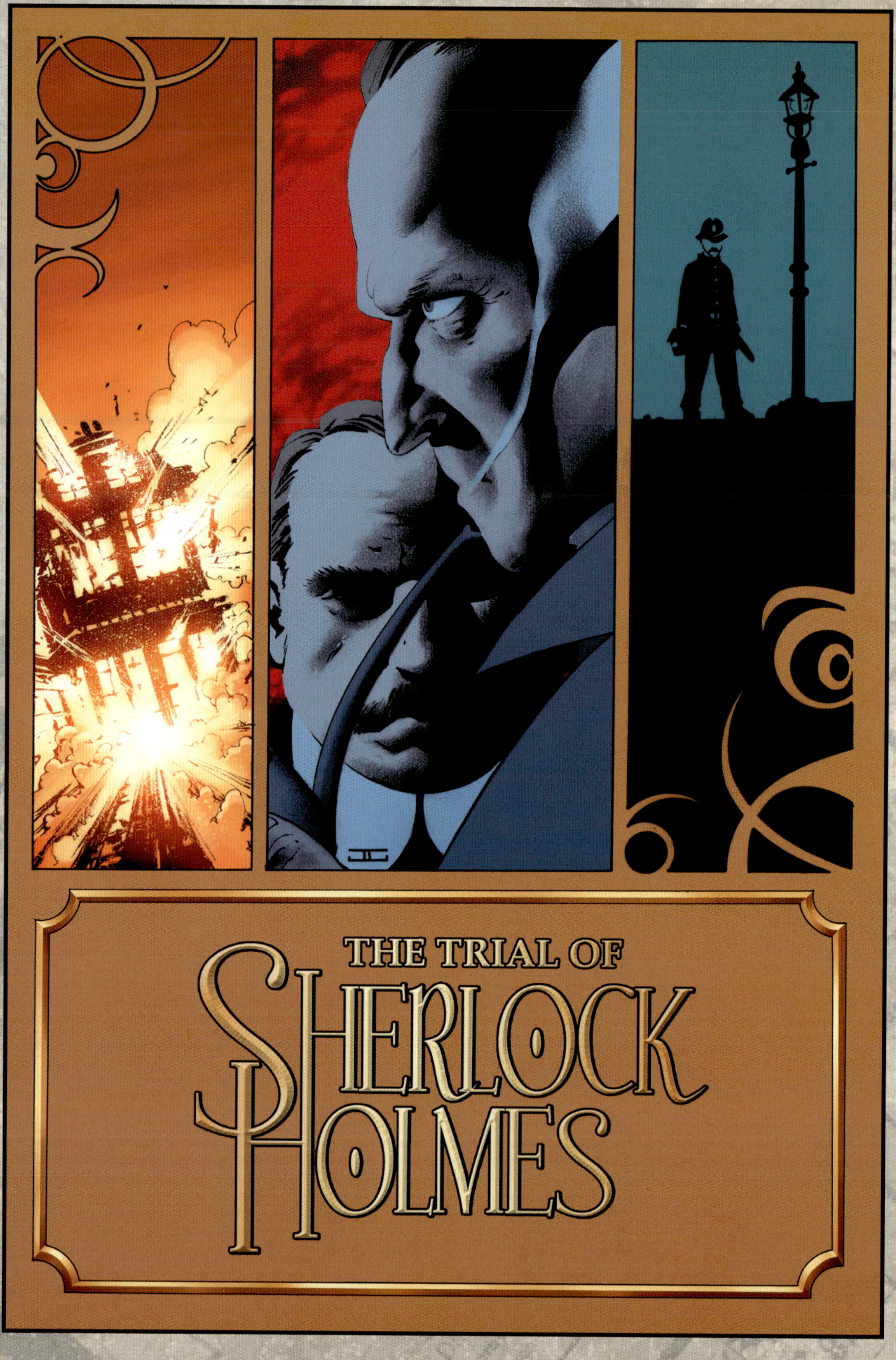

The Trial of Sherlock Holmes Issue 1 Cover by John Cassaday

LONDON'S EAST END, OCTOBER 1895.
CLICK
EH? BLAST!
FORGOT ME BLEEDIN' HAT...

BOOM
GAWD HELP US!
FIRE! FIRE!

Residents of a quarter of the city's East End were waked from their beds in the early hours of yesterday's morning by a considerable explosion.
The detonation occurred at the intersection of Challenger Lane and Doyle's Street, a quantity of explosives having been placed inside a warehouse by persons unknown.
Fortuity and the timely intervention of the local Fire Brigade saw to it that no lives were lost and further destruction of property avoided.
It is however fair to say that a number of residents suffered a dreadful shock to their nerves, some being scorch-ed by the immense heat.
Inspector Bradstreet of Scotland Yard has been charged with the task of tracing those responsible for the extraordinary crime and spoke thusly:
'Though no arrests have yet been made, rest assured that we are doing our utmost to find the culprits and bring them to justice.'

HERE WE ARE SIR, BAKER STREET.
WHOA THERE!
AH, DOMUS DULCIS DOMUS.
EXPLOSION!!!
221
DINGADINGDING

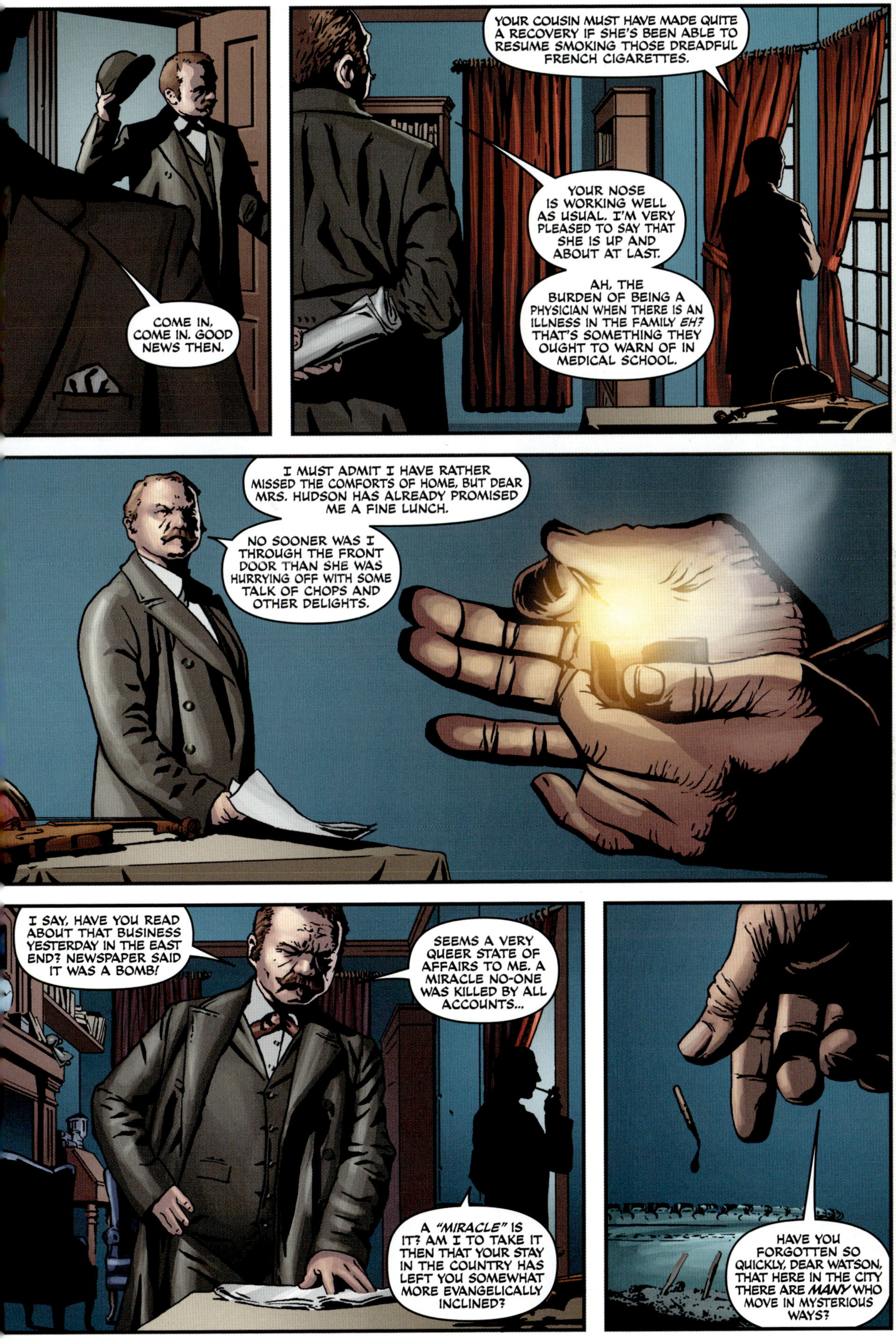
COME IN, COME IN. GOOD NEWS THEN.
YOUR COUSIN MUST HAVE MADE QUITE A RECOVERY IF SHE'S BEEN ABLE TO RESUME SMOKING THOSE DREADFUL FRENCH CIGARETTES.
YOUR NOSE IS WORKING WELL AS USUAL. I'M VERY PLEASED TO SAY THAT SHE IS UP AND ABOUT AT LAST.
AH, THE BURDEN OF BEING A PHYSICIAN WHEN THERE IS AN ILLNESS IN THE FAMILY *EH?* THAT'S SOMETHING THEY OUGHT TO WARN OF IN MEDICAL SCHOOL.
I MUST ADMIT I HAVE RATHER MISSED THE COMFORTS OF HOME, BUT DEAR MRS. HUDSON HAS ALREADY PROMISED ME A FINE LUNCH.
NO SOONER WAS I THROUGH THE FRONT DOOR THAN SHE WAS HURRYING OFF WITH SOME TALK OF CHOPS AND OTHER DELIGHTS.
I SAY, HAVE YOU READ ABOUT THAT BUSINESS YESTERDAY IN THE EAST END? NEWSPAPER SAID IT WAS A BOMB!
SEEMS A VERY QUEER STATE OF AFFAIRS TO ME. A MIRACLE NO-ONE WAS KILLED BY ALL ACCOUNTS...
A *"MIRACLE"* IS IT? AM I TO TAKE IT THEN THAT YOUR STAY IN THE COUNTRY HAS LEFT YOU SOMEWHAT MORE EVANGELICALLY INCLINED?
HAVE YOU FORGOTTEN SO QUICKLY, DEAR WATSON, THAT HERE IN THE CITY THERE ARE ***MANY*** WHO MOVE IN MYSTERIOUS WAYS?

NO DOUBT YOU HAVE ALSO READ RECENTLY OF THE IMPENDING VISIT OF *BARON ALBRECHT LOTHAIR*, ONE-TIME FAVOURITE GODSON OF THE LATE *PRINCE CONSORT*.
WHILE YOU WERE AWAY I RECEIVED WORD FROM BARON LOTHAIR HIMSELF REQUESTING THAT HE MIGHT CALL UPON US DURING HIS TRIP.
I SAY, HOLMES, HE ISN'T PROPOSING TO ENGAGE YOUR SERVICES IS HE? I DON'T KNOW IF YOU OUGHT TO GET INVOLVED IN ALL THAT BUSINESS.

THE NEWSPAPERS MERELY DREDGED UP THAT BUSINESS OF MORE THAN TWENTY YEARS AGO FOR FEAR OF RUNNING OUT OF THINGS TO WRITE ABOUT LOTHAIR'S VISIT.
THE PRESS ONLY REPORT UPON INCIDENTS THAT HAVE ALREADY OCCURRED, AND EVEN THEN THEY MANAGE TO MUDDY THE FACTS WITH OPINION AND SENSATIONALISM.
BARON LOTHAIR WISHES ONLY TO CALL UPON US AS AN ADMIRER OF OUR WORK. A FACT WHICH SEEMED TO RATHER AMUSE MY BROTHER...
THANK YOU FOR YOUR CONCERN DOCTOR, YOU HAVE ILLUSTRATED MY POINT PERFECTLY.

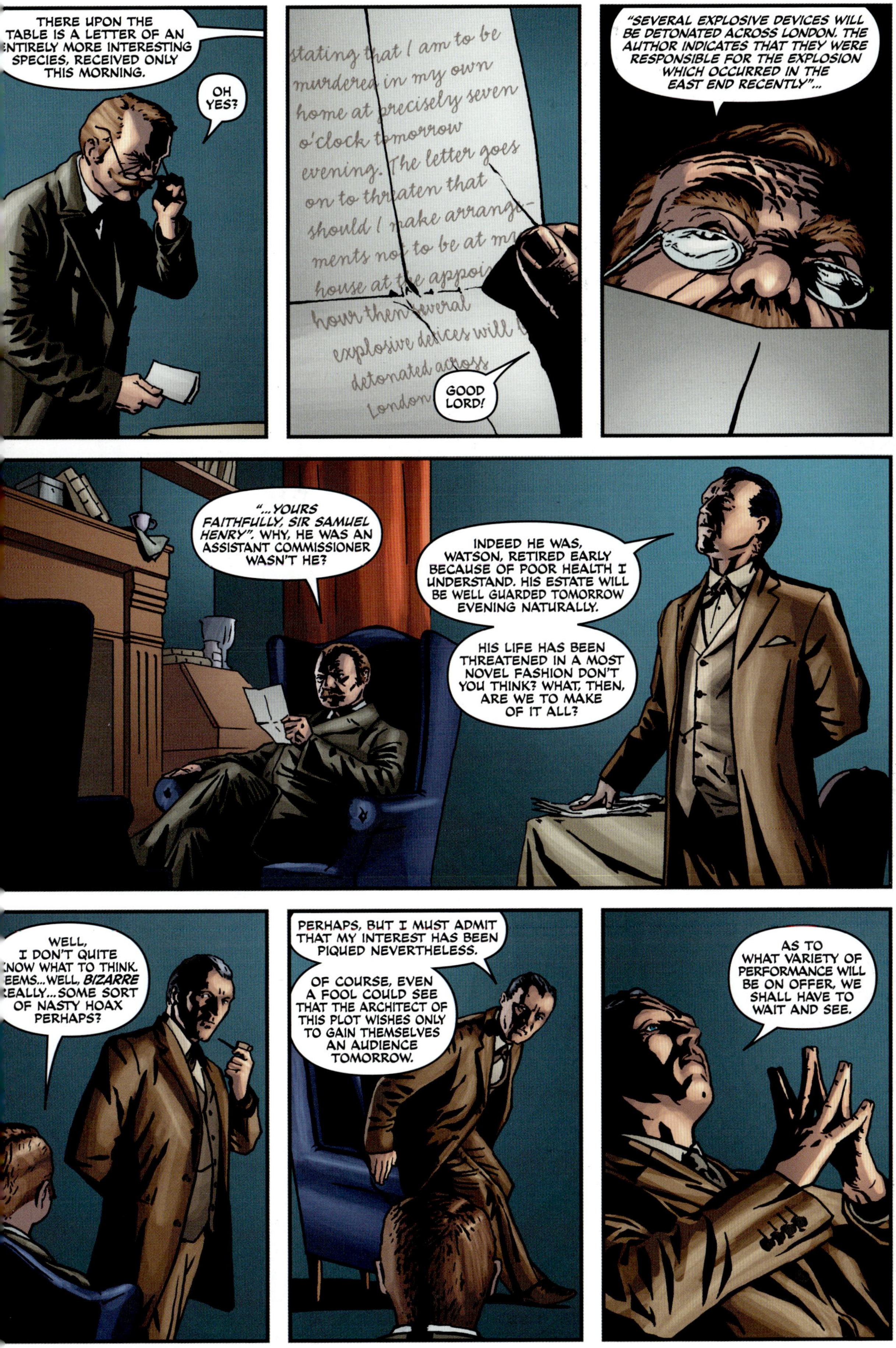
THERE UPON THE TABLE IS A LETTER OF AN ENTIRELY MORE INTERESTING SPECIES, RECEIVED ONLY THIS MORNING.
OH YES?
stating that I am to be murdered in my own home at precisely seven o'clock tomorrow evening. The letter goes on to threaten that should I make arrange-ments not to be at my house at the appoi hour then several explosive devices will b detonated across London
GOOD LORD!
"SEVERAL EXPLOSIVE DEVICES WILL BE DETONATED ACROSS LONDON. THE AUTHOR INDICATES THAT THEY WERE RESPONSIBLE FOR THE EXPLOSION WHICH OCCURRED IN THE EAST END RECENTLY"...
"...YOURS FAITHFULLY, SIR SAMUEL HENRY". WHY, HE WAS AN ASSISTANT COMMISSIONER WASN'T HE?
INDEED HE WAS, WATSON, RETIRED EARLY BECAUSE OF POOR HEALTH I UNDERSTAND. HIS ESTATE WILL BE WELL GUARDED TOMORROW EVENING NATURALLY.
HIS LIFE HAS BEEN THREATENED IN A MOST NOVEL FASHION DON'T YOU THINK? WHAT, THEN, ARE WE TO MAKE OF IT ALL?
WELL, I DON'T QUITE KNOW WHAT TO THINK. EEMS...WELL, *BIZARRE* EALLY...SOME SORT OF NASTY HOAX PERHAPS?
PERHAPS, BUT I MUST ADMIT THAT MY INTEREST HAS BEEN PIQUED NEVERTHELESS.
OF COURSE, EVEN A FOOL COULD SEE THAT THE ARCHITECT OF THIS PLOT WISHES ONLY TO GAIN THEMSELVES AN AUDIENCE TOMORROW.
AS TO WHAT VARIETY OF PERFORMANCE WILL BE ON OFFER, WE SHALL HAVE TO WAIT AND SEE.

SHOOTER'S HILL, SOUTHEAST LONDON, THE FOLLOWING EVENING.
I BELIEVE THIS IS THE PLACE.
DRIVER! STOP HERE PLEASE!
OFFICER, I TAKE IT THEN THAT THIS IS THE HOME OF SIR SAMUEL HENRY?
I AM NOT AT LIBERTY TO REVEAL THAT INFORMATION SIR.
AHA, I SHALL TAKE THAT AS A "YES" THEN.
NOW HANG ON A MINUTE... OH!

M-MY APOLOGIES SIR, I DIDN'T REALISE...
THINK NOTHING OF IT MY GOOD MAN.
HOLMES! GOOD TO SEE YOU. CUTTING IT A BIT FINE AREN'T YOU?
AH LESTRADE. YES, I'M AFRAID WE HAD SOME TROUBLE IN FINDING THE HOUSE.
IT IS A BIT OFF THE BEATEN PATH, I'LL GRANT YOU.
I ASSUME YOU KNOW THAT SIR HENRY IS SUFFERING WITH CONSUMPTION?
IT'S A MALICIOUS THING INDEED TO THREATEN A MAN SO CLOSE TO DEATH'S DOOR ALREADY, DON'T YOU THINK?
WELL, I QUITE UNDERSTAND WHY YOU'RE TAKING IT ALL VERY SERIOUSLY BUT...
LESTRADE! GOOD TO SEE YOU OLD MAN! ARE YOU KEEPING WELL?
DOING MY BEST, DOCTOR, DOING MY BEST.
INDEED, HOLMES, THIS WHOLE BUSINESS IS BEING TAKEN VERY SERIOUSLY. SIR HENRY IS STILL VERY WELL CONNECTED AND MUCH RESPECTED WITHIN THE FORCE.
PERHAPS WE SHOULD ADJOURN TO THE SITTING-ROOM BEFORE YOU START EXPOUNDING ANY DEFAMATORY THEORIES, YES?
MY DEAR FELLOW, AM I NOT ALWAYS THE VERY MODEL OF DISCRETION?
COME ALONG DOCTOR.
MAGNIFICENT TIMEPIECE...

HAVING BEEN AN ASSISTANT COMMISSIONER, SIR HENRY WOULD NATURALLY HAVE MADE ENEMIES.
OF COURSE, BUT WE'VE COME ACROSS NO *LIKELY* SUSPECTS.
IN MY EXPERIENCE IT IS SELDOM THE LIKELY SUSPECTS WHOM ONE SHOULD SUSPECT.
INSPECTOR, WHO IS THIS MAN? DIDN'T I TELL YOU THAT NO-ONE WAS TO SMOKE IN THIS HOUSE?
MRS. GAMMAGE, THIS IS MY GOOD FRIEND MR. SHERLOCK HOLMES. HE HAS KINDLY OFFERED TO HELP US WITH SIR HENRY'S... SITUATION.
MR. HOLMES IS IT? I RECKON AS I'VE HEARD YOUR NAME ALRIGHT.
STILL, I WON'T HAVE ANYONE LIGHT A PIPE IN THIS HOUSE. I'VE CARED FOR SIR HENRY LONG ENOUGH TO KNOW THAT SMOKE SETS HIM COUGHING.
MY APOLOGIES MADAM. YOU ARE SIR HENRY'S HOUSEKEEPER I TAKE IT?
I LOOK AFTER HIM, YES.
WELL THEN, YOU MAY REST ASSURED THAT WE ARE ALL DOING OUR BEST FOR HIM TODAY.
AHEM. QUITE A STRONG WILLED WOMAN THAT ONE?
INDEED, SHE'S HAD OUR BOYS TIPTOEING ROUND THE HOUSE ALL AFTERNOON.
NOW THEN, WITH REFERENCE TO SIR HENRY'S LETTER.
EARLIER THIS AFTERNOON AN ASSOCIAT OF MINE SUGGESTED I SHOULD CALL IN AT THE OFFICES OF THE COME NEWSPAPER...

"TURNS OUT THE EDITOR THERE HAD RECEIVED AN INTERESTING PIECE OF CORRESPONDENCE, ADDRESSED SIMPLY TO 'THE BOSS'.
"THE MEMO MADE REFERENCE TO THE DOYLE'S STREET EXPLOSION, AND AGAIN THREATENED FURTHER ACTION.
"HOWEVER, THIS LETTER MADE NO MENTION OF SIR HENRY.
Dear "Boss", Doyle's Street was the last warning. Baron Lothair is not welcome here. Almani-Lotharingen belongs to the French and Britannia had better remember whose side she is on, or next time will be the worse for everyone.
"IT WAS SOME NONSENSE ABOUT LOTHAIR, ALMANI-LOTHARINGEN AND ALL THAT BUSINESS IN THE PAPERS.
"THE CHAP THERE SEEMED QUITE DISAPPOINTED WHEN I SUGGESTED THAT HE SHOULDN'T PRINT THE LETTER AND CONFISCATED IT."
SAME AUTHOR AS SIR HENRY'S LETTER?
NOT A CHANCE. HIS WAS TYPED, THIS WAS A MESS. MIGHT AS WELL HAVE SIGNED IT "SAUCY JACKY." BLOODY HOAXERS.
AND WAS ANYONE THREATENED?
NOT SPECIFICALLY. JUST "BRITANNIA SHOULD REMEMBER WHOSE SIDE SHE IS ON."
EVERY CRACKPOT WILL BE CLAIMING RESPONSIBILITY FOR THE EXPLOSIONS, LOOKING TO PUT MORE WEIGHT BEHIND THEIR OWN GRIPES.
I HAD IT PASSED ON TO BRADSTREET ANYWAY. IT'S HIS CASE, NOT MINE.

TONIGHT, OF COURSE, I'LL BE GLAD IF WE'RE WASTING OUR TIME, UNDER THE CIRCUMSTANCES.
I THINK WE CAN ALL AGREE ON THAT INSPECTOR.
NOTHING WOULD PLEASE ME MORE THAN HAVING SIR HENRY'S SAFETY ASSURED, HOWEVER THIS SITUATION HAS ARISEN AT RATHER AN AWKWARD TIME.
AH, DETECTIVE INSPECTOR DAVIS SIR, I WAS JUST FILLING MR. HOLMES AND DR. WATSON IN ON A FEW DETAILS.
VERY PLEASED TO MEET YOU, DETECTIVE INSPECTOR. I BELIEVE I READ OF YOUR INVOLVEMENT IN THAT ANARCHIST MEUNIER'S ARREST A FEW YEARS AGO.
AND I, OF COURSE, HAVE READ OF YOUR EXPLOITS MR. HOLMES.
SPECIAL BRANCH IS TAKING THE THREAT OF MORE EXPLOSIONS SERIOUSLY THEN, FOR THEM TO GRACE US WITH YOUR COMPANY?

WELL, IT CERTAINLY WOULDN'T DO TO TAKE SUCH THREATS LIGHTLY.
HOWEVER, MY COLLEAGUES AND I NO LONGER EXCLUSIVELY DEAL WITH BOMBS, ANARCHISTS AND THE IRISH.
INDEED, THOUGH SIR HENRY IS SCARCELY *ROYALTY,* WHOM I BELIEVE ARE YOUR *OTHER* PRIMARY CONCERN.
YOU ARE CORRECT OF COURSE, I DO HAVE OTHER BUSINESS TO ATTEND TO ONCE THIS MATTER HAS BEEN DEALT WITH.
"CONFIDENTIALLY...
"THIS MORNING I WELCOMED BARON ALBRECHT LOTHAIR AND HIS PARTY ONTO BRITISH SOIL. PUBLICLY OF COURSE HE IS NOT EXPECTED UNTIL NEXT WEEK.
"MYSELF AND INSPECTOR LESTRADE SHALL BE IN CHARGE OF SECURITY FOR THE DURATION OF THE BARON'S VISIT."
LESTRADE? BUT...
BONG
DING DING DING DING DING
CHANG
BLESS ME! A QUARTER TO SEVEN ALREADY.
BONG BANG BONG
TING TANG TING TONG
YES, QUITE... *ASTOUNDING* ISN'T IT?
EVIDENTLY SIR HENRY'S PROXIMITY TO THE MERIDIAN HAS PROMPTED SOMETHING OF A FASCINATION FOR TIME KEEPING.

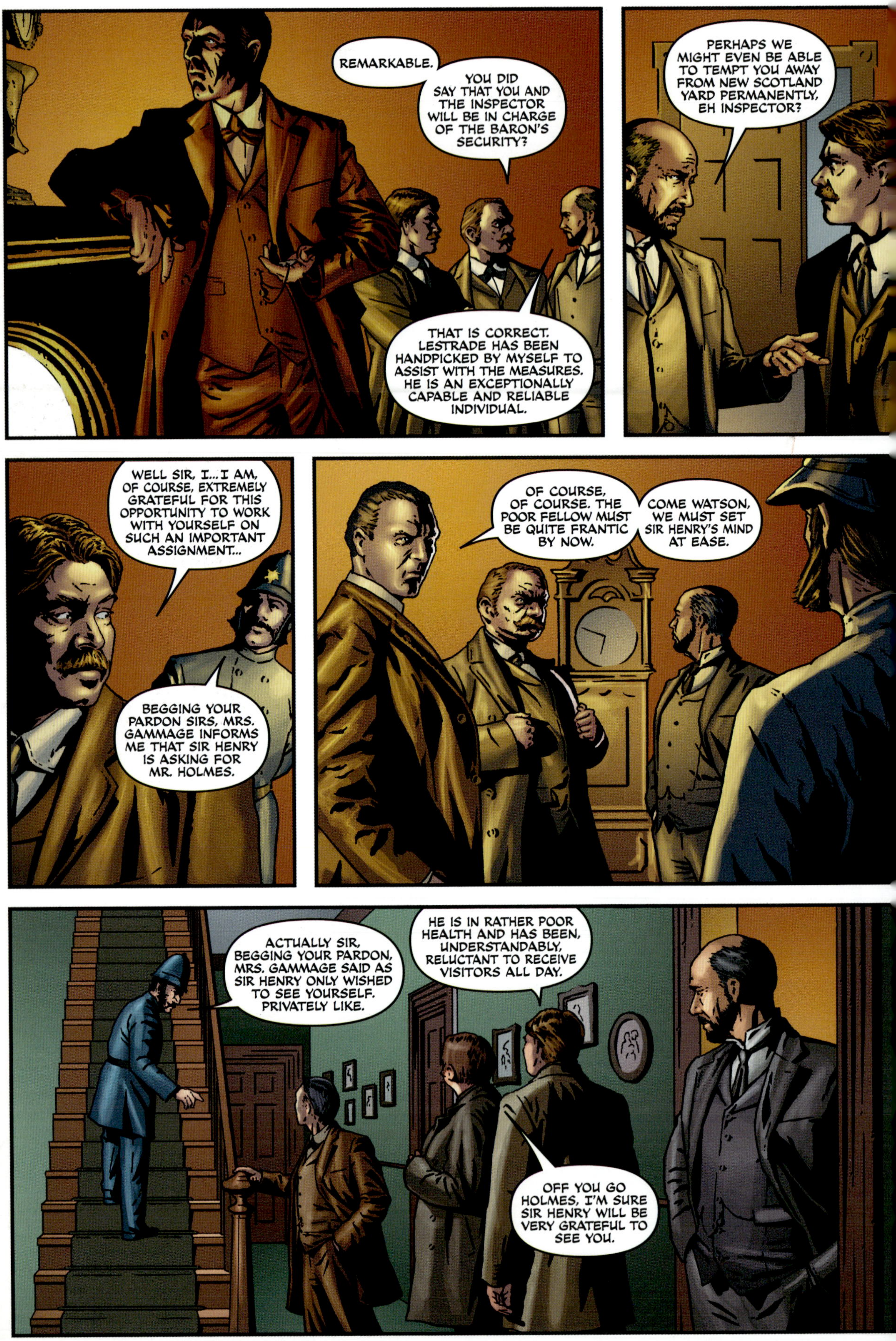
REMARKABLE.
YOU DID SAY THAT YOU AND THE INSPECTOR WILL BE IN CHARGE OF THE BARON'S SECURITY?
THAT IS CORRECT. LESTRADE HAS BEEN HANDPICKED BY MYSELF TO ASSIST WITH THE MEASURES. HE IS AN EXCEPTIONALLY CAPABLE AND RELIABLE INDIVIDUAL.
PERHAPS WE MIGHT EVEN BE ABLE TO TEMPT YOU AWAY FROM NEW SCOTLAND YARD PERMANENTLY, EH INSPECTOR?
WELL SIR, I...I AM, OF COURSE, EXTREMELY GRATEFUL FOR THIS OPPORTUNITY TO WORK WITH YOURSELF ON SUCH AN IMPORTANT ASSIGNMENT...
BEGGING YOUR PARDON SIRS, MRS. GAMMAGE INFORMS ME THAT SIR HENRY IS ASKING FOR MR. HOLMES.
OF COURSE, OF COURSE. THE POOR FELLOW MUST BE QUITE FRANTIC BY NOW.
COME WATSON, WE MUST SET SIR HENRY'S MIND AT EASE.
ACTUALLY SIR, BEGGING YOUR PARDON, MRS. GAMMAGE SAID AS SIR HENRY ONLY WISHED TO SEE YOURSELF. PRIVATELY LIKE.
HE IS IN RATHER POOR HEALTH AND HAS BEEN, UNDERSTANDABLY, RELUCTANT TO RECEIVE VISITORS ALL DAY.
OFF YOU GO HOLMES, I'M SURE SIR HENRY WILL BE VERY GRATEFUL TO SEE YOU.

AT LEAST THIS WILL ALL BE OVER SOON, THERE'S LITTLE CHANCE OF ANY SHADY CHARACTERS GETTING IN HERE TONIGHT.
ABSOLUTELY, AND WITH THE WORLD'S GREATEST DETECTIVE WATCHING OVER HIM, SIR HENRY COULD SCARCELY BE IN SAFER HANDS.
THIS WAY SIR.
THANK YOU OFFICER, I'M SURE I CAN FIND MY WAY FROM HERE.
YOU HAD BETTER GET BACK TO PATROLLING THE HOUSE EH?
VERY GOOD SIR.
KNOCK KNOCK
COME IN MR. HOLMES. RIGHT ON TIME.

LOOK ALIVE OFFICER! YOU'VE STILL GOT AT LEAST *TEN MINUTES* BEFORE YOU CAN RELAX.
YOU TELL HIM TO WIPE HIS BOOTS BEFORE HE COMES BACK IN HERE AS WELL!
ALL OFFICERS, STAY ALERT NOW.
ANY SIGN OF ANYTHING SUSPICIOUS, YOU BLOW YOUR WHISTLE IMMEDIATELY.
EVERYTHING SEEMS QUIET AND IN ORDER.
I SAY LESTRADE, VERY SAD BUSINESS ABOUT SIR HENRY'S HEALTH. I TAKE IT THIS IS HIS WIFE AND DAUGHTER?
CONSUMPTION IS SUCH A CRUEL DISEASE, THE WAY IT CAN SWEEP THROUGH A FAMILY. PEOPLE USED TO BELIEVE IT WAS A KIND OF CURSE YOU KNOW.
EVEN WITH MY TRAINING, IT'S EASY TO SEE HOW PEOPLE COULD BELIEVE SUCH THINGS...TERRIBLE THING REALLY...

TELL ME, WHEN DID HIS DAUGHTER...
I BELIEVE THAT SHE IS ALIVE DOCTOR. CONVALESCING ABROAD SOMEWHERE EVIDENTLY.
OH GOOD, I AM PLEASED. I HAVE READ THAT THE SICKNESS CAN BE SLOWED CONSIDERABLY GIVEN...
BANG
BLIMEY!
WHAT THE...?
GET A MOVE ON, MAN! GO!

BONG
DING DING DING DING DING
CHANG BONG
CLANG
TINGTANGTINGTON
BONG
CHANG

SIR HENRY? SIR HENRY CAN YOU HEAR ME SIR? ARE YOU INJURED?
HOLMES? HOLMES?!
PERHAPS THE SHOT CAME FROM OUTSIDE? A MARKSMAN AT THE WINDOW, LIKE MORAN LAST YEAR?
GET THAT BLOODY DOOR OPEN!
WHAK!

I... I DIDN'T... I DIDN'T KNOW WHAT TO DO...

HE'S DEAD...
HOLMES? YOUR PISTOL HOLMES, GIVE IT TO ME.
YES. YES, YOU TAKE IT LESTRADE...YOU TAKE IT.
LOOK HERE! LOOKS LIKE HE'S BEEN TRYING TO BURN SOMETHING.
LOCKED SIR, NO SIGN OF ANY FORCED ENTRY.
HOLMES? WHAT HAVE YOU DONE? WHY?
WATSON, I DIDN'T... I... IT ALL HAPPENED SO FAST... I... I DIDN'T KNOW HOW TO STOP HIM.

The Trial of Sherlock Holmes Issue 2 Cover by John Cassaday

NEW SCOTLAND YARD, MORNING.
"...MUST SURELY CONCUR THAT IF THEY WERE SEEN HERE TODAY THE YARD WOULD BE WIDE OPEN TO CRITICISM.
"THESE ARE EXCEPTIONAL CIRCUMSTANCES.
"SHERLOCK HOLMES STANDS ACCUSED OF MURDER, GENTLEMEN, AND THAT MEANS THAT NO-ONE IS ABOVE SUSPICION"
SIR BRADFORD, HOLMES IS *NOT* GUILTY. IT IS SIMPLY *IMPOSSIBLE!* YOU MUST KNOW THAT.
THE IDEA THAT LESTRADE AND I SHOULD BE FORBAD FROM *PROVING* THAT FACT...THAT I SHOULD BE PREVENTED FROM BEING HERE...IT'S JUST *OUTRAGEOUS!*
OUTRAGE IS WHAT I AM TRYING TO PREVENT DOCTOR.
I'M AFRAID DETECTIVE INSPECTOR DAVIS IS RIGHT, WATSON. THINGS DO NOT LOOK GOOD.
IF THIS DOES GO BADLY, YOU MUST REALISE THAT YOU TOO WILL UNDOUBTEDLY FALL UNDER SUSPICION.
LET SCOTLAND YARD DEAL WITH IT. KEEP YOUR DISTANCE FROM THE CASE AND FROM EACH OTHER. *YOU* MAY CONSIDER THAT AN ORDER, INSPECTOR.
SIR, WITH ALL DUE RESPECT, THIS IS *PREPOSTEROUS.*
THERE *MUST* BE AN EXPLANATION. IF I COULD JUST SPEAK WITH...
HAVE YOU NOT BEEN LISTENING INSPECTOR?
THIS IS NOT A CASE THAT MIGHT BE EXPLAINED AWAY AS A MERE MISUNDERSTANDING. THERE IS *EVIDENCE* OF A MOST COMPELLING NATURE.

"SIR SAMUEL HENRY, FORMER ASSISTANT COMMISSIONER OF THE METROPOLITAN POLICE, WROTE TO HOLMES, REQUESTING HIS PRESENCE ON THE FOLLOWING NIGHT."
SIR HENRY HAD RECEIVED AN ANONYMOUS, TYPED NOTE CONTAINING THE EXACT TIME AND LOCATION OF AN ASSASSINATION.
DISTURBINGLY, THE ASSASSINATION WAS HIS OWN.
"HE ALSO INFORMED SCOTLAND YARD.
"AS THE NOTE MADE MENTION OF THE DOYLE ST. BOMB, WE TOOK IT VERY SERIOUSLY INDEED..."
WE HAD HALF A SQUAD KEEPING WATCH IN THAT HOUSE. HALF A SQUAD OF MY BEST MEN.
"WHEN SEVEN O'CLOCK, THE STIPULATED HOUR, APPROACHED, SIR HENRY SUMMONED HOLMES.
"THE TWO WERE ALONE IN A LOCKED ROOM WHEN THE TIME CAME."
A GUNSHOT WAS HEARD FROM SIR HENRY'S ROOM.
"BY THE TIME WE BROKE INTO THE ROOM HE WAS ALREADY DEAD.
"MURDERED IN COLD BLOOD."
SHERLOCK HOLMES STOOD AT THE FOOT OF THE BED, A SMOKING PISTOL IN HIS HAND.
ALL RATHER LIKE ONE OF YOUR HISTRIONIC STRAND MAGAZINE STORIES IF YOU'LL FORGIVE MY SAYING SO DOCTOR.
THESE HOWEVER, ARE QUITE WITHOUT PRECEDENT.

THESE ARE THE PAPERS FOUND AT THE SCENE?
INDEED THEY ARE.
A FEW MOMENTS MORE AND THEY WOULD HAVE BEEN TOO BADLY BURNED TO DECIPHER.
WE MUST ASSUME THAT SIR HENRY COMPILED THE DOSSIER HIMSELF AS, SO FAR AS WE KNOW, NO ONE ELSE KNEW OF ITS EXISTENCE.
NO ONE EXCEPT FOR HOLMES THAT IS...
I HAVE HAD ENOUGH OF YOUR INNUENDOS SIR!
IF YOU HAVE SOMETHING TO SAY, THEN BY ALL MEANS COME OUT AND SAY IT AT ONCE!
AS YOU WISH DOCTOR.
PUT QUITE SIMPLY, IT IS THE CASE FILE OF THE INDIVIDUAL WHO, THANKS TO YOUR WRITINGS, THE WORLD KNOWS AS *"MORIARTY"*.
BUT *THIS* IS NO FICTION.
THESE DOCUMENTS SUGGEST THAT SHERLOCK HOLMES HAS LED A DOUBLE LIFE.
WHEN HE SPOKE OF A CRIMINAL GENIUS RIGHT HERE IN LONDON, HIDDEN IN PLAIN SIGHT...
...HE REFERRED TO HIMSELF.
"IT IS MY BELIEF THAT SIR HENRY FABRICATED THE THREAT UPON HIS OWN LIFE.
"HE ENGINEERED A SITUATION FROM WHICH HOLMES COULD NOT ESCAPE, AND THEN CONFRONTED HIM WITH HIS EVIDENCE.
"THE POOR FELLOW MUST HAVE EXPECTED HOLMES TO SURRENDER..."

CHANNEL ROW POLICE STATION.
MR. HO... UHM... SIR?
A MRS. HUDSON HAS JUST CALLED IN SIR. SAID SHE WAS YOUR LANDLADY?
THAT IS SO.
SHE BROUGHT THIS IN FOR YOU SIR. SERGEANT SAID HE COULDN'T SEE NO HARM IN IT, BUT WE DID HAVE TO CUT IT UP LIKE.
I TRUST YOU FOUND NO LOCK PICK NOR RASP FILE INSIDE? MRS. HUDSON IS A DISCRIMINATING COOK.
I'M SURPRISED THE SERGEANT RESISTED THE URGE TO TASTE A PIECE.
I EXPECT THAT YOU WOULD PREFER A TIDDY OGGY, YES?
WELL, YES... BUT HOW IN HEAVEN...?
AH, THERE'S STILL JUST A TOUCH OF CORNISH IN YOUR ACCENT. MARVELLOUS PLACE FOR A BOY TO GROW UP.
I SAY, HOW IS THAT OLD FELLOW NEXT DOOR? HE WAS MAKING QUITE A ROW LAST NIGHT.
OH HE'LL BE FINE SIR, I EXPECT HE'LL HAVE SLEPT OFF THE WORST OF THE DRINK BY NOW.
I'D BEST SEE TO HIM...
OF COURSE, DON'T LET ME KEEP YOU. GOOD-BYE.
YES, ERM, GOOD-BYE SIR.

KLIK
ARE YOU AWAKE IN THERE?
COME ON NOW, ON YOUR FEET.
WHASSAT?
'ERE, LEAVE ME BE EH BOSS? LEAVE ME BE A WHILE.
THIS AIN'T NO DOSS-HOUSE OLD FELLER. IT'S TIME YOU WERE ON YOUR WAY.
YOU'D DO WELL TO CAGG A DAY OR TWO.
HA! CAGG HE SAYS! CAGG!
AH YES, MR. MERRYN.
I TRUST OUR GUEST WAS PLEASED WITH HIS BREAKFAST.
NOTICE
WANTE
SEEMED SO, YES SIR.
YOU GOT RID OF *HER* THEN?

I ASSURE YOU MADAM THAT WE WILL INFORM YOU OF ANY DEVELOPMENTS BUT, AS THE INSPECTOR SAID, WE MUST ADHERE TO OUR ORDERS.
RIDICULOUS! THE WHOLE THING IS A SCANDAL SIR A SCANDAL!
YOU'LL BE LUCKY IF YOU DON'T FIND A MOB AT YOUR DOOR BEFORE THE DAY'S END. PEOPLE ARE NOT GOING TO STAND FOR THIS!
GOOD LORD! MRS. HUDSON?
DOCTOR? HAVE YOU COME TO SEE HIM TOO?
THEY WOULDN'T LET ME EVEN SPEAK WITH HIM. CAN YOU BELIEVE THAT?
MRS. HUDSON, YOU SHOULDN'T BE HERE...
COME ALONG, WE'LL TAKE A CAB BACK TO BAKER STREET.

...A THREAT TO THE REPUTATION OF THE FORCE.
NOT AT ALL INSPECTOR, ON THE CONTRARY IN FACT.
ASSISTING MYSELF WITH SECURITY DURING BARON LOTHAIR'S VISIT DEMONSTRATES THAT YOU ARE A COMPETENT AND TRUSTWORTHY OFFICER WHOSE ASSOCIATION WITH HOLMES IS... INCIDENTAL.
BEGGING YOUR PARDON SIR, BUT IF THAT IS THE CASE, WHY SHOULD I NOT BE ALLOWED TO SPEAK WITH HOLMES?
INSPECTOR LESTRADE, THESE ARE MOST UNPLEASANT CIRCUMSTANCES FOR ALL INVOLVED BUT I THINK IT WOULD BE BEST IF WE CONCENTRATED UPON THE JOB IN HAND.
PLEASE DO NOT MENTION HOLMES IN MY PRESENCE AGAIN. HIS CASE IS NOT YOUR CONCERN. DO YOU UNDERSTAND?
YES SIR. AS YOU WISH SIR.
GOOD. GOOD.
NOW THEN, WE MUST GET STARTED. WE HAVE A LONG DAY AHEAD OF US.

BUCKINGHAM PALACE, LATE EVENING.
...I WAS SURE IT WAS LORD CROSS BUT I SUPPOSE IT COULD HAVE BEEN GODALMING...
...GAVE A TRULY MAGNIFICENT PERFORMANCE AT ASCOT...
...I SHOULD IMAGINE THEY WOULD BE ONLY TOO DELIGHTED TO SHOW YOU ROUND...
...BY A FELLOW CALLED WELLS IN THE NEW REVIEW...
...A GOOD DEAL MORE REMOTE THAN WE ARE USED TO...
...THIS WAS MANY YEARS AGO YOU UNDERSTAND, BEFORE YOUR TIME, OBVIOUSLY...
...VERY ENJOYABLE DAY, I MUST SAY.

THERE IS SO MUCH I WISH TO DO UND SEE DURING MY VISIT HERE, I CONFESS I HARDLY KNOW WHERE TO BEGIN.
I INTEND TO SEE SAINT PAUL'S CATHEDRAL, WESTMINSTER, THE TOWER, THE GARDENS AT KEW...
I AM LIKE THE CHILD IN THE SWEETSHOP, AS YOU SAY.
HAVE YOU ANY INTEREST IN THE ZOO, BARON? SUCH A MENAGERIE!
...JOINED THE HUNT AT THE BEGINNING OF THE YEAR...
...PRACTICING CALISTHENICS I BELIEVE...
...NEVER SEEMED TO NOTICE...
...IT WAS CALLED UTOPIA, LIMITED...
...NO REAL CAUSE TO TAKE AN INTEREST IN SUCH THINGS...
...GRAND TOUR WHEN WE WERE OF HIS AGE...
ORD GOD ALMIGH...!
CLATTER
OH, I'M SORRY SIR, I QUITE FORGOT YOU WERE THERE.
HMM...
I DO APOLOGISE, I MUST GET ON.
YES. YES, I EXPECT YOU BEST HAD.

DOCTOR?
OH, I'M SORRY I DIDN'T REALISE THE HOUR...
DEAR ME, DOCTOR, I'VE NEVER KNOWN YOU TO LEAVE YOUR SUPPER.
I'M AFRAID I HAVEN'T MUCH OF AN APPETITE THIS EVENING.
WELL, I'LL ADMIT I HAVEN'T EATEN MUCH MYSELF BUT YOU NEED TO KEEP YOUR STRENGTH UP.
YOU GET SOME REST DOCTOR.
THINGS WILL LOOK BRIGHTER IN THE MORNING, I'M SURE.
I HOPE SO MRS. HUDSON, I HOPE SO.

Moriarty
COME ON MAN, THINK! WHAT WOULD HE DO? WHAT WOULD HE SAY?
"THE OBSERVATION OF TRIFLES"..."MY METHOD IS FOUNDED UPON THE OBSERVATION OF TRIFLES"...
Moriarty
WE HEARD THE SHOT *BEFORE* THE CLOCKS BEGAN TO CHIME. WHICH MEANS...
WHICH MEANS...
DAMN AND BLAST IT!
I'M SORRY HOLMES! I'M USELESS!
USELESS...

EVERYTHING IN ORDER HERE SIR. NOTHING SUSPICIOUS TO REPORT.
INSPECTOR, IF I DIDN'T KNOW BETTER I MIGHT THINK THAT YOU WERE BEING SARCASTIC.
YOU HAVE AFTER ALL SPENT A DAY IN THE COMPANY OF ROYALTY AND THEN PASSED AN EVENING INSIDE BUCKINGHAM PALACE.
I'VE NO DOUBT THAT MANY PEOPLE WOULD ENVY YOUR POSITION.
NEVER THE LESS IT HAS BEEN A LONG DAY HAS IT NOT?
I APPRECIATE THE WORK YOU HAVE DONE.
THANK YOU SIR. I'LL BID YOU A GOOD NIGHT THEN.

CLIMB IN, INSPECTOR. WE CAN'T HAVE YOU WALKING HOME ON A NIGHT LIKE THIS.
THANK YOU SIR BUT I'VE A MIND TO STRETCH MY LEGS. I FEEL A BIT OF STIFFNESS FROM BEING PARKED IN THAT CHAIR.
AS YOU WISH. SEE YOU IN THE MORNING THEN.
SIGH
WHOA THERE!
BAKER STREET...AS FAST AS YOU CAN.

DOCTOR WATSON?
ƎAHEMƐ
OH, I...I MUST HAVE DOZED OFF...WHAT TIME IS IT?
IT'S THE INSPECTOR SIR...
DOCTOR, I'M SORRY TO CALL ON YOU AT THIS HOUR. I AM IN NEED OF YOUR COOPERATION.
OF COURSE, OLD FRIEND OF COURSE.
I'M AFRAID THAT IT WILL INVOLVE BREAKING THE LAW...
...AND PERHAPS RUNNING A CHANCE OF ARREST.
I IMAGINE THAT WE ARE PRACTICALL RISKING THAT SIMPL BY YOUR COMING HERE.
AM I RIGHT IN THINKING THAT YOU PROPOSE A THOROUGH INVESTIGATION OF THE, *UHM*, THE CRIME SCENE?
I HAVE A CAB WAITING OUTSIDE.
221

SHOOTER'S HILL, SOUTHEAST LONDON.
EVENING OFFICER, OR IS IT MORNING NOW?
WHAT CAN I DO FOR YOU INSPECTOR?
AH, YOU KNOW WHO I AM THEN.
YES SIR, YOU ARE INSPECTOR LESTRADE OF SCOTLAND YARD.
I'M AFRAID I HAVE ORDERS NOT TO ALLOW YOU INSIDE THESE PREMISES.
WELL, I SUPPOSE I SHOULD BE FLATTERED THAT THEY'VE GONE TO ALL THIS TROUBLE.
YOU BEEN HERE LONG THEN?
A GOOD FEW HOURS SIR.

YOU BEEN HERE LONG THEN?
A GOOD FEW HOURS SIR.
FSSSS

TING TING TING TING TING
EH?
HELLO, WHAT'S THIS?
...STILL, COULD BE WORSE I SUPPOSE. THE FOG'S NOT SO THICK OUT HERE AND IT'S QUITE A PLEASANT VISTA.
TING TANG TING TONG
CHANG
BONG
BONG
...EVERY BLESSED QUARTER OF THE HOUR. I DON'T KNOW HOW ANYONE COULD GET ANY SLEEP WITH THAT RACKET GOING ON.
DING DING DING DING
BONG

CHANNEL ROW POLICE STATION.
LORD KNOWS WHY THEY DIDN'T JUST BREAK A WINDOW.
EVIDENTLY, THEY FANCIED THEMSELVES AS SOME KIND OF PROFESSIONAL CREW, ALL TOOLED UP AS THEY WERE.
STILL, THEY WAS MAKIN' A TERRIBLE RACKET. TRYING TO LEVER THE DOOR OFF ITS HINGES, IF YOU PLEASE.
WELL, SUPPOSE THEY WERE PLANNING ON THIEVING SOMETHIN' BIG LIKE A FANCY TABLE OR SOMETHIN', RIGHT? IT WOULDN'T FIT OUT A WINDOW NOW WOULD IT?
GAWD ALMIGHTY, YOU'RE AS BAD AS THEM.
YOU SEND ONE MAN IN THE WINDOW AND THEN HE COMES ROUND AND OPENS THE DOOR FROM *INSIDE*, DOESN'T HE?
WELL, 'SCUSE ME FOR...
'ERE, GET DOWN THE CELLS, *QUICK!*
...BUT HOW COULD HE?
STAND BACK! GIVE US SOME ROOM!

IT'S MERRYN! WHAT IN BLAZES IS GOING ON?
I WAS ON MY WAY OUT... I JUST... JUST LOOKED IN TO CHECK... HE SAID HE WAS FEELING FAINT...
I-I'M ALRIGHT... I JUST NEED... A FEW MOMENTS TO...
TAKE IT EASY MERRY, WHAT HAPPENED?
SOMEONE... *HE* MUST HAVE CLOCKED ME ON THE BACK OF THE HEAD...
OH GAWD, HE'S GONE HASN'T HE? SHERLOCK HOLMES HAS GONE!

The Trial of Sherlock Holmes Issue 3 Cover by John Cassaday

KNOCK KNOCK
KNOCK KNOCK KNOCK
ALRIGHT, ALRIGHT! I'M COMING!
DINGADING
JUST WHAT IS IT THAT YOU--?
OH...!
I'M SORRY TO DISTURB YOU AT THIS HOUR SIR.
I AM CURRENTLY IN PURSUIT OF A SUSPECT WHOM I BELIEVE MAY HAVE GAINED ENTRANCE TO YOUR PREMISES. MAY I COME IN?
W-WHY YES, OF COURSE...
Johansen's EST. 1850 THEATRICAL SUPPLIES
HARKER'S
DINGADING

KNOCK KNOCK
EH? OH, COME IN.
GOOD MORNING DOCTOR.
NOW THEN, AS YOU HARDLY ATE A THING YESTERDAY, I'VE COOKED YOU YOUR FAVOURITE BREAKFAST.
THANK YOU MRS. HUDSON, YOU ARE MOST KIND.
DEAR ME, YOU LOOK TIRED.
I'M AFRAID I DIDN'T SLEEP VERY WELL.
I DON'T SUPPOSE IT WOULD BE APPROPRIATE FOR ME TO ASK WHAT TIME YOU RETURNED HOME LAST NIGHT?
OR WHERE YOU AND THE INSPECTOR WENT?
I, *ERM*... I THINK IT WOULD BE BEST IF WE DIDN'T SPEAK ABOUT THAT.

I SEE...
AS I TOLD YOU, LESTRADE AND I HAVE BEEN FORBADE FROM INVESTIGATING THE, *UHM*, CASE.
"CASE", PAH!
WE ARE DOING ALL THAT WE CAN FOR HOLMES, MRS. HUDSON, I GIVE YOU MY WORD ON THAT.
IF YOU SAY SO DOCTOR. IT'S JUST THAT--
DINGADING
OH HEAVENS, WHO CAN *THAT* BE?
DINGADING
OH DEAR, I DO HOPE IT'S NOTHING URGENT.
"WHAT A DREADFUL THOUGHT. WHAT IF SOMEONE TURNED UP WITH A NEW CASE, AND MR HOLMES NOT HERE TO TAKE IT?"

--HEARD IT FROM ONE OF INSPECTOR GREGSON'S MEN SIR.
GREGSON? PAH!
WITH RESPECT SIR, DON'T YOU THINK THAT THE, UHM, SITUATION WITH MR. HOLMES WOULD BE GOSSIP ENOUGH?
I MEAN THERE'S NO REAL REASON WHY SOMEONE WOULD MAKE SOMETHING LIKE THAT UP.
PEOPLE DON'T NEED A REASON TO SENSATIONALISE THINGS THESE DAYS. THE DAMNED NEWSPAPERS HAVE SEEN TO IT THAT THE WHOLE NATION'S ADDICTED TO HYPERBOLE.
WELL SIR, I'M JUST TELLING YOU WHAT HE TOLD ME IS ALL.
LOOK, IF SHERLOCK HOLMES HAD ESCA--
LOOK ALIVE GENTLEMEN!
AHEM HER MAJESTY QUEEN VICTORIA OF GREAT BRITAIN AND IRELAND AND EMPRESS OF INDIA AND HIS LORDSHIP BARON ALBRECHT LOTHAIR OF ALMANI-LOTHARINGEN.
--WOMEN MAY VOTE IN LOCAL ELECTIONS, BECOME POOR LAW GUARDIANS, ACT ON SCHOOL BOARDS, BUT ARE THEY SATISFIED? I SHOULD SAY NOT.

AH, I SEE THAT WE STILL HAVE THE PLEASURE OF THE POLICE FORCE'S COMPANY.
I'M NOT SO SURE WE NEED THEM INSIDE THE PALACE. ARE MY GUARDS NOT ENOUGH?
YOUR MAJESTY, IF YOU WILL FORGIVE ME, YOU ARE YOURSELF A WOMAN AND PERFORM YOUR DUTIES AS WELL AS ANY MAN.
INDEED, BETTER THAN MANY MEN. IS IT NOT SO?
THAT I AM CAPABLE DOES NOT MEAN THAT I AM EQUAL.
NO, WERE WOMAN TO "UNSEX" THEMSELVES BY CLAIMING EQUALITY WITH MEN, THEY WOULD SURELY PERISH FOR LACK OF MALE PROTECTION.
BLIMEY...
GOD ALMIGHTY! YOU'D HAVE THOUGHT THEY COULD HAVE GIVEN US A BIT OF WARNING.
GOD HELP THE NEW WOMAN THAT RUNS INTO HER MAJESTY EH?
WHAT THE DEVIL ARE YOU DOING IN HERE?
I HOPE TO GOD NO-ONE OF ANY IMPORTANCE HAS SEEN YOU IN HERE.

EIGHT F'R A BOB YER MACKEREL!
GETCHER MACKEREL HERE, EIGHT FOR A BOB!
NEW WALL-FLEET OYSTERS!
FAIR LEMONS AND ORANGES! ORANGES AND CITRONS!
PRETTY PINS, PRETTY WOMEN!
...SO I TOLE 'IM IT WERE WORTH MORE'N THAT...
...AN' I CAN'T KEEP EM ALL, I GOT SIX O' MY OWN!
...SHE'LL DO IT FOR A HA'PENNY...
...SHE 'AD FOZZY JAW, POOR DUCK...
...I'LL BLEEDIN' *MURDER* YOU, YOU LITTLE SWINE!
...WELL I'D MARRY 'IM, EVEN IF 'E IS GERMAN! A BARON'S A BARON!

MISTER MANN SIR? I-I 'ADN'T SEEN YOU SIR, NOT FOR A WHILE...
I *HAVE* BEEN HERE, MRS. HARDWICK. *COFF* PERHAPS YOU DIDN'T HEAR ME COME IN?
Y-YOU'VE BEEN HERE SIR? BUT I SHOULD HAVE KNOWN ABOUT IT SIR...SURELY...
...AND IF I THOUGHT YOU WERE COMING BACK SIR, WELL I WOULDN'T HAVE... WELL, SIR...
MRS. HARDWICK, THE GUINEA I PAID YOU IN ADVANCE FOR THE RENTAL OF THIS ROOM, IS IT GONE NOW? SHOULD I PERHAPS HAVE GIVEN YOU MORE? *COFF-COFF*
OOH NO SIR! IT WAS PLENTY! THE ROOM IS YOURS SIR! WELL I SAY IT'S YOURS BUT...
...WELL SIR, THERE'S SOMEONE ELSE IN THERE...

YES? MAY I HELP YOU?
AH, MRS. HUDSON ISN'T IT? VERY NICE TO SEE YOU AGAIN.
AGAIN? I'M AFRAID YOU HAVE ME AT A BIT OF A DISADVANTAGE SIR.
WELL I'M ALMOST CERTAIN IT WAS YOU, MRS. HUDSON.
"I WAS OUTSIDE CHANNEL ROW POLICE STATION YES'D'Y MORNIN'.
"I SAW YOU BUMP INTO DOCTOR WATSON. WALKIN' AWAY FROM SCOTLAND YARD HE WAS."
OH! NO...NO SIR. I'M AFRAID YOU MUST BE MISTAKEN.
WHO ARE YOU IF I MAY ASK? AND WHAT IS YOUR BUSINESS?
ALFIE SPROATS MA'AM, FROM THE COMET.
A REPORTER? AND WHAT DO YOU WANT WITH ME MR. SPROATS?
WELL I WAS 'OPING TO SEE MR. HOLMES ACTUALLY, IF IT WOULDN'T BE PUTTIN' HIM OUT AT ALL?

NO SIR. NOT TODAY. I'M AFRAID MR. HOLMES IS VERY BUSY TODAY!
I UNDERSTAND. I'LL CALL BACK ANOTHER TIME.
WHEN MIGHT BE A GOOD TI--
SLAMM
NOT TO WORRY MRS. HUDSON. NOT TO WORRY. I'LL BE SEEIN' THE GREAT DETECTIVE SOON ENOUGH I'M SURE.
DOCTOR! DOCTOR WATSON, YOU WON'T BELIEVE IT!
IT WAS A REPORTER! FROM THE COMET, IF YOU PLEASE, ASKING IF HE MIGHT SEE MR. HOLMES!
YOU TOLD HIM IT WASN'T POSSIBLE?
I DID, BUT HE SAID HE SAW US YESTERDAY, OUTSIDE THE *POLICE STATION*...
TIME IS RUNNING OUT, MRS. HUDSON. WE MUST ACT!
"I MUST ACT!"

I'M SORRY SIR, THERE MUST HAVE BEEN SOME MISTAKE. ƎCOFFƐ THIS ROOM BELONGS TO ME.
I'M AFRAID YOU MUST SPEAK TO MY ASSOCIATE. HE DEALS WITH SUCH MATTERS.
VERY WELL SIR, ƎCOFFƐ IF YOU INSIST.
OF COURSE, MISMATCHED COMBATANTS ƎCOFF-COFFƐ NEED NOT ALWAYS MEAN A FOREGONE CONCLUSION...
IN MOST CASES ƎCOFFƐ THE SMALLER COMBATANT HAS AN IMMEDIA ADVANTAGE, IN THAT THEY POSSES A LOWER CENTRE OF GRAVITY THA THEIR ƎCOFFƐ ASSAILANT.
ONE MUST FIRST ƎCOFFƐ CREATE A PIVOT POINT, ACROSS WHICH THEIR CENTRE OF GRAVITY WILL PASS.
OOFFFF
THEN ALL THAT REMAINS IS A NUDGE IN THE CORRECT DIRECTION, AND GRAVITY DOES ALL YOUR HARD WORK FOR YOU.
WHMMP

MISS HARDWICK. ≈COFF-COFF≈ I NEED YOU TO SEND A BOY TO PAY A DEBT FOR ME.
GRAAAAAAAAH!
KRASH
AAAAAAAAAAAA
I THINK ≈COFF≈ YOU HAD BETTER GET SOMEONE TO HELP OUR VISITOR WITH HIS THINGS, MISS HARDWICK.
"I SHOULD HATE TO DELAY HIS LEAVING ≈COFF-COFF≈"

--BEGAN IN 1860. THE OCTAGONS WERE COMPLETED IN 1861 AND THE CENTRE SECTION IN 1862.
IT MAINLY HOLDS TENDER WOODY PLANTS FROM THE WORLD'S TEMPERATE REGIONS.
"JUBAEA CHILENSIS" ALTHOUGH ORNAMENTAL, IS ALSO CALLED THE CHILEAN WINE PALM. IT IS LOPPED UPHILL, AND THE LEAFY CROWN REMOVED TO FACILITATE THE REMOVAL OF SAP.
OVER MANY MONTHS, IT CAN YIELD UP TO NINETY GALLONS OF SAP WHICH CAN BE FERMENTED INTO PALM WINE OR CONCENTRATED INTO A SYRUP.
THIS PARTICULAR SPECIMEN WAS RAISED FROM SEED IN 1846, AND IS NOW THE TALLEST TREE UNDER GLASS IN THE WORLD.
WE ARE CURRENTLY AWAITING A NEW SPECIMEN, "ENCEPHALARTOS WOODII" FROM THE NGOYE FOREST, IN ZULULAND, MR. WOOD INFORMS US...

I BELIEVE THERE MAY HAVE BEEN SOME TROUBLE LAST NIGHT SIR.
OVER AT CHANNEL ROW SOMEONE SAID...
I'M NOT SURE WHAT YOU ARE REFERRING TO LESTRADE, BUT NEED I REMIND YOU THAT YOU ARE NOT PERMITTED TO SPEAK ABOUT THE HOLMES CASE?
JUST MAKING CONVERSATION SIR.
AND LASTLY, CAN ANYONE TELL ME WHAT WE GET FROM CINCHONA PUBESCENS? I'M CERTAIN YOU'LL ALL HAVE IT AT HOME...
PERFUME? NO WAIT, IS IT COCOA?
IF THERE WAS AN INCIDENT LAST NIGHT--
I RECOMMEND YOU CEASE THAT LINE OF QUESTIONING LESTRADE, IT IS IN YOUR OWN BEST INTERESTS.
TO THINK A PLANT COULD HOLD THE CURE FOR MALARIA! SUCH WONDERS ARE IN THE NATURAL WORLD.
BARON LOTHAIR, IT IS THE PURPOSE AND THE PRIVILEGE OF THE ROYAL BOTANICAL GARDENS TO DISCOVER EACH OF THOSE WONDERS FOR THE BETTERMENT OF MANKIND.
WELL SAID SIR! HEAR HEAR!

COMET NEWS
BARON LOTHAIR VISITS LONDON
BEAR LOOSE IN ST. PAUL'S CATHEDRAL!
SHERLOCK HOLMES IN SHOOTERS HILL MYSTERY
221
OOP! 'SCUSE ME OLD TIMER, I WEREN'T WATCHIN' WHERE I WERE GOIN'.
COFF DON'T MENTION IT SONNY *COFF*
DINGADING
YES?
OH, HOW MAY I HELP YOU THIS TIME MR. SPROATS?
JUST WANTED TO MAKE SURE YOU GOT A COPY OF THIS MRS. HUDSON.
LOAD O' NONSENSE I'M SURE, BUT I THOUGHT YOU COULD TAKE IT TO HIM...UPSTAIRS I MEAN.

"SHERLOCK HOLMES IN SHOOT"--
CRASSH
WHAT IN HEAVEN?
DEAR ME MRS. HUDSON! ALLOW ME TO INVESTIGATE.
OH MY GIDDY AUNT! WILL YOU LOOK AT THAT?
MY LOVELY PIE! RUINED! DO YOU THINK IT WERE BURGLARS? THEY COULD BE GETTING AWAY!
NOTHIN' 'ERE MRS. HUDSON, MUST'VE BEEN CATS...
'ERE! OLD TIMER! YOU 'ENT SEEN ANY BURGLAR LOOKIN' BLOKES 'AVE YER?
NOPE. *COFF* CAN'T SAY AS I HAVE. *COFF-COFF*
WELL, I DON'T KNOW WHAT I'M GOING TO SERVE FOR DINNER NOW.
IT'S A MYSTERY MRS. HUDSON. QUITE A MYSTERY.

I WILL HAVE TO COME BACK TO SEE THESE GLASSHOUSES WHEN THEY ARE COMPLETED UND WHEN THEY HAVE ALL THE NEW SPECIMENS.
OF COURSE BARON LOTHAIR, YOU WOULD ALWAYS BE MOST WELCOME.
MAY WE WALK TO THE ORANGERY NEXT BARON? I LOVE THE SMELL OF THE FRUITS!
BUT OF COURSE, THERE IS TIME FOR EVERYTHING TODAY!
IT IS SUCH A BEAUTIFUL TIME OF YEAR IS IT NOT?
PTUNK

WAS WAR DAS?
WAS IST LOS?
WAS IT A SHOT? MEIN GOTT!
IN THE TREES! HE'S IN THE BLOODY TREES!
LESTRADE! WOULD YOU *PLEASE* GET OFF BARON LOTHAIR?
THERE! THERE YOU CLOT! GET HIM!
LESTRADE? *INSPECTOR* LESTRADE OF SCOTLAND YARD?

EXCUSE MY INSOLENCE WON'T YOU, THIS IS RATHER PRESSING. I SHALL BE WITH YOU IN A MINUTE.
YOU HAVE HEARD ABOUT THE ARREST THEN?
OF COURSE. TERRIBLE BUSINESS. AWFUL MESS. WISH THERE WAS SOMETHING I COULD DO.
LESTRADE AND I... WE'VE BEEN TOLD NOT TO INTERFERE. WE CAN'T DO ANYTHING TO HELP HIM!
THERE'S THIS FELLOW, DI DAVIS, AND HE HAS BEEN VERY STERN ABOUT THE WHOLE THING.
HE SEEMS TO THINK HOLMES IS *GUILTY!*
I HAVE HEARD OF DAVIS YES. SPECIAL BRANCH. GOOD MAN.
LAST NIGHT LESTRADE AND I WENT UP TO SHOOTERS HILL--
STOP! I DON'T WANT TO HEAR ANY MORE!
WHATEVER YOU DID LAST NIGHT WAS HIGHLY ILLEGAL AND *I* CERTAINLY DO NOT WANT TO KNOW ABOUT IT.
I *CANNOT* KNOW!
BUT... BUT...
FEAR NOT DOCTOR. JUSTICE WILL PREVAIL. HAVE FAITH.

HAS ANYONE BEEN TO SEE YOU? AT BAKER STREET I MEAN?
BEEN TO...? THERE...THERE WAS A REPORTER THIS MORNING, BUT MRS. HUDSON SENT HIM AWAY.
A REPORTER EH? HEH. PROBABLY FOR THE BEST YOU GOT RID OF HIM THEN. CAN'T--
DONNG
AH, YOU MUST EXCUSE ME. IT IS TIME FOR MY LUNCH.
BUT *SURELY?* THE CASE...YOUR *BROTHER*...
PERHAPS WE COULD TALK WHILST YOU EAT?
I'M AFRAID NOT DOCTOR. I DINE ALONE. I AM A CREATURE OF HABIT.
THANK YOU SO MUCH FOR POPPING IN DOCTOR AND DO TRY NOT TO WORRY. I'M SURE EVERYTHING WILL BE FINE.
YES, BUT...
YOUR USUAL IS IT SIR? I'LL BRING IT OVER IN A MOMENT.

THANK YOU MY GOOD MAN. I SHALL BE SITTING IN THE SNUG.
YOU ARE LATER THAN USUAL.
WELL, YOU KNOW HOW THINGS CAN BE AT THE OFFICE.
I RECOMMEND THE PORT-WINE. IT IS BOTH NUTTY AND SPICY AND HAS YET TO BE WATERED DOWN.
HERE YOU ARE SIR, WILL THERE BE ANYTHING ELSE?
THANK YOU. A GLASS OF PORT PERHAPS?
IT CANNOT HAVE ESCAPED YOUR ATTENTION THAT I AM, AT PRESENT, IN RATHER A TIGHT SPOT.
INDEED, DEAR DOCTOR WATSON HAS JUST PAID ME A VISIT.
HE SAID THAT A *REPORTER* HAD VISITED BAKER STREET TODAY.
INDEED, I SAW HIM AND I HAVE SEEN THE NEWSPAPERS TOO.
WELL LITTLE BROTHER, HOW LONG BEFORE NEWS OF YOUR *ESCAPE* SEES PRINT?
I THINK IT WOULD BE BEST IF I ASKED THE QUESTIONS, MYCROFT, DON'T YOU?

The Trial of Sherlock Holmes

issue 4

The Trial of Sherlock Holmes Issue 4 Cover by John Cassaday

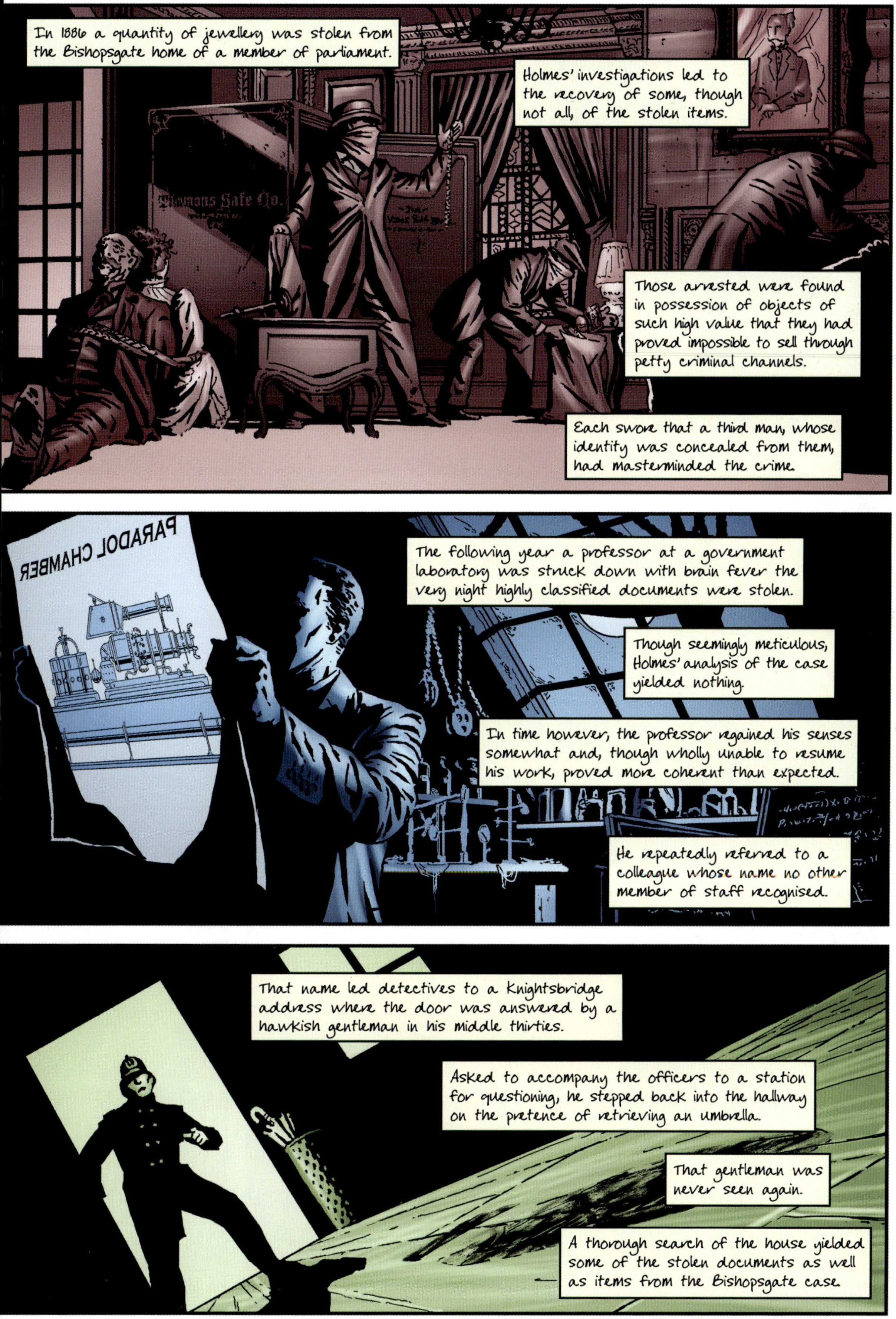
In 1886 a quantity of jewellery was stolen from the Bishopsgate home of a member of parliament.
Holmes' investigations led to the recovery of some, though not all, of the stolen items.
Those arrested were found in possession of objects of such high value that they had proved impossible to sell through petty criminal channels.
Each swore that a third man, whose identity was concealed from them, had masterminded the crime.
PARADOL CHAMBER
The following year a professor at a government laboratory was struck down with brain fever the very night highly classified documents were stolen.
Though seemingly meticulous, Holmes' analysis of the case yielded nothing.
In time however, the professor regained his senses somewhat and, though wholly unable to resume his work, proved more coherent than expected.
He repeatedly referred to a colleague whose name no other member of staff recognised.
That name led detectives to a Knightsbridge address where the door was answered by a hawkish gentleman in his middle thirties.
Asked to accompany the officers to a station for questioning, he stepped back into the hallway on the pretence of retrieving an umbrella.
That gentleman was never seen again.
A thorough search of the house yielded some of the stolen documents as well as items from the Bishopsgate case.

In addition to these...
KNOCK KNOCK
ENTER.
AH DAVIS. BACK AGAIN.
AFTER THIS MORNING'S NEWS, I DIDN'T THINK IT COULD GET ANY WORSE.
INDEED SIR.
SO, WHAT HAVE WE GOT ON THIS WOULD-BE ASSASSIN THEN?
IT IS POSSIBLE THAT THERE MAY HAVE BEEN MORE THAN ONE OF THEM SIR.
GO ON...
WELL SIR... I'VE GOT MY BEST MEN ON THE JOB SIR. THEY'RE OUT THERE GATHERING INFORMATION AS WE SPEAK.

DETECTIVE INSPECTOR, A MEMBER OF THE GERMAN ROYAL FAMILY WAS ALMOST SHOT ON BRITISH SOIL TODAY WHILE UNDER *YOUR* PERSONAL PROTECTION!
DO YOU HAVE *ANY* IDEA OF THE IMPACT SUCH AN INCIDENT COULD HAVE?
WHAT ABOUT THE WITNESSES?
THERE WERE VERY FEW SIR AND THE SHOTS WERE SO QUIET...A PRANK IS WHAT WE TOLD THEM. A CATAPULT MOST LIKELY.
AND WHAT ABOUT HOLMES?
THERE'S STILL NO NEWS AS YET I'M AFRAID SIR.
NOT GOOD ENOUGH!
THIS IS NOT WHAT I EXPECT FROM SPECIAL BRANCH. THIS IS NOT WHAT I EXPECT FROM *YOU.* THIS IS A BLOODY DISASTER!
I DON'T CARE HOW YOU DO IT BUT I WANT RESULTS AND I WANT THEM IMMEDIATELY! NOW GET OUT THERE AND DO YOUR JOB!

FWSHH
YOU SURE YOU'RE ALRIGHT MERRY? YOU'VE GOT A FACE LIKE A FIDDLE!
I DIN'T COME 'ERE T'TALK BILL, I CAME T'DRINK SO LEAVE ME BE.
FAIR ENOUGH. JUS' MAKIN' CONVERSATION LIKE.
AFTERNOON.
WHAT CAN I GET YOU THEN CONSTABLE?
LET ME SEE... HAVE YOU A PORT-WINE?
WELL I'LL BE...
IT'S YOU!

STOP 'IM! STOP 'IM I TELL YOU!
STOP 'IM!
GELD. French Bakery
GOTCHA!
MR. HOLMES YOU'VE JUST MADE MY DAY!

BUCKINGHAM PALACE, AFTERNOON.
WELL, NOW THAT YOU'RE SETTLED YOUR LORDSHIP...
I WISH TO THANK YOU INSPECTOR LESTRADE.
IT WAS NOTHI--
NO, NO, YOU ARE TOO MODEST INSPECTOR.
JUST DOING MY JOB YOUR LORDSHIP.
YOU MAY WELL HAVE SAVED MY LIFE THIS MORNING.
"IS THERE NO CLUE AS TO WHO THE GUNMAN COULD BE?"

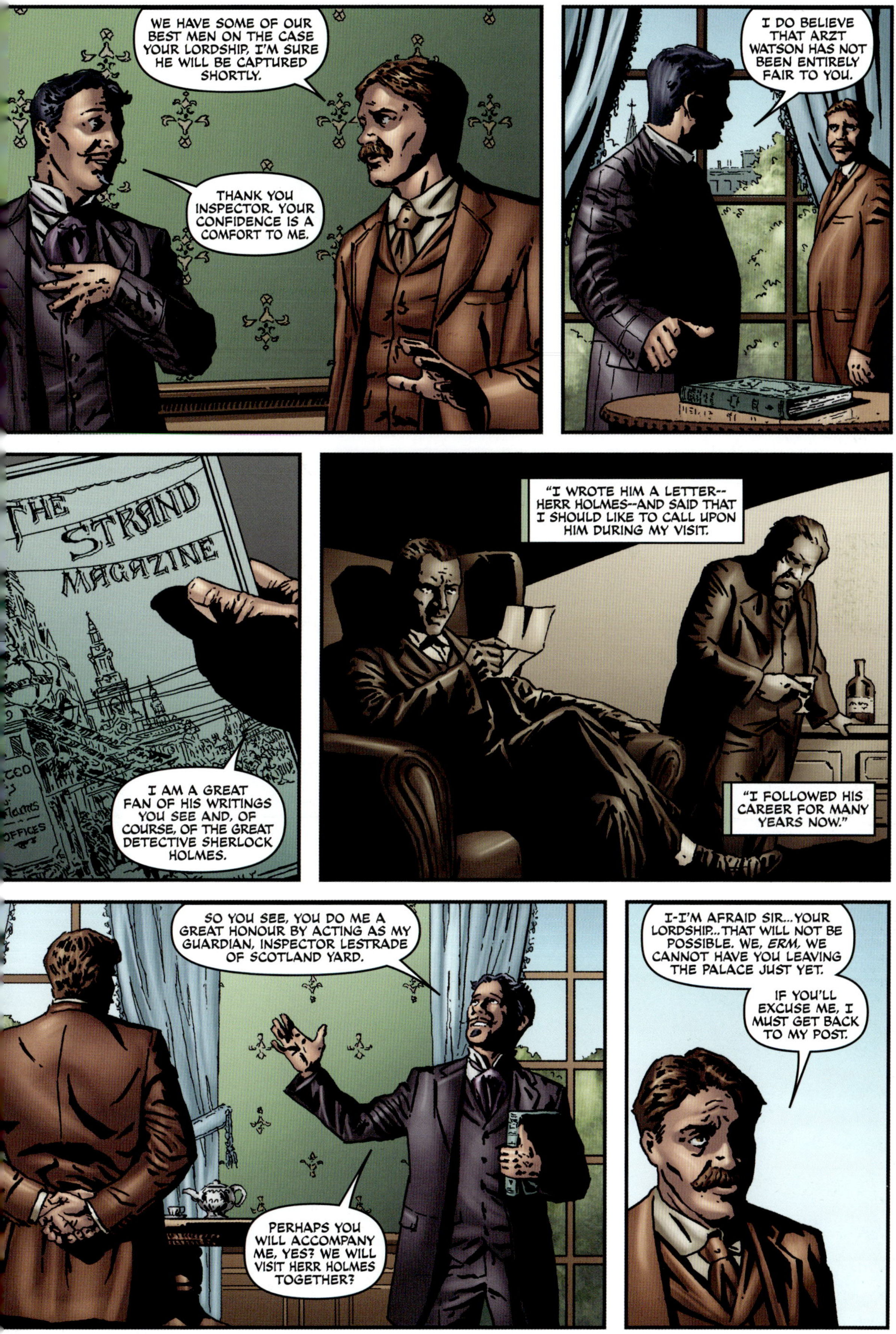
WE HAVE SOME OF OUR BEST MEN ON THE CASE YOUR LORDSHIP, I'M SURE HE WILL BE CAPTURED SHORTLY.
THANK YOU INSPECTOR. YOUR CONFIDENCE IS A COMFORT TO ME.
I DO BELIEVE THAT ARZT WATSON HAS NOT BEEN ENTIRELY FAIR TO YOU.
THE STRAND MAGAZINE
I AM A GREAT FAN OF HIS WRITINGS YOU SEE AND, OF COURSE, OF THE GREAT DETECTIVE SHERLOCK HOLMES.
"I WROTE HIM A LETTER-- HERR HOLMES--AND SAID THAT I SHOULD LIKE TO CALL UPON HIM DURING MY VISIT.
"I FOLLOWED HIS CAREER FOR MANY YEARS NOW."
SO YOU SEE, YOU DO ME A GREAT HONOUR BY ACTING AS MY GUARDIAN, INSPECTOR LESTRADE OF SCOTLAND YARD.
PERHAPS YOU WILL ACCOMPANY ME, YES? WE WILL VISIT HERR HOLMES TOGETHER?
I-I'M AFRAID SIR...YOUR LORDSHIP...THAT WILL NOT BE POSSIBLE. WE, *ERM*, WE CANNOT HAVE YOU LEAVING THE PALACE JUST YET.
IF YOU'LL EXCUSE ME, I MUST GET BACK TO MY POST.

...ALL OVER THE FLOOR. STEAK AND KIDNEY IT WAS TOO.
AND THAT AWFUL MAN SPROATS...OH! HAVE YOU SEEN THE NEWSPAPER?
EH? OH, NOTHING TO WORRY ABOUT I'M SURE MRS. HUDSON.
WELL IF YOU SAY SO DOCTOR.
IT... IT WILL ALL BE FINE...
WHAT THE DEVIL?
BUT IT CAN'T BE...
My Dear Watson,
Firstly I must apologise, for the presence of this note, and the absence of that other object, will doubtless have caused you some considerable shock.

I would have preferred speaking to you in person of course but unfortunately it was not possible.
SALT
I entered the house secretly whilst Mrs. Hudson was engaged in conversation with a newspaper reporter.
Opening your drawer, I found the bullet which I knew at once must have been removed from the house in Shooters Hill.
HEYNEMAN'S PUNCH
You were wise to take it old man, for, if someone meant to tamper with the evidence, they would certainly have done away with it.
I feel however that the time when such interference was likely is now passed. The crime scene shall be restored to its correct condition.
This is important above all else, as you shall soon understand.
Below you shall find a list of instructions which you are to follow to the letter.

SCOTLAND YARD.
'AVE I GOT ANY COMMENT? GET OUT OF IT!
BLEEDIN' NEWSPAPERMEN.
NICE AND SECURE ARE THEY? I HOPE SO!
JUST YOU WAIT THERE. A MAN'LL BE OUT TO PAY YOU SHORTLY.
WAS THAT...?

...SHERLOCK HOLMES!
WELL I'LL BE...
...YOU...YOU'VE BROUGHT HIM IN, IN HANDCUFFS IN THE MIDDLE OF THE AFTERNOON! GAWD ALMIGHTY MERRYN, ANYONE COULD HAVE SEEN YOU!
BUT SIR I...
I'M AFRAID THAT CAN'T BE HELPED NOW SERGEANT. BESIDES, SUCH THINGS CANNOT BE KEPT SECRET INDEFINITELY.
WANTED
VERY DECENT OF YOU TO SAY SO I'M SURE, MR. HOLMES.
ALL THE SAME, CONSTABLE, YOU'D BEST SHOW OUR GUEST TO HIS CELL QUICK SMART!
RIGHT YOU ARE SIR!

...SAID YOU'D UNDERSTAND THE IMPORTANCE.

INDEED I DO, DOCTOR, AS YOU KNOW. MR. HOLMES AND I DISCUSSED THE ROLE OF SUCH PRACTICES IN THE FUTURE OF THE FORCE SEVERAL TIMES.
HMM.

AND YOU UNDERSTAND THAT NO-ONE CAN KNOW OF MY INVOLVEMENT.
I AM UNDERTAKING THE WORK ENTIRELY OF MY OWN VOLITION HAVING RECEIVED NO ORDERS TO THE CONTRARY. THE CASE BEING INDISPUTABLY ONE OF INTEREST.
THANK YOU, HOPKINS. THANK YOU.
ANYTHING FOR MR. HOLMES, DOCTOR.
GREAT SCOTT!

CONFIDENTIAL
Commissioner of Police of the Metropolis New Scotland Yard
Sir, Further to our meeting earlier today I enclose the following report detailing the actions taken by those under my immediate command.
Officers began by contacting informants who had proven useful in former cases.
The information gathered from these meetings was then passed on to several separate squads of officers who conducted their investigations simultaneously.
Given the potentially political nature of the attempted crime, I chose to focus largely upon suspects of foreign origin.
Alphonse Bordeaux--who painted a portrait of the Greenwich Park bomber--was amongst the first arrested.
Feeling that the Frenchman's anarchist associations would make him an apt source of information he was questioned thoroughly.
Intelligence gathered from Bordeaux led officers to a number of addresses within the city where asylum seeking countrymen of his were still in residence.
If the attempted crime was indeed political in intent, those French refugees now in custody may yet prove amongst our strongest of leads.

Concurrently, officers made enquiries about foreign persons who had recently arrived in London or who had been acting in a suspicious manner.
Two Chinamen of obvious wealth who had lately been seen in the capital's slums were found to be dealers in fireworks visiting on business.
Whilst the public proved generally eager to assist, there were unavoidably several such occurrences.
This I mention chiefly because on one or two occasions officers were threatened with formal complaint.
Most notably in the case of an elderly Swiss gentleman who professed to a weak heart and noted the name of the senior attending officer.
In closing, please rest assured that I shall inform you of any and all developments as they occur.
I remain, Sir,
Your most obedient Servant.
≥SIGH≤

THE MALL. EVENING.
OI! WHAT'S THE BLEEDIN' 'OLD UP?
WHAT'S OCCURRING?
ITS ALL STUCK SIR, SOMETHING'S 'APPENED UP AHEAD.
BY GOD! THE BEAST'S GAWN MAD!
HERE, COME ALONG! TAKE THE RAIL! WE'LL ALL LIFT TOGETHER!
BORDEUX & SONS. C^TD

THAT'S IT! IT'S MOVING! GET HIM! GET THE BOY!
AAAH! MY LEGS! OH IT 'URTS SIR!
BAD BUSINESS EH? POOR LAD.
YES...
HOLMES ARRESTED
DEAR GOD!

"IT RAINS ON THE JUST..."
"...AND ON THE UNJUST."
WILL MR. HOLMES BE GETTING ANY SPECIAL TREATMENT? WHAT ABOUT MEALS?

WHAT'S GOING ON? WHAT ARE THIS LOT DOING HERE?
THEY TURNED UP AFTER THE LATE EDITION SIR...
COMMISSIONER SIR! HAVE YOU ANY COMMENT ON THE STORY SIR? WHAT IS HOLMES BEING HELD FOR?
GET RID OF THOSE MEN. TELL THEM THEY CAN EXPERIENCE A NIGHT IN THE CELLS FIRST HAND IF THEY DON'T MOVE!

≥AHEM≤
COMMISSIONER BRADFORD TO SEE YOU SIR.
MR. HOLMES.
COMMISSIONER. NICE OF YOU TO CALL IN.
I WISH THE CIRCUMSTANCES WERE MORE PLEASANT OF COURSE.
OH, THANK YOU CONSTABLE.
FACT IS, WERE IT NOT FOR ALL THIS BUSINESS WITH SIR HENRY...WELL I RATHER THINK WE'D BE SEEKING YOUR ADVICE.
REGRETTABLY SIR, I AM IN NO POSITION TO OFFER ANY ASSISTANCE.
CLOSE THAT DOOR WOULD YOU CONSTABLE? I WILL CALL WHEN I'M FINISHED HERE.

WE'RE IN A TIGHT SPOT HERE, HOLMES. THE CASE AGAINST YOU...IT DOESN'T LOOK GOOD.
THE FACT IS THERE'S BEEN AN ATTEMPT ON BARON LOTHAIR'S LIFE. WE...WE NEED YOUR HELP.
JUST EXPLAIN IT TO ME HOLMES. ALL I NEED IS AN EXPLANATION AND WE CAN SEE ABOUT SORTING THIS MESS OUT.
COME NOW, COMMISSIONER, WE BOTH KNOW WE'RE BEYOND THAT NOW.
THE BUSINESS OF THE ESCAPE NEEDN'T COME OUT. YOU DIDN'T GET FAR. BESIDES, IT WOULDN'T LOOK GOOD...
HOW NOBLE OF YOU TO SPARE CONSTABLE MERRYN ANY EMBARRASSMENT.
WHAT HAPPENED IN THAT ROOM? WHO DID THIS TO YOU?
VINDICATE YOURSELF, MAN! GIVE ME A NAME!
I AM INNOCENT, COMMISSIONER. OF THAT YOU CAN BE CERTAIN, BUT I CANNOT GIVE YOU THE GUILTY PARTY.
THERE IS NO NAME. NO PERSON TO TAKE MY PLACE IN THIS CELL.
EVERYTHING WAS SET IN MOTION THE VERY MOMENT I READ SIR HENRY'S LETTER.
NEWS OF MY ARREST, MY CONNECTION TO THE CRIME, MUST BY NOW BE PUBLIC KNOWLEDGE.
SO YOU SEE, THERE REALLY IS NO ALTERNATIVE.
I MUST BE TRIED FOR THE MURDER OF SIR SAMUEL HENRY.
I WILL DEFEND MYSELF AND I WILL CLEAR MY NAME PUBLICALLY.
THERE IS NO OTHER COURSE OF ACTION OPEN TO ME.

DINGADING DINGADING DINGADING DINGADING
DEAR ME!
JUST WHAT DO Y--OH IT'S YOU INSPECTOR. I THOUGHT THERE MUST BE A FIRE...SUCH A CARRY ON--
MRS. HUDSON, I NEED TO SEE WATSON.
LESTRADE? WHAT'S WRONG MAN? WHAT WAS ALL THE NOISE ABOUT?
WE NEED TO TALK, WATSON. IT'S ALL BEEN KEPT FROM US, BUT NOW IT'S COMING OUT!
YES, I SAW THE LATE EDITION...BUT YOU MUSTN'T COME HERE. IF ANYONE SAW YOU, IT WOULD MAKE THINGS WORSE!
BUT WE HAVE TO DO SOMETHING! WE HAVE TO HELP HIM!
WE *CAN'T*, LESTRADE. WE CAN'T DO IT. NO MATTER WHAT, WE MUST KEEP OUR DISTANCE.
DAVIS IS RIGHT; WE'RE TOO CLOSE TO THE CASE. YOU MUST SEE THAT.
IF YOU GO DISOBEYING ORDERS, BREAKING THE LAW...WE'RE ONLY GOING TO MUDDY THE WATERS.
I CANNOT BELIEVE I AM HEARING THIS, JOHN! FROM YOU OF ALL PEOPLE!
PLEASE, LESTRADE. FOR ALL OUR SAKES, FORGET ABOUT IT. THERE REALLY IS NOTHING YOU CAN DO.

The Trial of Sherlock Holmes
issue 5

The Trial of Sherlock Holmes Issue 5 Cover by John Cassaday

A most unique trial begins today at London's Old Bailey.
A man stands accused of murder. Shocking enough perhaps, but regrettably common in this day and age, when the streets teem with garrottes and thugees.
This is no ordinary miscreant however, for he is none other than the world famous consulting detective, Mr. Sherlock Holmes, of London's own Baker Street.
Mr. Holmes is understood to have been among those in attendance at a house in Shooters Hill some few evenings ago.
A grave misdeed was done that night, a man slain in cold blood.
Sir Samuel Henry--former Assistant Commissioner of Police of the Metropolis--was that poor, unfortunate soul.
Sir Henry's life had apparently been threatened openly and in addition to Mr. Holmes, some dozen or so police officers were in attendance.

The exact nature of the tragic killing has not yet been made entirely apparent.
Nevertheless, Holmes' part is evidently believed to have been a pernicious one.
Crowds of some considerable size are expected both inside and outside the court today.
Their members hoping to learn more about the wholly unprecedented and extraordinary trial.
THE GREAT DETECTIVE ON TRIAL
ORDER! ORDER IN COURT!
I WILL HAVE SILENCE IN THIS COURTROOM!
NOW, WILL THE CLERK OF THE ARRAIGNS PLEASE READ THE INDICTMENTS.

MR. SHERLOCK HOLMES, YOU ARE CHARGED WITH THE MURDER OF SIR SAMUEL HENRY.
HOW DO YOU PLEAD?
NOT GUILTY.
VERY WELL MR. HOLMES. YOU SHALL RECEIVE A FULL TRIAL IN ACCORDANCE WITH THE LAWS OF THIS LAND.
I UNDERSTAND, MR. HOLMES, THAT YOU WISH TO DEFEND YOURSELF. SO BE IT THEN.
MR. GILL WILL LEAD FOR THE PROSECUTION. YOU MAY PROCEED SIR.

DETECTIVE LESTRADE? I'VE BEEN LOOKING ALL OVER FOR YOU SIR!
I DO APOLOGISE. IS THERE A PROBLEM?
IT'S BARON LOTHAIR SIR. HE WISHES TO SPEAK WITH YOU MOST URGENTLY.
HE MENTIONED THE TRIAL...
COULD YOU PLEASE TELL HIS LORDSHIP, WITH ALL DUE RESPECT, THAT I AM HERE SOLELY FOR HIS *PROTECTION.*
NO-*ONE* IS TO LEAVE THE PALACE UNTIL HER MAJESTY AND HIS LORDSHIP TRAVEL TO BALMORAL TOMORROW.
Y-YES SIR. VERY GOOD SIR.

KNOCK KNOCK
YOUR LORDSHIP, I'M AFRAID INSPECTOR LESTRADE IS CURRENTLY INDISPOSED AND SENDS HIS APOLOGIES.
WILL THERE BE ANYTHING ELSE, YOUR LORDSHIP?
NO. THANK YOU.
THE GREAT DETECTIVE ON TRIAL

INSPECTOR LESTRADE, SIR! YOU MUST COME AT ONCE!
I HALF EXPECTED TO SEE HIS LORDSHIP WITH YOU, SIR. I-I THOUGHT HE MIGHT HAVE GONE OFF LOOKING FOR YOU, YOU SEE?
HE WAS IN HERE, SIR. WHEN I LEFT HIM.
HAVE YOU MENTIONED THIS TO ANYONE ELSE?
NOT YET, SIR. NO. I THOUGHT--
GOOD.
"HE PICKED JUST THE RIGHT TIME. WITH EVERYTHING BEING PACKED UP FOR THE JOURNEY TOMORROW, THERE'LL BE PLENTY OF COMINGS AND GOINGS."
BUT SIR, WHERE CAN HIS LORDSHIP HAVE GONE?
I BELIEVE I KNOW *EXACTLY* WHERE HE IS HEADING.

WAS GESCHIEHT?
DRIVER! WHY ARE WE SLOWING DOWN?
IT'S THE CROWD, YOUR LOR--SIR. I-I COULD TRY TO ANOTHER ROUTE?
NO, NO, I HAVE LEGS!
‹HE IS OUT ON THE STREET!›
‹SURELY NOW IS THE TIME, WHILE HE IS ALONE...›
‹PATIENCE, MY FRIEND. WE KNOW WHERE HE IS GOING, DO WE NOT?›
‹IN ANY CASE, FOR OUR PURPOSE, WE REQUIRE AN AUDIENCE...›

...COMPILED THE DOSSIER OVER MANY YEARS.
HE KEPT HIS SUSPICIONS TO HIMSELF UNTIL, FEARING DEATH THROUGH ILL HEALTH, HE DECIDED AT LAST TO CONFRONT HOLMES.
WE MUST ASSUME THAT SIR HENRY FABRICATED THE THREAT UPON HIS LIFE TO GUARANTEE POLICE ATTENDANCE.
THEN WHEN THE TIME CAME, HE SUMMONED HOLMES TO HIS ROOM.
SIR HENRY MUST HAVE EXPECTED HIM TO BOW TO THE BETTER MAN AND CONFESS ALL TO THE ATTENDING OFFICERS.
INSTEAD, *ENRAGED,* HOLMES DREW HIS PISTOL AND *SHOT* HIM!
HE MURDERED AN HONOURABLE MAN IN COLD BLOOD.
AND, HAD IT NOT BEEN FOR THE ACTIONS OF DAVIS, HE WOULD HAVE DESTROYED THE DOSSIER!
AHEM THANK YOU MR. GILL.
MR. HOLMES, YOU MAY NOW SPEAK IN YOUR OWN DEFENCE.
THANK YOU VERY MUCH, YOUR HONOUR. AND THANK *YOU,* MR. GILL, THAT WAS MOST ENTERTAINING.

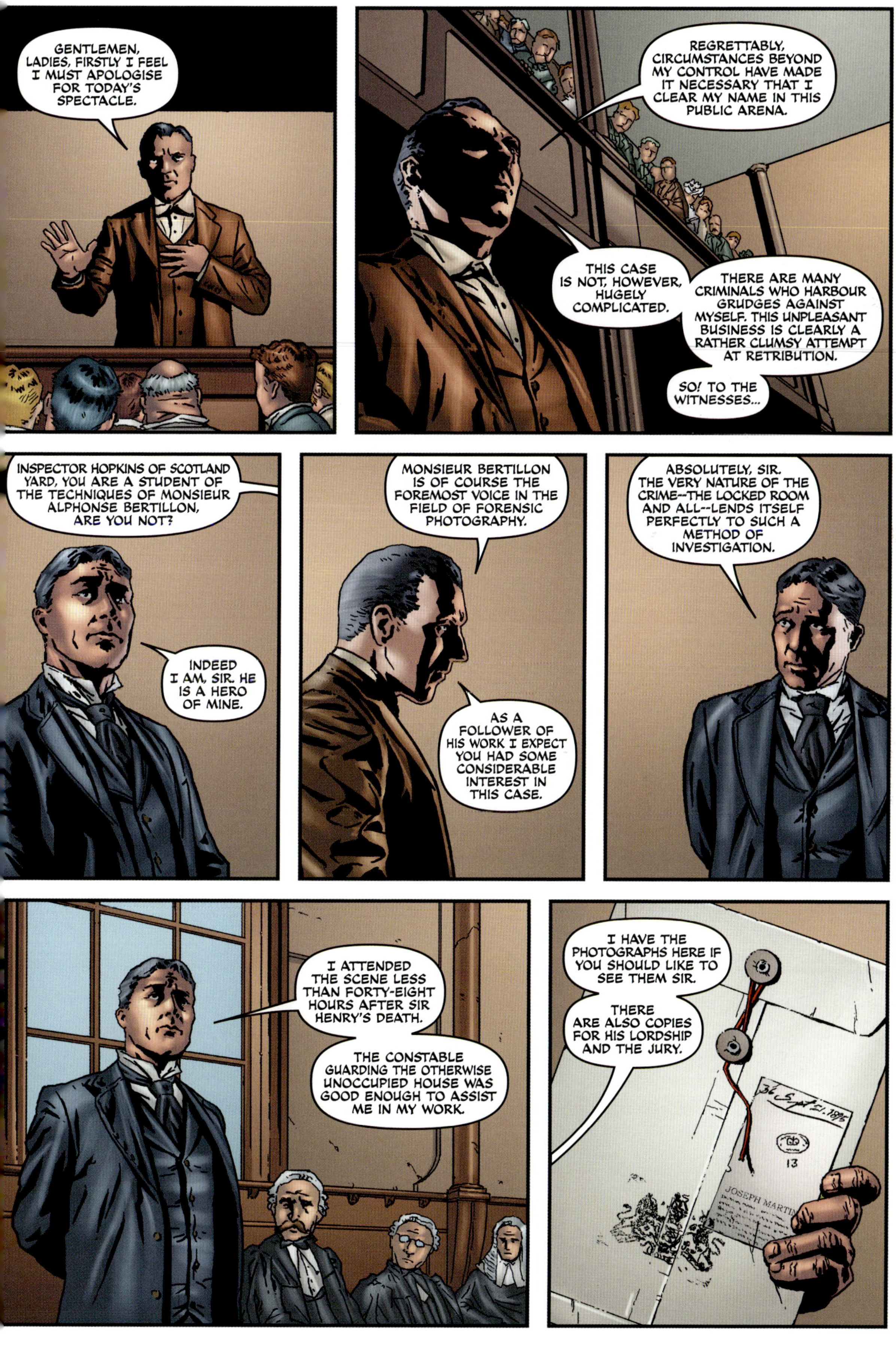
GENTLEMEN, LADIES, FIRSTLY I FEEL I MUST APOLOGISE FOR TODAY'S SPECTACLE.
REGRETTABLY, CIRCUMSTANCES BEYOND MY CONTROL HAVE MADE IT NECESSARY THAT I CLEAR MY NAME IN THIS PUBLIC ARENA.
THIS CASE IS NOT, HOWEVER, HUGELY COMPLICATED.
THERE ARE MANY CRIMINALS WHO HARBOUR GRUDGES AGAINST MYSELF. THIS UNPLEASANT BUSINESS IS CLEARLY A RATHER CLUMSY ATTEMPT AT RETRIBUTION.
SO! TO THE WITNESSES...
INSPECTOR HOPKINS OF SCOTLAND YARD, YOU ARE A STUDENT OF THE TECHNIQUES OF MONSIEUR ALPHONSE BERTILLON, ARE YOU NOT?
INDEED I AM, SIR. HE IS A HERO OF MINE.
MONSIEUR BERTILLON IS OF COURSE THE FOREMOST VOICE IN THE FIELD OF FORENSIC PHOTOGRAPHY.
AS A FOLLOWER OF HIS WORK I EXPECT YOU HAD SOME CONSIDERABLE INTEREST IN THIS CASE.
ABSOLUTELY, SIR. THE VERY NATURE OF THE CRIME--THE LOCKED ROOM AND ALL--LENDS ITSELF PERFECTLY TO SUCH A METHOD OF INVESTIGATION.
I ATTENDED THE SCENE LESS THAN FORTY-EIGHT HOURS AFTER SIR HENRY'S DEATH.
THE CONSTABLE GUARDING THE OTHERWISE UNOCCUPIED HOUSE WAS GOOD ENOUGH TO ASSIST ME IN MY WORK.
I HAVE THE PHOTOGRAPHS HERE IF YOU SHOULD LIKE TO SEE THEM SIR.
THERE ARE ALSO COPIES FOR HIS LORDSHIP AND THE JURY.
13
JOSEPH MARTIN

...HURRY! COME ALONG...
...MORE 'N THE SHINSCRAPER FER 'IM...
...OF COURSE HE'S INNOCENT...
...SINCE WILDE'S IN THE SPRING...
...WHOLE GAGGLE O' BLEEDIN' MILTONIANS...
‹BUT THERE IS VERY LITTLE CHANCE HE CAN HAVE ARRIVED BEFORE US!›
‹BUT EVEN IF SOMETHING IS UNLIKELY, THAT DOES NOT MAKE IT IMPOSSIBLE.›
‹GO! QUICKLY! I NEED TO KNOW IF HE IS ALREADY WITHIN.›

OVER THERE! THERE!
WHICH ONE, INSPECTOR LESTRADE SIR?
AH RIGHT, THE BOATER! I SEE 'IM SIR!
WELL? LOOK ALIVE MAN! GET SOME BLOODY MEN OVER THERE.
PEEEEEEP

AHEM MR. HOLMES?
MY APOLOGIES, YOUR HONOUR. THE SCENE OF ANY CRIME HOLDS A PECULIAR FASCINATION FOR ME.
"SO THEN: MOTIVE! MR. GILL DECLARES MINE TO BE THE ATTEMPTED CONCEALMENT OF NUMEROUS OTHER CRIMES.
"CRIMES HEINOUS ENOUGH TO KILL FOR."
YET MR. GILL HAS NOT PROVIDED EVIDENCE LINKING ME TO A SINGLE OTHER CRIME.
CLEARLY THEN, THE DOCUMENTS ARE NOT WORTH KILLING FOR.
TO THE CRIME SCENE THEN. INSPECTOR. WOULD YOU PLEASE EXPLAIN WHAT IS SHOWN IN THE PHOTOGRAPHS MARKED F AND G?
BULLET HOLES, SIR.
THEIR LOCATIONS?
ONE IN THE FLOORBOARDS NEAR THE FIREPLACE, AND ONE IN THE PLASTERWORK NEAR THE WINDOW. BULLETS RECOVERED FROM BOTH, SIR.
AND PHOTOGRAPH E?
IT SHOWS THAT DESPITE ALL OTHER CLOCKS BEING SYNCHRONISED PERFECTLY, THOSE IN THE BEDROOM RAN THREE MINUTES FAST.
DETECTIVE INSPECTOR DAVIS, DID YOU FIND ANYTHING NOTEWORTHY ABOUT THE TIMEPIECES DURING YOUR VISIT?
HM? WELL THEY WERE NUMEROUS... AND NOISY AS I RECALL.
CLOCKS MUST CHIME INSPECTOR, HOW ELSE MIGHT THEY TELL US THE HOUR?
THEY STRUCK EXCEEDINGLY LOUDLY. ON THE QUARTER AS WELL AS THE HOUR.
AND PICTURE A INSPECTOR HOPKINS?
THE "GOD'S-EYE-VIEW" SIR. A PICTURE TAKEN FROM CEILING HEIGHT LOOKING DOWN AT THE WHOLE ROOM. BERTILLON'S FINEST INNOVATION.

YOU WILL OBSERVE, YOUR HONOUR, THE LARGE QUANTITY OF BLOOD SOAKED INTO THE BEDCLOTHES...
AH! OF COURSE... THE HOUSEKEEPER!
MRS. GAMMAGE WAS, OTHER THAN MYSELF, THE LAST PERSON TO SEE SIR HENRY ALIVE. BUT WHERE IS SHE?
CAN ANYONE HERE TELL ME HER WHEREABOUTS?
YES SIR! I AM MR. BORD, SIR HENRY'S SOLICITOR. SHE HAS JUST LATELY GONE ABROAD SIR.
ABROAD?
YES SIR, TO CARE FOR SIR HENRY'S DAUGHTER. SADLY, SHE SUFFERS FROM CONSUMPTION AND RESIDES IN A CHARITABLE HOSPICE IN ITALY.
SAD INDEED. THANK YOU, SIR.
RETURNING TO THE BED LINEN THEN, I CALL DR. WATSON...
WATSON?
IT SEEMS HE IS NO LONGER HERE. VERY WELL, IS SIR HENRY'S PHYSICIAN HERE?
I AM, SIR. DR. SHOWERS, AT YOUR SERVICE.
"TELL ME, DOCTOR, IN YOUR PROFESSIONAL OPINION, WHAT IS THE LONGEST A MAN MIGHT LIVE IF SHOT IN THE STOMACH?"
IF THE BULLET PENETRATED ONLY THE ABDOMEN AND THE STOMACH, I SHOULD SAY FIFTEEN MINUTES AT THE MOST.
FIFTEEN MINUTES.
THANK YOU VERY MUCH, DOCTOR.

"NOW, LET US RETURN ONCE MORE TO THE BEGINNING.
"IT IS SUGGESTED BY MR. GILL THAT SIR HENRY FABRICATED THE THREAT UPON HIS OWN LIFE.
"MAKING MENTION OF THE RECENT DOYLE STREET BOMBING, AND THREATENING FURTHER ACTION TO GUARANTEE A POLICE PRESENCE WITHIN HIS HOME."
HIS LETTER TO ME STRESSED THE PECULIAR AND NOVEL NATURE OF THE ALLEGED THREAT UPON HIS LIFE, THUS GUARANTEEING MY OWN ATTENDANCE.
IN THESE DETAILS I CONCUR WITH MR. GILL.
"WHEN THE CLOCKS CHIMED A QUARTER TO SEVEN, INSPECTOR LESTRADE, WATSON, DETECTIVE INSPECTOR DAVIS AND I WERE TOGETHER IN THE SITTING ROOM.
"*FIFTEEN MINUTES* BEFORE SIR HENRY WAS SCHEDULED TO DIE."
WHEN I WAS SUMMONED TO SIR HENRY'S ROOM I WAS SHOCKED TO FIND HIM IN A TERRIBLE STATE.
THE ROOM WAS STIFLING YET HE WAS BURIED BENEATH LAYERS OF BEDCLOTHES.
HE SLURRED HIS WORDS AS HE BID ME LOCK THE DOOR.
I OBSERVED SOME CHARRED PAPERS UPON THE HEARTH, BUT MY ATTENTION WAS FOCUSSED UPON SIR HENRY HIMSELF.
ALMOST AT ONCE THE CLOCK ON THE MANTLE BEGAN TO STRIKE.
I GLANCED AT THE TIMEPIECE, AND WHEN I LOOKED BACK, SIR HENRY HAD FLUNG HIS BEDCLOTHES ASIDE.

"HE WAS SOAKED IN BLOOD, A PISTOL IN HIS SHAKING HAND.
"BEFORE I COULD SAY ANYTHING, HE FIRED A SHOT INTO THE FLOOR AT MY FEET--THE VERY SHOT THAT WAS HEARD THROUGHOUT THE HOUSE.
"SIR HENRY FELL BACK IN OBVIOUS PAIN AND I STEPPED FORWARD TO DISARM HIM JUST AS THE CLOCKS IN THE HOUSE BEGAN TO CHIME.
"IT SHOULD BE NOTED THAT DURING THE WEEKS PRIOR TO THIS CASE, MY COMPANION WATSON WAS OUT OF LONDON VISITING A RELATIVE."
DURING THAT PERIOD I WAS, AS USUAL, CALLED UPON DAILY BY VARIOUS PEOPLE SEEKING COUNCIL.
ONE SUCH VISITOR HAD EVIDENTLY SEIZED THE OPPORTUNITY TO RELIEVE ME OF MY WEAPON.
"STANDING IN THAT HELLISHLY HOT ROOM, I REALISED WITH CONSIDERABLE SHOCK THAT THE PISTOL WAS MY OWN.
"CONTRARY TO WATSON'S WRITINGS I AM NOT *WHOLLY* BEYOND BEWILDERMENT.
"IT WAS IN THIS CONFUSED STATE THAT I WAS FOUND, THE GUN IN MY HAND."

SOME DAYS LATER.
...YOUR OWN BROTHER TO THE GALLOWS.
COME COME NOW, OLD MAN, WE BOTH KNEW IT WOULD NEVER COME TO THAT.
YOU MENTIONED YOUR FRIEND THE INSPECTOR EARLIER, HOW IS HE?
LESTRADE IS RECOVERING EXCELLENTLY.
HE WILL RETAIN HIS RANK DESPITE HIS MISTAKES. I SUPPOSE I SHOULD THANK YOU...?
NOT AT ALL. HIS HEROICS HAVE EVIDENTLY STOOD HIM IN GOOD STEAD.
AND THE INTREPID DR. WATSON?
THE GOOD DOCTOR IS WELL AND SENDS HIS REGARDS.
REMARKABLE PIECE OF LUCK HIS BEING UP ON THE ROOF...
PITY THAT OTHER CHAP GOT AWAY THOUGH.
I FORGOT TO MENTION, WATSON TELLS ME THAT AS THE GUNMAN FELL, HE CRIED OUT--IN GERMAN!

WELL THAT SEEMS RATHER UNLIKELY DOESN'T IT?
THE WAR OF THE SEVENTIES IS STILL RATHER A SORE POINT. HAD THE BARON BEEN KILLED IT WOULD NATURALLY BE DECLARED A SUCCESS FOR *FRANCE.*
NATURALLY. BUT THE FRENCH ARE BLAMED FOR A GREAT MANY THINGS THESE DAYS.
THE EXPLODING OF *EMPTY* GOVERNMENT OWNED WAREHOUSES FOR EXAMPLE...
THE ASSASSIN'S NATIONALITY IS PRACTICALLY IMMATERIAL.
HAD HE SUCCEEDED, MATTERS WOULD HAVE COME TO A HEAD IN ALMANI-LOTHARINGEN, AND THEN GERMANY AND FRANCE WOULD BE AT WAR.
AND WHERE WOULD THAT LEAVE *BRITAIN?*
BUT IF HE *WERE* A GERMAN...?
WELL, IT'S NO REAL SECRET THAT THE FRENCH HAVE BEEN BUILDING UP THEIR MILITARY.
THEORETICALLY, GERMANY MIGHT THINK THAT, IF A WAR WAS COMING, SOONER MIGHT BE BETTER THAN LATER.
STRIKE *BEFORE* THE FRENCH CAN.

HAD I NOT BEEN *INCONVENIENCED*, I MIGHT HAVE HELPED THE BARON.
BUT YOU DIDN'T WANT THAT DID YOU?
EACH MAN ABIDES BY HIS OWN ETHICS, SHERLOCK.
YOU WILL NOT STOP UNTIL YOU HAVE EXPOSED THE ROOT OF A PROBLEM AND DIPLOMACY BE DAMNED.
YOU KNEW ABOUT THE ASSASSINS FROM THE BEGINNING, AND FELT YOU COULD NOT RISK MY REVEALING THEIR ORIGIN.
BRITANNIA'S LOYALTIES MUST REMAIN UNTESTED, IS THAT IT?
I BELIEVE WE HAVE REACHED A STALEMATE.
ANOTHER GAME?
NOT TODAY, BROTHER. NOT TODAY.
END

Liverpool Demon

issue 1

Liverpool Demon Issue 1 Cover by Francesco Francavilla

LIVERPOOL'S DOCKLANDS, AUGUST 1888.
'EY! WATCH IT, WILL Y'?
I SAY!

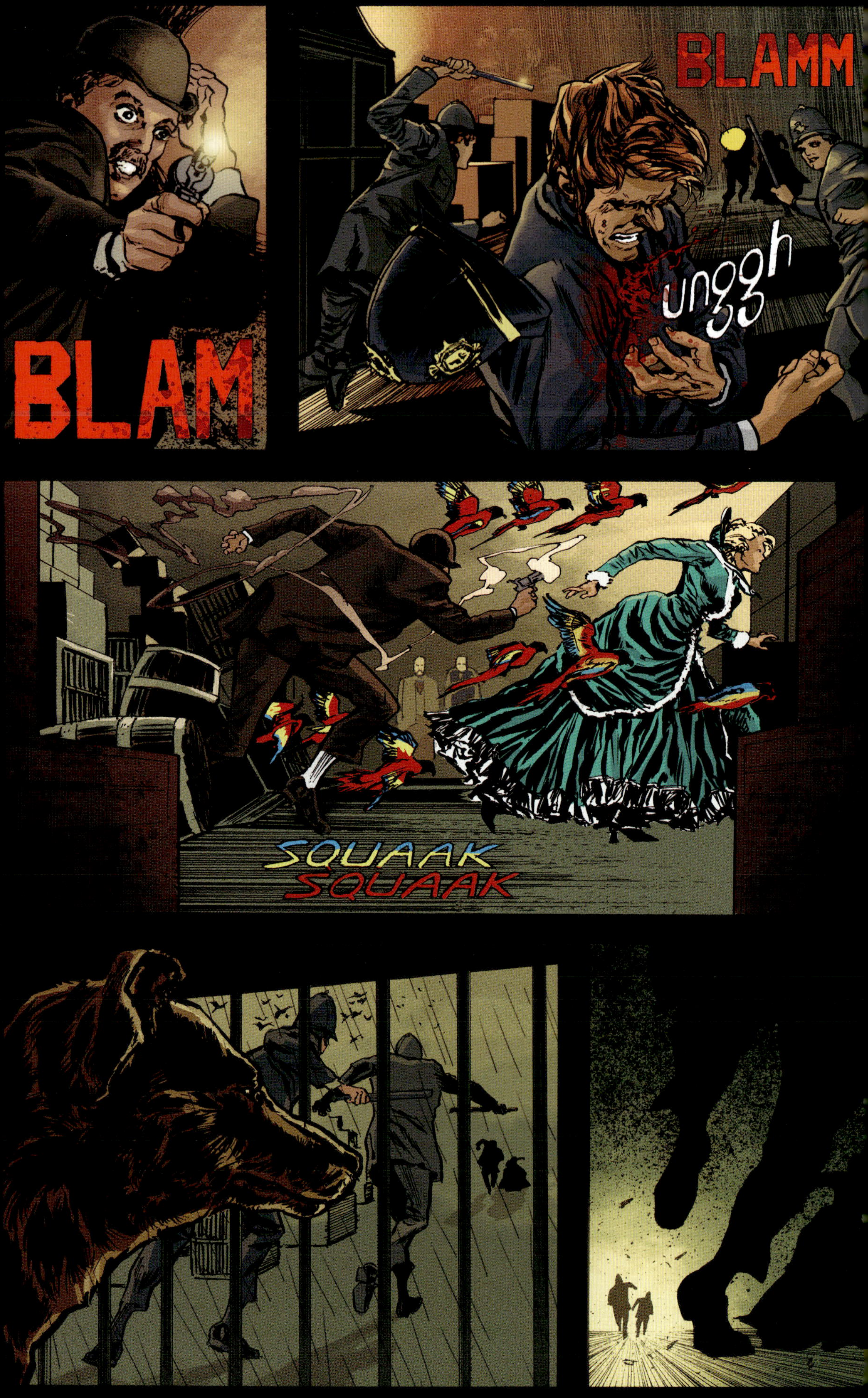
BLAM
BLAMM
unggh
SQUAAK
SQUAAK

A LINE!
FOR GOD'S SAKE, THROW US A LINE!
I HAVE IT! I HAVE IT!
SO SORRY TO DISAPPOINT YOU, OFFICERS...
BUT WE HAVE A BOAT TO CATCH.
BLAMM

I ADVISE THAT YOU BOTH REMAIN VERY STILL.
DR. WATSON HERE MUCH PREFERS SAVING LIVES TO TAKING THEM.
YOU FOOL!
MY HAND! MY HAND!
I'M SO GLAD YOU'RE HERE AT LAST. WHEN THE GANGPLANK WENT UP WITHOUT YOU ABOARD, WELL, I THOUGHT THE WORST.
I SEE YOU WERE IN FACT DELAYED BY THE LOCAL CONSTABULARY.
YOUR NEW *FRIEND* MUST BE RATHER LESS DISCREET THAN YOU, EH MRS. BICKERDYKE?
THOUGH, OF COURSE, YOU AREN'T REALLY MRS. BICKERDYKE, ARE YOU?
SNIK
SNIK
SNAKK
YAAAAH!
AHA! THE *NAVAJA*, A MOST DISTINCTIVE SPANISH BLADE. I'VE READ OF IT IN THE *"MANUAL OF THE BARATERO,"* OF COURSE.
I SHOULD REALLY HAVE KNOWN IT BY ITS SOUND.
YOU ARRIVED IN HULL AS FRÄULEIN STOLLER.
YOU TRAVELLED IN THE HOLD WITH A SHIPMENT OF POTASH, WHICH MARKED YOUR DRESS.
THE SAME DRESS FOUND ON MRS. BICKERDYKE'S CORPSE.

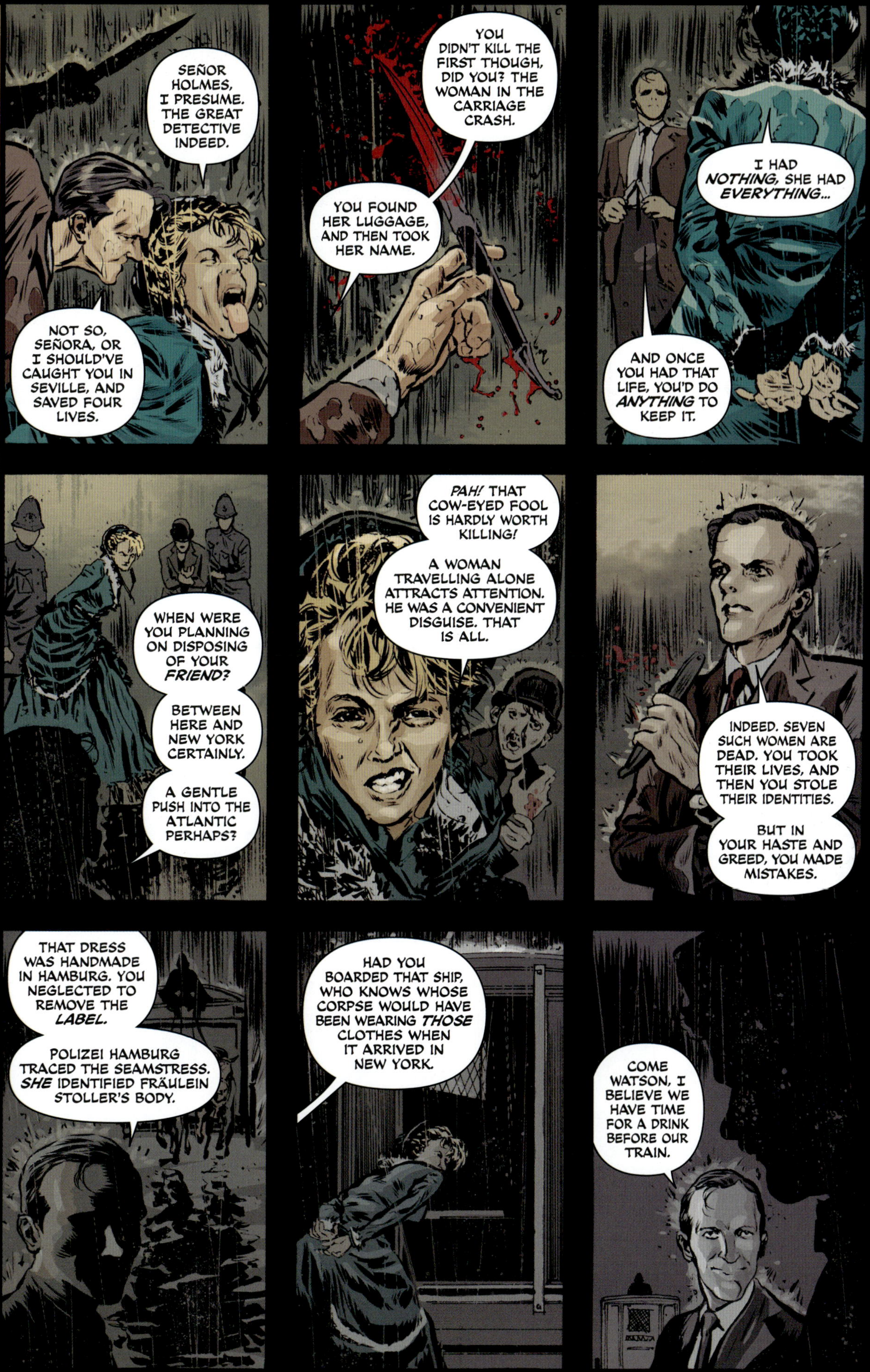
SEÑOR HOLMES, I PRESUME. THE GREAT DETECTIVE INDEED.
NOT SO, SEÑORA, OR I SHOULD'VE CAUGHT YOU IN SEVILLE, AND SAVED FOUR LIVES.
YOU DIDN'T KILL THE FIRST THOUGH, DID YOU? THE WOMAN IN THE CARRIAGE CRASH.
YOU FOUND HER LUGGAGE, AND THEN TOOK HER NAME.
I HAD *NOTHING*, SHE HAD *EVERYTHING*...
AND ONCE YOU HAD THAT LIFE, YOU'D DO *ANYTHING* TO KEEP IT.
WHEN WERE YOU PLANNING ON DISPOSING OF YOUR *FRIEND?*
BETWEEN HERE AND NEW YORK CERTAINLY.
A GENTLE PUSH INTO THE ATLANTIC PERHAPS?
PAH! THAT COW-EYED FOOL IS HARDLY WORTH KILLING!
A WOMAN TRAVELLING ALONE ATTRACTS ATTENTION. HE WAS A CONVENIENT DISGUISE. THAT IS ALL.
INDEED. SEVEN SUCH WOMEN ARE DEAD. YOU TOOK THEIR LIVES, AND THEN YOU STOLE THEIR IDENTITIES.
BUT IN YOUR HASTE AND GREED, YOU MADE MISTAKES.
THAT DRESS WAS HANDMADE IN HAMBURG. YOU NEGLECTED TO REMOVE THE *LABEL.*
POLIZEI HAMBURG TRACED THE SEAMSTRESS. *SHE* IDENTIFIED FRÄULEIN STOLLER'S BODY.
HAD YOU BOARDED THAT SHIP, WHO KNOWS WHOSE CORPSE WOULD HAVE BEEN WEARING *THOSE* CLOTHES WHEN IT ARRIVED IN NEW YORK.
COME WATSON, I BELIEVE WE HAVE TIME FOR A DRINK BEFORE OUR TRAIN.

GREAT NORTH WESTERN HOTEL, AFTERNOON.
"...REALLY SEE HOW SHE COULD HAVE EXPECTED TO GET AWAY WITH IT FOR ANY REAL PERIOD OF TIME.
"I MEAN, SHE COULDN'T HAVE GONE ON KILLING."
MY DEAR WATSON, SHE HAD ONLY TO FIND THAT PERFECT VICTIM AMONGST HER FELLOW PASSENGERS, AND SHE WOULD HAVE HAD NO *NEED* TO GO ON.
I-I BEG YOUR PARDON SIRS.
I HAVE THE PACKAGE YOU REQUESTED FROM THE CHEMIST, MR. HOLMES.
AH, EXCELLENT. THANK YOU VERY MUCH.
THERE'S NO NEED TO GLARE AT ME SO, IT IS MERELY TINCTURE OF IODINE AND A DRESSING FOR MY ARM.
MY *PHYSICIAN* NEGLECTED TO BRING HIS BAG, YOU SEE.
NOW THEN, WHAT TIME MAY WE DEPART FOR LONDON?
THE NEXT TRAIN IS TWO-FIFTEEN, THE FOLLOWING AT HALF PAST THREE.
THE LATTER SHOULD HAVE US BACK BEFORE TEN.

VERY WELL. I SUPPOSE WE MUST DINE ON THE TRAIN.
I'D BETTER SEND A TELEGRAM TO MRS. HUDSON TO LET HER KNOW WHEN WE'LL ARRIVE HOME.
YOU CAN SEND IT WHEN WE COLLECT OUR LUGGAGE.
AHEM I WAS RATHER HOPING YOU'D LEND A HAND.
THERE WE ARE, GOOD AS NEW!
AN EXCELLENT JOB, SIR. THANK YOU.
GOOD HEAVENS. LIKE A MONSOON.
I BELIEVE THE LOCAL PHRASE IS *"RAINING STAIR RODS"*.
EXCUSE ME, SIR, I DO BEG YOUR PARDON. MY NAME IS DENBY...

AM I ADDRESSING MR. SHERLOCK HOLMES?
DO FORGIVE ME, BUT I BELIEVE I'VE SEEN YOUR PICTURE IN THE NEWSPAPERS. THAT BUSINESS DOWN IN SUSSEX?
YOU ARE INDEED, MR. DENBY.
WHICH MEANS YOU THAT IT *IS* YOU! JOHN WATSON! AS I LIVE AND BREATHE.
DENBY? NOT...DANIEL DENBY?
THE VERY SAME! AND HERE YOU ARE ASSISTING THE WORLD FAMOUS CONSULTING DETECTIVE!
WELL, THIS IS EXTRAORDINARY! I HAVEN'T SEEN YOU SINCE--
SEVENTY-TWO. I FAINTED CLEAN AWAY WORKING ON THAT CADAVER, YOU REMEMBER?
OH, ALLOW ME TO INTRODUCE MY COLLEAGUES, THIS IS MR. FALLON...
...AND MR. LECK.
I COULDN'T HELP BUT OVERHEAR THAT YOU ARE PLANNING ON LEAVING ON THE THREE-THIRTY TO LONDON?

IT SEEMS A POOR SHOW THAT YOU COME ALL THIS WAY AND ARE THEN SUBJECTED TO A RAILWAY SUPPER!
MIGHT I SUGGEST THAT YOU DELAY YOUR LEAVING BY AN HOUR OR TWO AND ALLOW US TO TAKE YOU BOTH TO DINNER?
AH, WELL...
COME NOW, JOHN, I INSIST. YOU CAN STILL CATCH A TRAIN TO LONDON THIS EVENING.
THERE IS AN EXPRESS WHICH WILL HAVE YOU BACK IN THE CAPITAL BEFORE MIDNIGHT.
WE CAN DINE AT MY CLUB. IT'S NOT FAR IN A CAB AND THEY HAVE A VERY REASONABLE SELECTION OF SCOTCHES.
I'LL SEND A MESSAGE AND ENSURE THEY HAVE EVERYTHING JUST SO.
WELL NOW, WHAT DO YOU SAY HOLMES?
DENBY AND I WERE AT UNIVERSITY TOGETHER YOU SEE... AND, *UHM,* WE'VE NO PRESSING BUSINESS BACK AT HOME.
HOW CAN WE REFUSE?
HOW INDEED.

PEEEEEP
YAAH!
PEEEEEEP
BURST 'IM! BURST THE BASTARD!
DO 'IM! DO 'IM PROPER!
'AVE IT, YER BLOODY CRUSHER!
GRAAH!
DOSE THE BUGGER! DOSE 'IM!
HEC! HEC! THE SLOPS LADS! THE SLOPS!
MAKE WAY! OR DO YOU WANT A SCUTCHIN?
DIRTY CRUSHERS!
JESUS FLYNN, WHAT 'AVE THEY DONE TO YE?

CAN YOU 'EAR ME, FLYNN? YOU POOR SOD, ARE YOU IN THERE?
THEY LEGGED OFF, OFFICER...DOWN TOWARD *TITHEBARN STREET!*
THERE WAS SIX OF 'EM... WE SEEN 'EM DO IT!
YOUNG 'UNS THEY WERE, OFFICER, ALL FIVE OF 'EM!
IF ANY O' Y'S BOYS WANTS T' HOLD ON HERE AWHILE, I'LL BE DELIGHTED T' HELP Y'S RECALL THE EVENTS AS THEY HAPPENED.
IT SEEMS *PC FLYNN* HERE WAS SET UPON BY SOME *REAL* TOUGH LADS.
IT'D TAKE A FEW BIG BOYS TO MANAGE HIM, WOULDN'T IT?
PC FLYNN. ON HIS *OWN.*
IT WAS HIS OWN FAULT! DIRTY CRUSHER!
HE'S NOT *S'POSED* TO BE HERE!
OH HE ISN'T, IS HE?
WELL MAYBE YOU CAN STAY AROUND AND EXPLAIN THAT A WHILE.
I THINK I'D LIKE THAT VERY MUCH.

IT WAS NOT SPIRITS FROM BEYOND WHICH GAVE ME THOSE MESSAGES.
MR. DENBY SITS AWKWARDLY, SUGGESTING AN EARLY HIP FRACTURE, WHICH, SET INCORRECTLY, HEALED SLOWLY AS A RESULT.
MR. LECK'S SHOES SHOW A RESIDUE FROM WALKING ON WET YORK STONE.
MR. FALLON WEARS A DANDIFIED WAISTCOAT AND CRAVAT MORE SUITED TO A GENT TEN YEARS HIS JUNIOR.
HIS WEDDING BAND IS UNSCUFFED, AND HE DISGUISES HIS GREY WHISKERS WITH TINTED MOUSTACHE WAX.
AHEM WELL NOW...
WHAT BUSINESS DID YOU SAY YOU WERE ENGAGED IN?
A TRAM-LINE, WAS IT?
IT'S AN OVERHEAD RAILWAY. IT WILL BE THE FIRST OF ITS KIND IN GREAT BRITAIN OR EUROPE!
AH, I BELIEVE THERE IS SUCH A THING IN NEW YORK, IS THERE NOT?
THERE IS INDEED, ALTHOUGH IT IS NOT WITHOUT ITS FLAWS. WE HOPE TO IMPROVE UPON IT.
LIVERPOOL SHALL HAVE THE MOST MODERN TRAIN LINE IN THE WORLD! AND WHY NOT, WHEN THE RAILWAY ITSELF WAS BIRTHED HERE?

INDEED. THE LIME STREET CUTTING-- THE ONE THE LONDON TRAINS PASS THROUGH-- WAS PART BUILT BY JOSEPH WILLIAMSON, THE MOLE OF EDGE HILL HIMSELF!
STEPHENSON'S ROCKET RAN ON THOSE VERY TRACKS!
AND NOW, INSTEAD OF TUNNELLING BELOW-GROUND, WE SHALL LIFT THE RAILWAY INTO THE SKIES!
WELL, MOSTLY...
GENTLEMEN, IT SOUNDS LIKE A MARVELLOUS INNOVATION.
I'M SO GLAD YOU THINK SO, DOCTOR.
PERHAPS YOURSELF, AND MR. HOLMES OF COURSE, MIGHT EVEN ATTEND THE GRAND OPENING?
"IT SHOULD BE QUITE A SPECTACLE."
GOOD LORD! HE'S FAINTED CLEAN AWAY!
HE WAS LOOKING OUT OF THE WINDOW...
WHAT THE DEVIL DID HE SEE?

SCRITCH SCRITCH
KRAKK
SLAM
WHAT ON EARTH...?
HELLO?
IS THERE ANYBODY THERE?
KAKRAKK
MY WORD!
CLICK

ALISTAIR, YOU OLD FOOL. SCARED OF YOUR OWN SHADOW.
KRAK
LORD IN HEAVEN!
B-BUT HOW...?
MAY...MAY GOD HAVE MERCY UPON YOUR SOUL.

...CLINGING TO THE WALL...
...EYES LIKE BALLS OF FIRE...
...LEAPT A HUNDRED FEET OR MORE...
...THE VERY DEVIL...
...UP THERE WATCHING US...
...EASILY CARRY A PERSON AWAY...
HOLMES, HOLD ON! WE DON'T EVEN KNOW WHAT THIS IS ALL ABOUT!
WHATEVER IT IS, IT HAS TO BE A GREAT DEAL MORE INTERESTING THAN AN OVERHEAD RAILWAY!

BLAMM
I'LL FIX THE BLIGHTER!
KAKRAK
ptang
MY GOD! THERE IT IS!
THE TILES! LOOK OUT!
IT MEANS TO KILL US ALL!
QUICK, FETCH A LADDER! A LADDER!
CRACK
...WHERE IT WENT...
...IMPS OUT O' HELL...
...COULD BE SURROUNDED BY 'EM...
J-JESUS CHRIST ALMIGHTY...

Liverpool Demon Issue 2 Cover by Francesco Francavilla

SO, WHERE DOES THAT LEAVE US?
LIME STREET
WELL, SIR, WE COULD SEND TO DERBY ROAD FOR AN ENGINE TO PUMP IT OUT...
AND HOW LONG WILL THAT TAKE?
WELL, THEY ARE MOST OFTEN BUSY, SIR.
IF THEY *CAN* SEND AN ENGINE, IT'LL STILL TAKE HOURS TO SHIFT THE WATER.
WELL THEN, IN THE MEANTIME, YOU'D BETTER SEND FOR SOME BUCKETS.
BUCKETS, SIR?
TO BAIL THE WATER OUT, MAN. WE'VE AT LEAST GOT TO *SEEM* TO BE DOING SOMETHING.
LADIES AND GENTLEMEN, I REGRET TO ANNOUNCE THAT, DUE TO YESTERDAY'S RAINFALL, THERE WILL BE NO SERVICE FROM LIME STREET TODAY.
MY SINCEREST APOLOGIES.
IF YOU ARE ABLE TO MAKE YOUR WAY TO MANCHESTER, I'M TOLD THAT THERE IS NO SUCH PROBLEM THERE.
ONCE AGAIN, MY APOLOGIES.

MR. HOLMES! WATSON!
I MUST APOLOGISE, GENTLEMEN. I FEEL RESPONSIBLE.
IF IT WEREN'T FOR MY DELAYING YOUR LEAVING YESTERDAY...AND THE RAIN, OF COURSE...IT'S BAD ENOUGH YOU WERE FORCED TO STAY OVERNIGHT...
OH, NOT AT ALL, DENBY. YOU WEREN'T TO KNOW.
AT LEAST LET ME PAY FOR YOUR CAB TO MANCHESTER.
NO, NO, WE WOULDN'T HEAR OF IT. WOULD WE, HOLMES?
HOLMES?
AH, THERE HE IS.
MUST HAVE SPOTTED SOMETHING IN THE NEWSPAPER.
AN ACCOUNT OF YESTERDAY'S DARING ARREST, NO DOUBT.
I SAY, HOLMES, ANYTHING IN THERE ABOUT THE BICKERDYKE CASE?
HM?
OH, NOT MUCH.
YOU DO SURPRISE ME.

siderable commotion was caused yesterday in Everton on a rumou
ring-heeled Jack" was pursuing his antics in that neighbourhood. T
talk of a great cloaked or winged figure seen leaping from rooftop
op during last evening's fierce electrical storm. No less than four ladi
overcome and had to be revived by means of smelling salts or simila
even told of seeing the creature breathe fire, but the police have been
to find any ground for the suggestion that a "demon" was at work,
lieve some foolish person has been playing pranks. Yet many might
hat the perplexing event which occurred not one mile distant in Edge
night literally bears marks of diabolism. Alerted by a sound from
he Reverend at Saint Mary's Church unlocked his chapel and there
ed the corpse of an elderly gentleman showing all the marks of
en mauled as if by some clawed beast. Lurid stories of the
orious "Spring-heel Jack" who some years ago
d children of London will doubtl
d it is to be hoped that
or from this
"ALERTED BY A SOUND FROM WITHIN, THE REVEREND AT SAINT MARY'S CHURCH UNLOCKED THE CHAPEL...
"...DISCOVERED THE CORPSE OF AN ELDERLY GENTLEMAN WHICH BORE ALL THE MARKS OF HAVING BEEN MAULED AS IF BY SOME CLAWED BEAST."
SORRY, HOLMES? I-I DIDN'T QUITE CATCH THAT.
FETCH THE LUGGAGE, WATSON, WE MUST CHECK BACK INTO THE NORTHWESTERN, IMMEDIATELY.

...ROLLED A YOUNG LAD, FRESH ASHORE FROM THE MATILDA BRIGGS AN' COME AWAY WITH NEAR ENOUGH *EIGHT GUINEAS!*
...'S WHY I NEVER LAY A BET, SEE...
...'E CAN'T SEPARATE THEM AND GULLY GETS 'IS NECK RIPPED OUT.
...CAME HOME AN' FOUND SHE'D DRANK THE LOT...
ALRIGHT, ALRIGHT, SHUT IT NOW.
SO, WE'RE MISSIN' A FEW TODAY, AREN'T WE? WHY'S THA'?
BECAUSE THEY'RE BLOODY STUPID!
BECAUSE THEY DECIDED TO GIVE A COPPER THE BOOT WHEN THEY SHOULD'VE JUST ACTED NICE LIKE.
HE SHOULDN'T 'VE BEEN THERE, TRUE ENOUGH, BUT THA' ISN'T THE POINT.
EVEN IF A BLUEBOTTLE'S SOMEWHERE HE'S BEEN *TOLD* HE'S NOT SUPPOSED T', SO LONG AS YOUR HAND'S NOT DIPPIN' A POCKET, BE NICE.
THEY HATE THA' WORSE THAN ANYTHING.
I'M SHORT-HANDED NOW, JUST 'CAUSE SOMEONE FANCIED A ROW.
I AM *NOT* HAPPY.

MICK, TAKE A FEW LADS OVER TO HITCHCOCK'S.
HE WON'T BE EXPECTIN' ANOTHER VISIT SO SOON, SO BE GENTLE LIKE.
DON'T WANT ANY MORE *ACCIDENTS,* DO WE?
Y'LL NEED A WAGON AN' A DRIVER MOST PROBABLY, EH MICKY?
I'M SURPRISED TO FIND YOU, DRUMMOND.
HADN'T THAT DEMON IN THE PAPERS COME TO CLAIM *YOUR* SOUL?
WELL, WELL, MISS GOLDSMITH.
IT'LL TAKE MORE THAN ONE OF 'EM TO DRAG ME DOWN, I PROMISE YE'.
BUT WHAT'S THIS? FOR ME? YOU DIDN'T 'AVE TO DO THA'.
YES, I DID. MY GIRLS'VE HAD ENOUGH OF A NIGHT OF IT WI'OUT YOUR LOT TURNING UP DEMANDIN' OF 'EM.
FEELS A LITTLE *LIGHT* T' ME, MAGGIE.
THINGS AIN'T BEEN RIGHT SINCE YOUNG LIZZY LOST HER EYE. SHE'S DOIN' HER BEST, DRUMMOND. SHE REALLY IS.
I DIDN'T THINK THEY WERE PAYIN' T' LOOK AT HER EYES.
EH, LADS?

LIVERPOOL CITY POLICE MAIN BRIDEWELL, EARLY AFTERNOON.
IF, ERM, IF YOU WOULDN'T MIND SIGNING HERE, SIR. JUST A FORMALITY.
YES, YES OF COURSE.
RIGHT THEN, IF YOU'LL FOLLOW ME PLEASE, GENTLEMEN.
CORONER SHOULD REALLY'VE BEEN BY TO COLLECT 'IM BY NOW BUT... WELL, THIS AIN'T LONDON, EH?
INDEED.
I DON'T SUPPOSE ANYONE THOUGHT TO TAKE ANY PHOTOGRAPHS OF THE SCENE BEFORE THEY REMOVED THIS UNFORTUNATE GENTLEMAN?
PHOTOGRAPHS? W-WHY WOULD ANY--
NEVER MIND, NEVER MIND.

AND A NAME?
OH, YES, SIR, WE KNOW WHO HE IS. OLD TOM CHRISTIAN.
HE WAS A PI-- A DRUNK SIR. W-WE 'AD HIM IN MANY'S THE TIME...
IS-IS THAT STRICTLY NECESSARY, SIR?
YES.
AND THE WOUNDS ARE ON HIS BACK, YES?
AHA.
YOU WERE SAYING?
EH? WELL, HE WAS SUPPOSED TO HAVE BEEN FROM A WELL-TO-DO FAMILY... MIND YOU, HE TOLD A GOOD YARN...
HE DOES NOT LOOK LIKE A MAN OF MEANS.
NO, THE MONEY-- IF THERE REALLY WAS ANY--WAS LONG GONE. THE WAY HE TOLD IT, HIS FATHER WAS QUITE THE GENTLEMAN, THOUGH.
ANY RELATIVES THAT YOU KNOW OF?
WIFE? CHILD? SIBLINGS?
NO, SIR, HE WAS ALL ALONE.
"LAST O' THE CHRISTIANS," HE'D SAY, AND SOON GET ROUND T' SOME BUSINESS ABOUT ***CHRISTIAN*** CHARITY...
THE WOUNDS HAVE BEEN MADE WITH CURVED, CLAW-LIKE WEAPONS OF SOME SIZE, I BELIEVE.
DEFINITELY NOT BLADES. SEE HERE HOW THE FLESH HAS BEEN TORN RATHER THAN CUT?

YOU KNOW, IT DOES RATHER REMIND ME OF SOMETHING I SAW OUT IN INDIA.
OF COURSE, THE CLAWS WOULD HAVE TO BE...
OF COURSE. THE PRIEST MUST HAVE *FORGOTTEN* TO MENTION A TIGER.
THE ATTENDING OFFICERS, TOO. STILL, EASY ENOUGH TO OVERLOOK, EH?
I WAS MERELY OFFERING MY PROFESSIONAL OPINION.
IF *THAT* IS YOUR OPINION, WATSON, YOU CAN KEEP IT.
IT-IT'D 'AVE TO BE BIG THOUGH, WOULDN'T IT? GIANT, REALLY.
I'M SORRY? WAS THERE ANY EVIDENCE OF A GIANT BEAST?
WELL, NOT EXACTLY, SIR.
BUT THEN THERE WOULDN'T BE, WOULD THERE?
OH, SO YOU ALSO HAVE A THEORY? DO TELL US.

WELL, I MEAN, SPRING HEELED JACK...HE'S LIKE A GHOST OR A DEVIL OR SOMETHIN', ISN'T HE?
SO...WELL...HE, *ERM*, MIGHT'VE BEEN ABLE TO PASS THROUGH THE WALL, OR...OR SOMETHIN'?
WONDERFUL. YOU'VE CRACKED THE CASE, OFFICER. CONGRATULATIONS.
NEVERTHELESS, FORMALIST THAT I AM, I BELIEVE I SHALL CONTINUE WITH MY OWN ENQUIRIES.
I ASSUME YOU HAVE ALREADY NOTICED THIS, WATSON?
WHY YES, IT'S SAND, THE WHOLE BODY IS COATED WITH IT.
IN TRUTH, HE LOOKS MORE LIKE A MAN WHO HAD BEEN IN THE SEA--OR THE RIVER, I SUPPOSE--RATHER THAN CAUGHT IN A STORM.
MY THOUGHTS EXACTLY.
AND YET, SAINT MARY'S IS AT LEAST TWO MILES FROM THE MERSEY.

SERGEANT, I WOULD LIKE TO SPEAK WITH THE OFFICER WHO ATTENDED THE MURDER AT SAINT MARY'S CHURCH LAST EVENING.
THAT'D BE WARDY, I THINK. HE'S NOT 'ERE NOW.
WELL, DO YOU THINK YOU COULD FIND OUT WHERE HE IS?
IT'S RATHER IMPORTA--
NOW, DIDN'T THE SERGEANT JUST SAY HE'S NOT HERE?
HE'LL BE OFF DOING REAL POLICE WORK.
OUT ON THE STREET LIKE.
I SEE. AND YOU ARE?
I'M INSPECTOR THORNTON, AND THIS IS MY STATION.
WHO ARE YOU?
PLEASED TO MEET YOU, INSPECTOR.
MY NAME IS SHERLOCK HOLMES AND THIS IS MY COMPANION DR. WATSON.

AH, THE FELLAS WHO CAME TO SEE THE MORTAL REMAINS.
HAVE A GOOD LOOK, DID Y'?
DID YOU ATTEND THE SCENE AT ALL, INSPECTOR?
I DID NOT. WHY WOULD I?
BETWEEN THE NAVVIES AND THE CORNERMEN, THE WHORES AND THE CRACKSMEN, WE ARE *BUSY*, MR. HOLMES. VERY, *VERY* BUSY.
WE CAN'T DROP EVERYTHING EVERY TIME AN OLD DRUNK DIES.
IF Y'S WANT T' GO BOTHERING ANYONE ABOUT WHAT THEY SAW, THEN THE VICAR IS Y'R MAN.
I'M SURE *HE'LL* BE GLAD TO TALK T' YOU.
WELL, THANK YOU VERY MUCH FOR YOUR HELP, INSPECTOR.
WE SHOULD BE ON OUR WAY THEN.
AR DO BHEALACH, MR. HOLMES. A AMADÁN.
GOOD DAY, INSPECTOR.

M-MR. HITCHCOCK, SIR?
CHOCK
YES, MATTHEW, WHAT IS IT?
S-SOMEONE TO SEE YOU, SIR...
IF IT'S CAPTAIN TAGGART'S BOYS, TELL 'EM HE'LL GET HIS MONEY BEFORE THE NEXT TIDE.
NOT TAGGART'S BOYS, MR. HITCH. WE AIN'T SO GENTLEMANLY AS CAP'N TAGGART'S LOT.
I-I TOLD YOU YESTERDAY I HAVEN'T--
YESTERDAY MR. DRUMMOND WAS FEELIN' *GENEROUS.*
TODAY? WELL...

MR. DRUMMOND WANTS HIS MONEY, MR. HITCH. HE WANTS IT NOW.
LEAVE THAT ALONE!
PLEASE, GENTLEMEN, MR. DRUMMOND WILL GET HIS MONEY!
KLANGGGG
KELLOW, THAT'S ENOUGH! HOW'M I SUPPOSED TO TALK TO MR. HITCH WITH THIS RACKET?
MR. HITCH, YOU ARE A VERY LUCKY MAN INDEED. YOU WILL THANK YOUR LUCKY STARS.
MR. DRUMMOND HAS THOUGHT OF ANOTHER WAY FOR YOU TO REPAY SOME OF YOUR DEBT.

...THESE DAYS THE PARISH IS IN GREAT NEED, AND IT IS ONLY A MATTER OF TIME RE--
BOOOOMMMMM
GOOD LORD!
THE VERY SAME!
IT WAS THAT VERY SAME NOISE I HEARD! MR. WATSON, THE FIEND HAS STRUCK AGAIN!
HALLO? MR. HOLMES, ARE YOU ALL RIGHT?
HOLMES? HOLMES, ARE YOU THERE?
HOLMES! ARE YOU THERE, HOLMES?
SHOUT OUT, MAN!
PERHAPS IT WAS THE SLAM OF A DOOR?
HE...HE MAY HAVE SIMPLY STEPPED OUTSIDE A MOMENT.
WHERE IN GOD'S NAME HAS HE GONE TO?
AHEM
WHERE INDEED?

I DON'T UNDERSTAND IT, REVEREND. CAN YOU REMEMBER WHEN WE SAW HIM LAST?
HE WAS WITH US UNTIL WE WENT TO YOUR STUDY, WASN'T HE?
I, *AH,* I THINK HE WAS, YES...BUT AFTER THAT...*UM.* I COULDN'T SAY...
DR. WATSON, I REALLY MUST APOLOGISE...
APOLOGISE FOR WHAT, REVEREND?
WHAT HAVE YOU DISCOVERED OUTSIDE, WATSON? ANYTHING OF USE?
I-I, *UM,* NO, NO, HOLMES... NOTHING REALLY.
NO MATTER, I BELIEVE I HAVE LEARNED ALL I CAN FROM SAINT MARY'S TODAY.
MANY THANKS, REVEREND, YOU HAVE BEEN MOST USEFUL, MOST USEFUL INDEED.
EXTRAORDINARY...

GO ON! GE'IM! GE'IM!
GRRRR
COME ON!
BITE DOWN, Y' BLOODY GUMMER!
KILL 'IM!
BASTARD'S TURNED FELON!
RIP 'IS NECK OUT!
RRRARRRGH
GRRARRGH
BENDIGO WINS!
NOW PAYING ALL BETS ON BENDIGO!
NEVER MIND, EH LAD? HE DID HIS BEST. PUT ON A GOOD SHOW LIKE.
WHHNNN

'ELLO JIMMY.
DRUMMOND!
I-I... I MEAN, I DIDN'T EXPECT YOU TO...DIDN'T KNOW YOU WERE HERE LIKE.
JUST ARRIVED, JIMMY, JUST ARRIVED.
I-I'M VERY SORRY ABOUT GULLY... HE WAS A FINE DOG. A GREAT FIGHTER.
MY LADS DID THEIR BEST Y'KNOW. TRIED TO GET THE POWDER ON AN' SEPARATE 'EM...
SOMETIMES THAT'S JUST HOW THE GAME GOES THOUGH, EH?
I-I MEAN...WELL, IT WASN'T RIGHT LIKE AND I KNOW YOU LOST A BIT OF MONEY...
SO...WELL, I MEAN, IF YOU GET YOURSELF ANOTHER BEAST LIKE.
WELL, I-I'D BE HAPPY TO GIVE YOU GOOD ODDS. Y'KNOW, FAIR'S FAIR.
VERY KIND OF Y', JIMMY, VERY KIND.
I DO HAPPEN TO 'AVE A NEW BEAST WI' ME 'ERE TONIGHT, AS IT HAPPENS.
AH, WELL THEN, L-LET'S GET 'IM IN THE PIT THEN, EH?
W-WHAT'S THE NAME?
I CALL 'IM SAVAGE.

WILLIAM BROWN MUSEUM, LATE EVENING.
"NOW THEN, WHERE'S THAT PRISEBAR? AHA!"
WONDERFUL!
KREEEEEEE
...SOME PECULIAR AUSTRALIAN BEAST, NO DOUBT.
WHO'S THERE?
EH?
OH, I'M SORRY, SIR.
I DIDN'T MEAN TO STARTLE YOU...
HA. NO, NO, THAT'S QUITE ALRIGHT, ARTHUR.

I MIGHT HAVE KNOWN YOU WOULDN'T LEAVE 'TIL YOU'D UNPACKED THE LOT.
IT'S A FASCINATING COLLECTION. WE REALLY ARE LUCKY!
IF YOU SAY SO, SIR. DON'T WORK *TOO* LATE NOW, WILL YOU?
I WON'T. GOOD NIGHT.
AAAARRRGH
KLINK
WHAT THE DEVIL...?

Liverpool Demon Issue 3 Cover by Francesco Francavilla

THE BANK OF THE RIVER MERSEY, EARLY MORNING.
'ERE, LOOK AT THIS!
A PENNY!
RRR
LE' ME SEE.
GE' OFF!
RAFF RA RAFF
OI! WHAT'S UP WITH WINSTON?
RAFF RA RAFF
L-LOOK THERE...
HAOOOOOoooo
IT'S... IT'S...
...SPRING HEELED JACK!

GREAT NORTHWESTERN HOTEL, BREAKFAST TIME.
MR. WATSON, ISN'T IT?
IT'S DOCTOR, ACTUALLY.
HOW CAN I HELP YOU, INSPECTOR THORNTON?
ACTUALLY, I WAS LOOKING FOR Y'R MAN, HOLMES.
I'M AFRAID MR. HOLMES ISN'T HERE.
HE WENT OUT SOME TIME AGO.
ALREADY? AT THIS HOUR? D'YOU KNOW WHEN HE'LL BE BACK?
I'M AFRAID NOT. HE'S ALWAYS LIKE THIS WITH A NEW CASE.
HE WAS AWAKE AT FIVE THIS MORNING--
NOT SO, WATSON!

I ROSE AT FOUR--I MERELY CALLED UPON *YOU* AT FIVE TO BORROW YOUR PEN.
AND HERE YOU ARE, ONLY JUST SITTING DOWN TO BREAKFAST!
LUCKILY, THE CENTRAL LIBRARY'S CHIEF BIBLIOGNOST WAS NOT AS DIFFICULT TO WAKE AS YOUR GOOD SELF.
THE COLLECTION THERE IS QUITE IMPRESSIVE.
INCIDENTALLY, AS I LEFT THE LIBRARY, I NOTICED A NUMBER OF OFFICERS FAILING TO APPEAR INCONSPICUOUS OUTSIDE THE MUSEUM.
IS SOMETHING AMISS, INSPECTOR?
WELL, FACT IS, THERE'S BEEN ANOTHER MURDER, MR. HOLMES.
HAS THERE INDEED?
WAITER, COULD YOU SEE THESE BOOKS GET TO ROOM *THREE-OH-SEVEN*, PLEASE?
COME ALONG, WATSON. THIS IS NO TIME FOR EATING!
YOU, TOO, INSPECTOR.
TÁ AN CLUICHE AR COIS!

WILLIAM BROWN MUSEUM.
FUNNY, I THOUGHT SPRING HEELED JACK WAS SUPPOSED T' GO AFTER YOUNG GIRLS LIKE.
CONSTABLE, IF YOU--OR ANYONE ELSE--MENTIONS SPRING HEELED BLOODY JACK AGAIN, Y'LL FEEL MY BOOT UP Y'R ARSE. UNDERSTOOD?
SIR.
CHRISTOPHER CONNOR. WORKING LATE LAST NIGHT UNPACKING ALL THIS STUFF AN' SETTING UP FOR THE EXHIBITION. IT WAS HIS OWN PET THING, SO I'M TOLD.
NIGHT-WATCHMAN WAS THE LAST T' SEE THE LAD ALIVE, NOT LONG BEFORE IT HAPPENED.
HE HEARD A SCREAM, CAME RUNNING, AN' FOUND HIM LIKE THIS.
INTERESTING...

HIS NECK HAS BEEN BROKEN. BLUNT INSTRUMENT BY THE LOOK OF IT.
AND THE WOUNDS? THEY'RE THE SAME AS OUR MAN AT THE CHURCH.
WELL, THEY ARE SIMILAR--
SIMILAR?
THE CONFIGURATION OF WOUNDS IS *DIFFERENT,* THE NUMBER OF WOUNDS IS *DIFFERENT,* THESE WERE INFLICTED CAREFULLY AND DELIBERATELY WHILST THE OTHERS WERE QUICK AND VICIOUS.
I WAS ABOUT TO SAY THAT THEY'RE *SIMILAR* IN AS MUCH AS THE SAME SORT OF SHARP-ENDED, CURVED WEAPON APPEARS TO HAVE BEEN USED.
ANY SIGNS OF A FORCED ENTRY, INSPECTOR?
A NICE, NEAT, LITTLE, CIRCULAR HOLE IN A SHUTTER, JUST BIG ENOUGH FOR A FELLA TO GET HIS HAND IN AND RAISE THE BAR.
PROPER OLD FASHIONED JOB LIKE.
HE'S NO AMATEUR CRACKSMAN, THIS ONE.
SO FAR AS WE CAN TELL, NOTHING'S MISSING.
NOT TRUE, INSPECTOR.
SOMETHING IS DEFINITELY MISSING.

THE DOCKLANDS.
...PERHAPS THE INTENTION WAS TO MURDER MR. CONNOR FROM THE OUTSET, AND THE KILLER SIMPLY TIRED OF WAITING FOR HIM TO EXIT THE MUSEUM?
MERE SUPPOSITION! YOU ARE PUTTING THE CART BEFORE THE HORSE AS ALWAYS, MY FRIEND.
FOR WHAT REASON? BY WHOM? BESIDES, WHY WOULD THEY HAVE THE MEANS TO BREAK IN SO EFFICIENTLY IF THAT WAS NOT THEIR ORIGINAL INTENTION?
SUCH CONJECTURE MERELY CROWDS THE MIND AND CLOUDS THE JUDGEMENT. DATA IS WHAT WE NEED, NOT SUPPOSITIONS!
THE MATILDA BRIGGS, SIRS.
PERHAPS WE MIGHT FIND SOME ANSWERS HERE, EH?
I HOPE SO, WATSON, I HOPE SO.

GOOD MORNING, SIRS. WOULD IT BE POSSIBLE TO SPEAK WITH THE CAPTAIN OF THIS VESSEL?
AN' WHO'S ASKIN', THEN?
THIS IS OFFICIAL POLICE BUSINESS WE'RE ON, SO JUST YOU WATCH Y' TONE.
IS THAT SO?
JENKS!
I SEE WE HAVE SOME VISITORS.
YOU WERE ABOUT TO SHOW 'EM ABOARD, I'M SURE?
A VERY GOOD MORNING TO YOU GENTS.
I'M CAP'N TAGGART, AND *THE MATILDA'S* MY TUB.

YOU'LL HAVE TO EXCUSE JENKS.
HE'S A GOOD MAN, A FINE FIRST MATE, BUT DRY LAND... WELL, IT DOESN'T REALLY AGREE WITH HIM.
OF COURSE, I KNOW WHO YOU ARE. SAW YOU TWO CHASING THAT COUPLE DOWN NOT TWO DAYS AGO.
TRUTH IS, I'M QUITE HONOURED TO HAVE THE GREAT DETECTIVE-- AND YOUR SELF OF COURSE, DOCTOR--VISIT MY HUMBLE LITTLE SHIP.
AND THAT SHOT! WELL, YOU'RE QUITE THE MARKSMAN, DOCTOR!
AH, WELL...
A NASTY BUSINESS THAT, PRETTY YOUNG THING BEHIND ALL THEM KILLINGS?
MAKES ME GLAD I DON'T TAKE PASSENGERS. SOME OF THEM WOULD BE MORE TROUBLE THAN THE BEASTS.
WE'RE BALANCING THE NEW CARGO BEFORE WE CLEAR OUT FOR GUAM.
SUNLIGHT SOAP, TATE AND LYLE TREACLE--THE BEST OF BRITISH, SENT TO THE ENDS OF THE EMPIRE!

IT'S NOT FAR NOW, I SHOULD'VE SENT A BOY OVER TO THE MUSEUM WITH IT AS SOON AS WE FOUND IT...
BUT, YOU KNOW HOW IT IS.
OF COURSE, CAPTAIN, YOU'RE A BUSY MAN.
HERE WE ARE, GENTS.
THE MATE DISCOVERED IT, THOUGHT IT WERE AN EMPTY ONE, SOMEHOW MIXED UP WITH THE REST.
BUT THEN HE MOVED IT AND REALISED THERE WAS SOMETHIN' INSIDE, SO WE OPENED IT UP.
KRKxx
GAVE MY BOYS QUITE A TURN, IT DID.

GOOD GOD. HOW BIG IS IT?
WELL, IT'S A PANTHER... A BIG JUNGLE CAT LIKE.
TELL ME *ONE* O' THESE IS DRUMMOND!
SAID THEY BROUGHT THE BEAST 'ERE T' FIGHT LIKE.
THE KID WHO STOPPED THE BOBBY THIS MORNIN'--POOR LAD BARELY GOT OUT ALIVE--IT'S HIM WHO PUT DRUMMOND AND HIS BOYS IN IT.
GIVE ME SOME *GOOD* NEWS HERE, CONSTABLE!
OH, ERM, 'FRAID NOT, SIR. KELLOW AND RYAN FROM 'IS CREW THOUGH.
WHO'S HERE FROM THE ZOO, THEN?
WHO'S HELPIN' US CATCH THE THING?

W-WE DON'T KNOW WHICH ONE IT'S FROM, SIR, SO...
JAYSUS! SEND SOMEONE TO FIND OUT!
WELL, SIR...
I MEAN, I DON'T THINK THERE'LL BE TIME NOW, LIKE.
LIKE I SAID, THEY'VE GOT IT CORNERED IN BELEM COURT NOW.
WELL, WHY CAN'T THEY JUST KEEP IT THERE? DID WE NOT GET EVERYONE OUT?
WE...WE DIDN'T GET ANYONE OUT, SIR. WE COULDN'T RISK IT.
IT'S BEEN DONE BAD BY THE DOGS, SIR. IN A TERRIBLE WILD STATE. THE MEN ARE GOING TO BRING IT DOWN WITH RIFLES.
INSPECTOR?
I KNEW IT WAS YOU, INSPECTOR THORNTON! I RECOGNISED YOUR VOICE FROM THE END OF THE ENTRY, SIR.
KATHLEEN, I DEFINITELY DO NOT HAVE TIME FOR THIS.
I HAVE SOMETHING TO TELL YOU, SIR. SOMETHING *IMPORTANT.*
SEE, I KNOW WHO KILLED TOM CHRISTIAN.

RIGHT, I'LL--
IT'S ON THE MOVE!

SAVE US! FOR GOD'S SAKE, SAVE US!
MY BABY! TAKE MY BABY!
AAAGH! IT'S COMING! IT'S GOING TO GET 'IM!
HOLD YOUR FIRE!

OH GOD, IT'S 'ERE!
GRRAHRRR
AAAGGGHHH
FIRE!
BLAM BLAM BLAMM
SPK
ZPP
ZPP
CEASE FIRE!

MAIN BRIDEWELL.
THE CELLS ARE RAMMED. THE CROWD WE BOOKED FOR DOING P.C. FLYNN ARE--
KATHLEEN PUGH SAYS ONE OF 'EM MURDERED TOM CHRISTIAN.
SO, WE'RE KEEPING 'EM.
WHAT A BLOODY WEEK! WHAT'S NEXT?
WILL I BE STRUCK BY LIGHTNING P'RHAPS?
SIGH
RIGHT...
The Liverpool Dem
Considerable commo
yesterday in Everton on
"Spring Jack"
A WINGED DIABHAIL TEARS ROUND THE CITY, KILLS TWO UNCONNECTED MEN AND LEAVES ONE IN A LOCKED CHURCH, THE OTHER IN THE MUSEUM.
BOTH OF 'EM WITH DIRTY GREAT CLAW MARKS ON 'EM.
"'COURSE THERE'S BEEN A FRIGGIN' JUNGLE CAT ON THE LOOSE SO THAT RULES OUT OLD JACK. CASE CLOSED. MYSTERY SOLVED."
YET PANTHERS CAN'T WALK THROUGH WALLS OR BREAK INTO MUSEUMS AN' IT SOUNDS LIKE THE BEAST ONLY GOT AWAY LAST NIGHT...
"KATHLEEN PUGH TELLS ME SHE SAW TOM CHRISTIAN DOOR KNOCKIN' ON RAT LANE AN' TWO OF DRUMMOND'S LADS--KELLOW AN' GERAGHTY--THREATENING HIM."

"SO, DID DRUMMOND'S FELLAS SET THE PANTHER ON TOM?
"KELLOW'S UNDONE--HIM AN' THE OTHERS MAULED BY THE CAT ITSELF. THEY OBVIOUSLY HAD NO CONTROL OF IT. DEAD END.
"BESIDES, I ARRESTED GERAGHTY MYSELF AFTER FLYNN WAS ATTACKED THE NIGHT BEFORE LAST.
"HE WAS ALREADY IN THE CELLS WHEN OLD TOM TURNED UP IN SAINT MARY'S."
THE MARKS ON THE TWO BODIES DON'T MATCH UP ANYWAY...
...THE BEAST'D HAVE TO BE TWICE THE SIZE O' THE CAT AN' CONNOR'S ARE DIFFERENT TO TOM'S.
SO, WHAT'S THAT? THREE CLAWED THINGS ON THE LOOSE?
FOUR, IF Y' COUNT THE SPRING HEELED FELLA...UNLESS HE KILLED ONE OF 'EM... DAMNŪ AIR!
AT LEAST I'VE AN IDEA WHAT WENT ON WI' THE DOG FIGHT.
DRUMMOND'S GOING T' PAY FOR WHAT HAPPENED IN BELEM COURT. I'LL SEE TO THAT PERSONALLY!
THE CAT'S NOT FROM HENGLER'S CIRCUS, NOR WALTON ZOO...
...WHICH LEAVES THE TRAVELLING CIRCUS--WHO'RE ALWAYS A PAIN IN THE ARSE--AND HITCHCOCK T' SPEAK WITH.
WHICH STILL GIVES ME NO LEADS FOR EITHER CHRISTIAN OR CONNOR'S KILLINGS.
NOT SO, INSPECTOR!
I DO APOLOGISE FOR EAVESDROPPING, BUT I KNOW HOW INFURIATING IT CAN BE TO BE INTERRUPTED WHEN THINKING.
I BELIEVE THERE'S ONE AVENUE YOU'VE OVERLOOKED.

'COURSE, KATHLEEN DIDN'T MENTION EXACTLY WHICH PLACE TOM'D CALLED AT...
SUPPOSE WE JUST GET KNOCKIN', EH?
OH, I BELIEVE WE CAN NARROW IT DOWN, INSPECTOR.
THERE ARE, WHAT, A SCORE OF DOORWAYS?
NOW, WHICH MIGHT OLD TOM CHRISTIAN HAVE KNOCKED UPON?
FIRSTLY, WE MAY DISCOUNT THOSE DOORS WHICH LOOK AS THOUGH THEY WOULD NOT *WITHSTAND* BEING KNOCKED UPON.
NEXT, WE RULE OUT THOSE DOORS WHICH HAVE OBVIOUSLY NOT BEEN KNOCKED UPON OR OPENED FOR SOME TIME.
THAT IS *CLEARLY* THE DOOR TO A BROTHEL.
WHICH REALLY ONLY LEAVES US WITH...
...THIS ONE!
NOK NOK NOK
KREEEK
I'M AFRAID YOU'RE LA--*OH!*
GOOD EVENING. WE'RE HERE CONCERNING THE DEATH OF A GENTLEMAN LAST SEEN AT THIS ADDRESS TWO DAYS AGO. A MR. CHRISTIAN.
TOM?
DEAD?

THE SPIRITS ARE WITH US.
WITNESS THE LIGHT BY WHICH THEY MAKE THEMSELVES KNOWN.
AMAZING.
HEAVENS! SOMETHING JUST TOUCHED MY LEG!
BE CALM, THE SPIRITS ARE FRIENDLY. DO NOT BREAK THE CIRCLE.
NOW, DOES ANYONE HAVE--
MR. JOHNSON, YOU'RE UNDER ARREST FOR THE MURDER O' THOMAS CHRISTIAN.

Liverpool Demon Issue 4 Cover by Francesco Francavilla

...ON THE LOOSE FOR ALL I KNOW...WHO KNOWS WHAT'S TO BECOME OF ME NOW...POLICE'RE BOUND TO COME KNOCKING SOONER OR LATER...
I 'AD NO CHOICE...NO CHOICE AT ALL...BUT WHO'S GOING TO BELIEVE THAT?
SHOULD'VE KNOWN I COULD NEVER PAY IT BACK. THEY'D NEVER LET ME, EVEN IF I COULD...NEVER LET ME GO.
SCHLUK
HA HAKK HA HA
ANIMALS ARE CLOSE TO STARVING AS IT IS...WHO KNOWS WHAT'D HAPPEN IF... IF...
HAK HA HA HA
BUT THEN, WHAT'S TO HAPPEN TO *ME* IF I STAY?
I SHOULD GET OUT OF LIVERPOOL ONCE AND FOR ALL...GET OUT WHILE I STILL CAN!
NOT THINKIN' OF LEAVIN' US ARE Y', MR. HITCH?
D-DRUMMOND... I...
ONLY I'VE GOT MESELF INTO A BIT OF BOTHER LIKE AND I WAS 'OPIN' YOU'D 'ELP.
US BEIN' *FRIENDS* AN' ALL.

YOU MAY AS WELL COME CLEAN, JOHNSON. THE LONGER THIS TAKES, THE ANGRIER I'M LIKELY T' GET, SEE?
Y'R LAD HERE'S ALREADY TOLD US THAT TOM CAME T' SPEAK WITH YOU THE DAY BEFORE LAST.
HE SAYS YOU ARGUED. SOMETHING ABOUT SOME MONEY Y' OWED THE OLD MAN F'R INFORMATION.
JARROD? WHAT HAVE YOU SAID?
I ONLY TOLD THEM THE TRUTH!
OLD TOM WAS A FRIEND OF MINE, AND...AND THEY SAY HE'S BEEN MURDERED AND, WELL, YOU WERE SO *ANGRY* WITH HIM!
...I...I HEARD HIM THREATEN TO TELL PEOPLE WHAT YOU'D BEEN ASKING HIM ABOUT.
ALL HE WANTED WAS ANOTHER BOB OR TWO.
AND WHAT *HAD* YOU BEEN ASKING TOM CHRISTIAN ABOUT, MR. JOHNSON?
MEDIUMSHIP CANNOT BE TURNED OFF AND ON LIKE A TAP.
SPIRITS, LIKE THE LIVING, CANNOT *ALWAYS* BE RELIED UPON.
SO, FROM TIME TO TIME, IT IS, REGRETTABLY, NECESSARY TO RESORT TO OTHER MEANS.

BY "OTHER MEANS", YOU MEAN NOT ONLY THE RIDICULOUS FAKERY WE WITNESSED EARLIER, BUT ALSO THE GATHERING OF INFORMATION, YES?
A MAN OF CHRISTIAN'S YEARS BEING AN IDEAL SOURCE OF SEEMINGLY LOST DATA.
I DID CONSULT MR. CHRISTIAN ON CERTAIN MATTERS...
...HE HAD LONG SINCE TOLD ME ALL HE KNEW, AND YET STILL EXPECTED PAYMENT.
SO, HE WAS OF NO FURTHER USE TO YOU, EH? AND THEN HE THREATENED TO EXPOSE YOUR CHARLATANRY!
I AM NOT A MURDERER, SIR, BUT NEITHER AM I A CHARITY!
MR. CHRISTIAN AND I HAD AN ARRANGEMENT, BUT OUR BUSINESS HAD BEEN CONCLUDED.
HE WAS NO THREAT TO ME, MERELY AN ANNOYANCE.
WHAT BUSINESS? WHAT INFORMATION?
INDEED!
THAT IS PRECISELY WHAT I SHOULD LIKE TO KNOW!

MR. HITCHCOCK! THIS IS THE POLICE!
HITCHCOCK!
HITCH COCK'S MENAGERIE
NOK NOK NOK NOKK
MR. HITCHCOCK! WE NEED T' SPEAK WITH YOU!
NOK NOK NOKK
IT'S NO USE HIDIN' IN THERE!
NOK NOKK
SHUT YER BLOODY NOISE! KEEPIN' HONEST FOLK AWAKE.
IT'S NO USE BANGIN' ON THAT DOOR!
HE'S OBV'USLY DONE A BUNK, AT LAST.

AND WHY WOULD HE DO THAT, THEN?
WHY? JUS' LOOK AT THE STATE O' THE PLACE!
PLACE LIKE THAT CAN'T COMPETE WI' THE LIKES OF HENGLER'S, CAN IT? SHOULD'VE PACKED IT IN YEARS AGO!
OWES MONEY OUT LEFT, RIGHT AND CENTRE. EVEN OWES ME A PENNY OR TWO!
"I'VE SEEN SOME RIGHT ROUGHS COMIN' AN' GOIN' RECENTLY, TOO.
"POOR LAD MUST BE IN SOME PROPER TROUBLE T' BE ALLOWIN' 'IS GOODS T' BE CARRIED OFF LIKE."
GOODS? WHAT SORT OF GOODS?
'OW SHOULD I BLOODY KNOW? Y' THINK I'VE GOT NOTHIN' BETTER T' DO THAN SPYIN' ON FOLK?
THEY TOOK A BIG CRATE FULL 'O SOMETHIN' 'EAVY...
...LAST NIGHT I THINK. AYE, LAST NIGHT IT WAS.
THEY 'AD A TERRIBLE JOB WI' IT, TOO.

TOK TOK TOK
IT'S RARE YOU REVISIT THE SCENE OF A CRIME, HOLMES, DO YOU THINK YOU MISSED SOMETHING LAST TIME?
I MISSED NOTHING, WATSON. A SECOND VISIT WAS ALWAYS GOING TO BE NECESSARY.
YES? AH! MR. HOLMES...
I AM SORRY TO BOTHER YOU, REVEREND, ESPECIALLY AT THIS HOUR.
COULD WE COME IN?
THIS IS ABOUT TOM CHRISTIAN, I ASSUME?
YOU ARE CORRECT, REVEREND.
I HAD TO WAIT UNTIL THE TIDE TURNED BEFORE RETURNING.
NOW, SOMEWHERE HERE...THERE SHOULD BE...
THIS IS A CHURCH, HOLMES! SHOULDN'T WE RESPECT THAT?
AH! HERE WE ARE...
TK

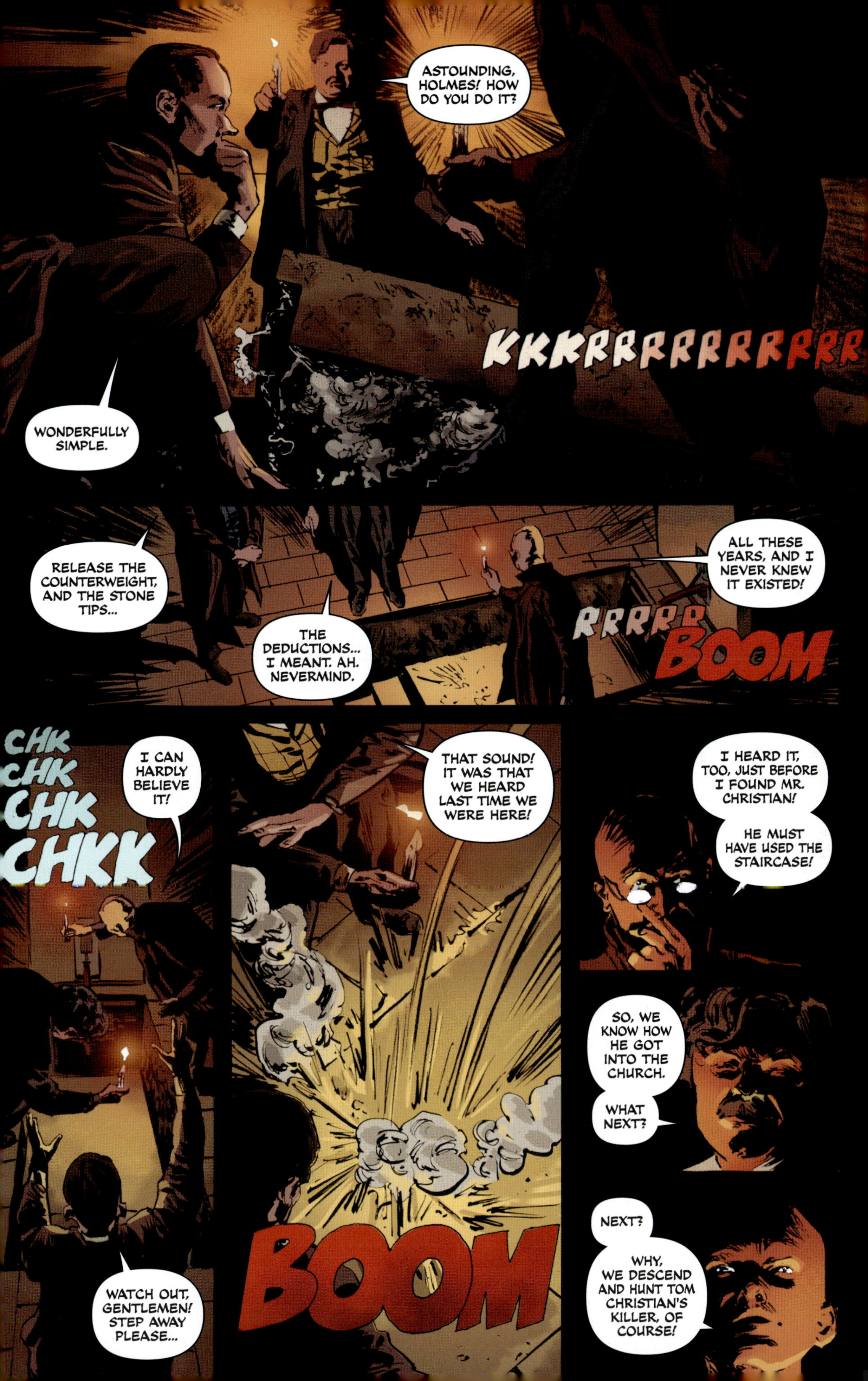
ASTOUNDING, HOLMES! HOW DO YOU DO IT?
KKKRRRRRRRRRRRR
WONDERFULLY SIMPLE.
RELEASE THE COUNTERWEIGHT, AND THE STONE TIPS...
THE DEDUCTIONS... I MEANT. AH. NEVERMIND.
ALL THESE YEARS, AND I NEVER KNEW IT EXISTED!
RRRRR
BOOM
CHK
CHK
CHK
CHKK
I CAN HARDLY BELIEVE IT!
WATCH OUT, GENTLEMEN! STEP AWAY PLEASE...
THAT SOUND! IT WAS THAT WE HEARD LAST TIME WE WERE HERE!
BOOM
I HEARD IT, TOO, JUST BEFORE I FOUND MR. CHRISTIAN!
HE MUST HAVE USED THE STAIRCASE!
SO, WE KNOW HOW HE GOT INTO THE CHURCH.
WHAT NEXT?
NEXT?
WHY, WE DESCEND AND HUNT TOM CHRISTIAN'S KILLER, OF COURSE!

I HAVE NEVER SEEN THE LIKE! SUCH CRAFTSMANSHIP IS ASTONISHING...
TAKE CARE, IT'S DAMP AND RATHER SLIPPERY UNDERFOOT.
"THE TUNNELS LOCATION WAS OBVIOUS FROM THE REVEREND'S DESCRIPTION OF MR. CHRISTIAN'S DISAPPEARING FOOTPRINTS.
"IT WAS APPARENT, HOWEVER, THAT I MUST ALLOW TIME ENOUGH FOR THE FLOOD-WATERS TO RECEDE BEFORE EXPLORING PROPERLY."
YOU'VE KNOWN ABOUT THIS PASSAGE ALL THIS TIME? WHY DIDN'T YOU SAY SOMETHING, MAN?
Recollections of Old Liverpool
Churches of Lancashire
THE STREETS OF LIVERPOOL
"FORGIVE ME, WATSON, BUT HAD I DONE SO, YOU WOULD HAVE BEEN DRAWN UNCONTROLLABLY INTO FANCIFUL AND *DISTRACTING* SUPPOSITION.
"I SOON FOUND RECORD OF THE WORKS OF MR. JOSEPH WILLIAMSON, OR *'THE MOLE',* AS HE WAS LATER KNOWN. A GRAVEN TRIBUTE TO WHOM ADORNS THE NARTHEX OF THE CHURCH, ABOVE."
EXCAVATIONS CONTINUED UNTIL HIS DEATH, LESS THAN FIFTY YEARS AGO, AND YET THE TUNNELS HAVE ALREADY PASSED INTO THE REALM OF *LEGEND.*
CONSEQUENTIALLY, PRECIOUS LITTLE DATA ON THE LABYRINTH'S EXACT LOCATION, OR EXTENT, EXISTS.
BUT CHRISTIAN KNEW ENOUGH TO CREATE A MAP.
ON WHICH HE INDICATED A RIVERWARD PATH, EVIDENTLY MISUNDERSTANDING JOHNSON'S INTEREST IN TUNNELS LEADING TO THE DOCKS.
SAINT MARY'S, HOWEVER, DID *NOT* FEATURE ON HIS MAP.

GREAT SCOTT!
THIS IS UNBELIEVABLE, HOLMES! THE WORKMANSHIP IS EXQUISITE, AND YET HERE IT ALL IS, BURIED WHERE NO-ONE CAN SEE IT.
FROM WHAT I HAVE READ, OLD WILLIAMSON LIKED IT THAT WAY. THESE CATACOMBS WERE NOT CREATED TO IMPRESS.
WELL, WHY DO IT THEN? WAS HE MAD? DID HE FANCY IT HIS VERY OWN KINGDOM?
THERE MAY BE SOME TRUTH IN THAT.
HOWEVER, THE CONSTRUCTION OF TUNNELS ALSO GAVE EMPLOYMENT TO MANY VETERANS OF THE NAPOLEONIC WAR.
WITHOUT WILLIAMSON, WHO KNOWS HOW THOSE MEN, AND THEIR FAMILIES, WOULD HAVE SURVIVED?
A PHILANTHROPIST THEN? REMARKABLE!

KUNKK
SKIK
"SIR?"
KKRAKKKK
SIR, I'M NOT SURE WE SHOULD...
I'VE TEN CORPSES, EIGHT OF WHOM WERE KILLED BY A GREAT BASTARD PANTHER.
Y'R MAN SAYS A CRATE LEFT HERE LAST NIGHT, SO THE CAT *HAD* T' BE HITCHCOCK'S.
I AM *NOT* LETTING HIM FECK OFF!
SECURE THIS ENTRANCE!
IT--IT'S ALL A BIT MUCH REALLY, ISN'T IT? THE MURDERS, THEN THE BEAST ON THE LOOSE, AND NOW THIS!
WHO NEEDS SPRING HEELED JACK, EH? THE NEWSPAPERMEN WILL HAVE A RIGHT MERRY TIME OF IT!
WON'T THEY JUST. BLOODY JACKALS.

RRR
WHA...
HITCHCOCK? ARE YOU THERE? THIS IS INSPECTOR THORNTON OF THE CITY POLICE.
HELLO HELLO
HELLO
JAYSUS! CLAMHACH PEARÓID!
KLANGKK

ARE YOU SURE YOU KNOW WHICH WAY WE'VE COME, HOLMES?
THESE PASSAGES DO NOT TALLY WITH MR. CHRISTIAN'S MAP AS YET, BUT FEAR NOT.
WE ARE NOT LOST!
SHOULDN'T WE HAVE A THREAD LIKE ARIADNE?
BREADCRUMBS, AT THE VERY LEAST...
HA! NOT AT ALL, NOT AT ALL.
A BASIC KNOWLEDGE OF LIVERPOOL GEOGRAPHY IS ALL WE REQUIRE.
I BELIEVE THESE STAIRS SHOULD BRING US OUT IN CANNING...
IF YOU SAY SO. IT WOULD BE PLEASANT TO HAVE SOME FRESH AIR AGAIN.
HERE WE HAVE ANOTHER COUNTERWEIGHT MECHANISM.
IT'S RATHER DAMP. I IMAGINE WE ARE LOWER DOWN IN THE WATER TABLE...
KLUNK
TK TK TK TK TK
ONE PULLS THE CHAIN WHICH ENGAGES THE COUNTERWEIGHT...

SPLOOOSHHHH
WHAT'S HAPPENING?
THE FLOOD! IT MUST HAVE FILLED THE CHAMBER ABOVE US!
WATSON! QUICKLY TAKE HOLD!
HOLMES! *HOLMES!*
NGAA
NO
WATSON!

NOT SO CLEVER NOW, ARE Y', PADDY?
WHO EVER 'EARD OF AN IRISH COPPER, ANYWAY? SOUNDS LIKE THE KICK-OFF F'R A BAD JOKE.
ACTIN' ALL HIGH AN' MIGHTY, WHEN YOUR LOT'RE THE WORST O' THE SCUM.
Y'R A BLOODY TRAITOR T' Y'R OWN KIND.
STRIKIN' AN OFFICER O' THE LAW IS A SERIOUS OFFENSE, MR. DRUMMOND.
KKKRANG
BUT STRIKIN' AN IRISHMAN...
WHOKK
...WELL, THAT'S VERY SERIOUS!

PAKK
BOK
ARAWK
AWRK
KRAANNGGG
TANG

HOW MANY'RE DEAD, OR GOOD AS, BECAUSE OF YOU?
PAKK
THAT STUPID STUNT WI' THE CAT'S NOT THE HALF OF IT, IS IT?
SCUM LIKE YOU FEEDIN' OFF DECENT FOLK. THOSE WHO KNOW NO BETTER, THOSE WHO DON'T HAVE A CHOICE.
WELL, Y'VE SLIPPED UP AT LAST, AN' HERE I AM--*THE LAW*--READY AN' WAITIN' FOR Y'.
KRAK
NOT SO CLEVER NOW, ARE Y'? *EH? EH?*
SKKRAKKK
WHMPP
WHMPP
WELL, *HUFF* HASN'T THIS BEEN A NICE LITTLE *HUFF* TRIP T' THE ZOO, EH?
BUT *HUFF* Y' KNOW WHAT, INSPECTOR? *HUFF* TH' BEST BIT'S YET T' COME.

'CAUSE NOW, *HUFF* IT'S FEEDIN' TIME!
AHAHAHA
HAKK HAAK
HA HA HA HA

HHHULGG
HAKK
"WHAT THE HELL WAS THAT?"

DID YOU SEE IT? IT WAS ENORMOUS!
WHERE IS IT? I SAW IT PASS THAT MAST THERE!
HELP! HELP ME!
KOF
PLASHHH
GUAA!
KOF KOF
AAAGHH
LOOSE THE NETS! LOOSE THEM!
GOD ALMIGHTY! IT HAS US! IT HAS US!

Liverpool Demon Issue 5 Cover by Francesco Francavilla

LIVERPOOL'S DOCKLANDS, AUGUST 1888.
BOOM
'EY! WATCH IT, WILL Y'?
I SAY!

STOP...STOP LAUGHING...
HAH HAH HA HAHHAHA HA HAK HA
...LAUGHING... OFFICERS WAITING... WAITING OUTSIDE...
HA! IT'S TOO LATE. FAR, FAR TOO LATE.
GOODBYE INSPEC--
STOP!
D-DON'T YOU EVEN MOVE!
TOO MANY PEOPLE ARE DEAD ALREADY. THERE'S BLOOD ON M-MY HANDS BECAUSE OF YOU.
I-I WON'T LET YOU DO THIS.
HA HA HAK HAA

OH, YES YOU WILL.
HE DIDN'T COME 'ERE F' ME. HE'S 'ERE TO ARREST THE FELLA WHO THAT CAT BELONGED TO.
I'M DOIN' YOU A FAVOUR.
BESIDES, YOU HAVEN'T GOT THE BAWBLES, AN' Y' KNOW IT.
YOU'RE WEAK, HITCHCOCK. EASY PICKIN'S.
WHY D' Y' THINK WE LOANED YOU THE MONEY IN THE FIRST PLACE?
THORNTON 'ERE KNOWS. 'E GETS IT.
IT'S SURVIVAL OF THE FITTEST.
KILL OR BE KILLED.
AN' YOU'RE NO KILLER. ARE Y', HITCHOCK?
NOT LIKE ME!
KRAKKK

THE BALTIC FLEET PUBLIC HOUSE.
BALTIC FLEET
...THOUGHT 'E WAS A GONER, WE DID!
COUGHED UP A GALLON O' THE MERSEY, AN' GOD KNOWS A TASTE'D KILL MOST OF US!
MIND YOU, I WAS NEARLY IN THERE M'SELF. BETTER A BELLY FULL O' RIVER THAN BE CARRIED OFF BY SPRING HEELED JACK, EH?
PLSSHHHH
COULD'VE TORCHED THE LOT WITH ONE FLAMIN' BREATH...
AN' THEN IT JUST MELTED AWAY, LIKE. INTO THE SHORELINE.
IT WASN'T A DEMON. I...I THINK IT WAS AFTER THE FISH.
AFTER THE *FISH?* YOU'VE HAD A FAIR CRACK ON THE HEAD, MATE. YOU'RE NOT THINKIN' RIGHT.
IT WAS A *BAT.* SOME KIND OF...OF GIANT BAT.
AND IT DIDN'T *"MELT AWAY"*. IT MUST BE ROOSTING SOMEWHERE, IN SOME HIDDEN CAVE. PERHAPS EVEN ONE OF WILLIAMSON'S TUNNELS.

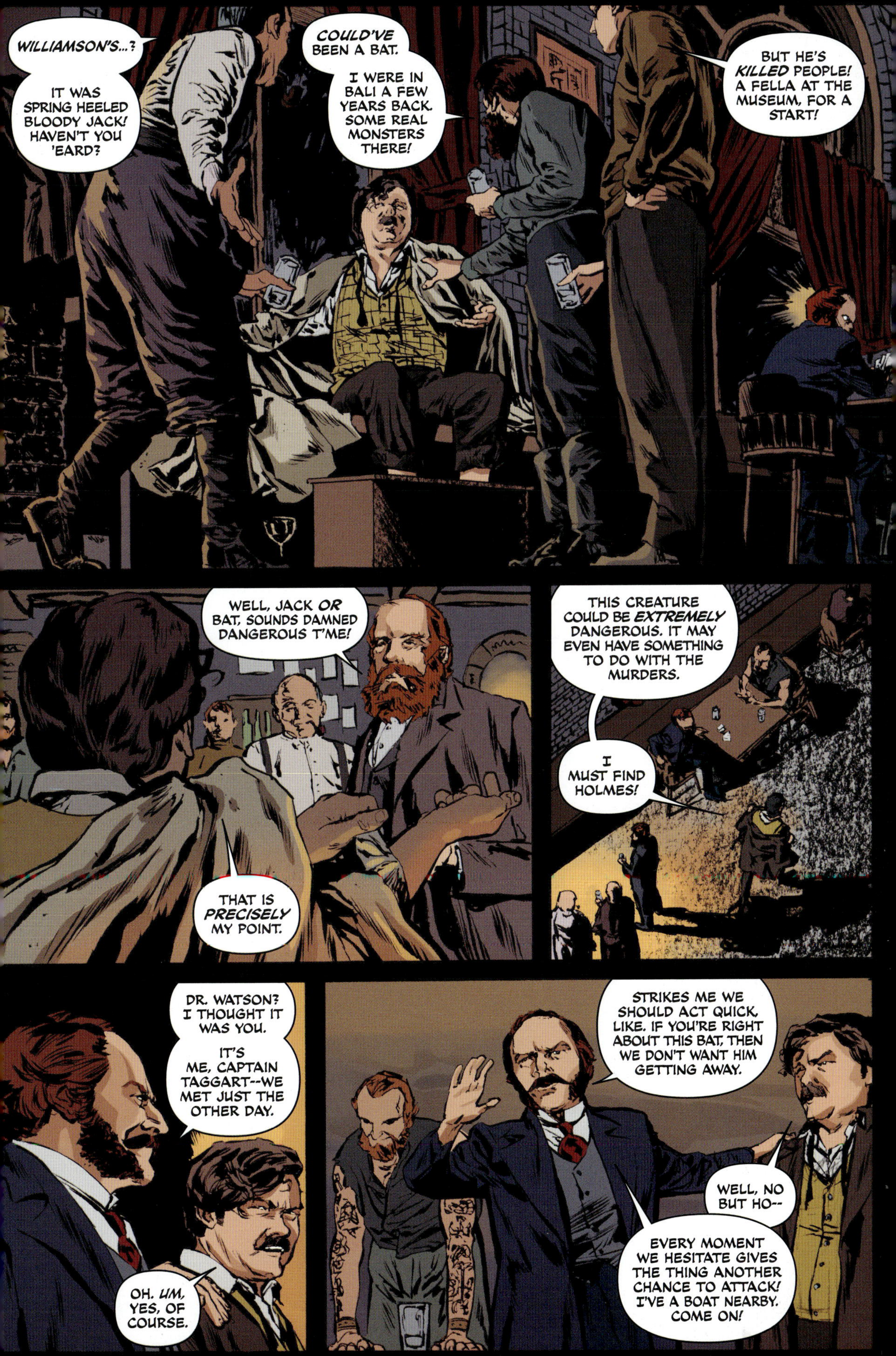
WILLIAMSON'S...?
IT WAS SPRING HEELED BLOODY JACK! HAVEN'T YOU 'EARD?
COULD'VE BEEN A BAT.
I WERE IN BALI A FEW YEARS BACK. SOME REAL MONSTERS THERE!
BUT HE'S KILLED PEOPLE! A FELLA AT THE MUSEUM, FOR A START!
WELL, JACK OR BAT, SOUNDS DAMNED DANGEROUS T'ME!
THAT IS PRECISELY MY POINT.
THIS CREATURE COULD BE EXTREMELY DANGEROUS. IT MAY EVEN HAVE SOMETHING TO DO WITH THE MURDERS.
I MUST FIND HOLMES!
DR. WATSON? I THOUGHT IT WAS YOU.
IT'S ME, CAPTAIN TAGGART--WE MET JUST THE OTHER DAY.
OH. UM, YES, OF COURSE.
STRIKES ME WE SHOULD ACT QUICK, LIKE. IF YOU'RE RIGHT ABOUT THIS BAT, THEN WE DON'T WANT HIM GETTING AWAY.
WELL, NO BUT HO--
EVERY MOMENT WE HESITATE GIVES THE THING ANOTHER CHANCE TO ATTACK! I'VE A BOAT NEARBY. COME ON!

IF WE BEAR LEFT UP AHEAD, IT SHOULDN'T BE MUCH FURTHER.
I 'EARD STORIES ABOUT THESE TUNNELS WHEN I WAS A LAD BUT I NEVER THOUGHT...I MEAN, I DIDN'T *BELIEVE*...
YES, IT IS INCREDIBLE, ISN'T IT? WATSON WAS EQUALLY IMPRESSED BEFORE HE...
THAT IS, BEFORE I LOST HIM.
WE ARE FOLLOWING THE PATH TAKEN BY THE WATER I LOOSED, WHICH WOULD BE THE PATH WATSON WAS CARRIED ALONG.
WE CAN ONLY HOPE THAT HE HAS NOT WANDERED OFF AND GOT HIMSELF LOST.
IF HE IS IN ANY STATE TO WALK AT ALL.
TH-THERE COULD BE ANYONE DOWN HERE!
ANYONE, OR...OR ANY*THING!*
HA! HAVE I BEEN CAST AS THESEUS THEN? OR PERHAPS VIRGIL?
NO, THERE IS NO MINOTAUR DOWN HERE.

AHA! I RECOGNISE THIS. I SAW ITS PAIR IN THE BRIDEWELL'S LAYING OUT ROOM.
THIS IS TOM CHRISTIAN'S SHOE.
NOT FAR NOW.
SOON IT WILL BE TIME FOR YOU TO TURN BACK. AND MAKE SURE THAT YOU CARRY OUT MY INSTRUCTIONS *EXACTLY.*
THE ARROWS WILL GUIDE YOUR WAY.
THERE IS NOT A MOMENT TO LOSE.
TIME AND TIDE TARRY FOR NO MAN!
MINOTAUR?
HERE, WATCH YOUR FEET, THE BOULDER THERE IS LOOSE.
I SEE IT SIR, THANK YOU.

I'LL GET TO YOU IN JUST A MOMENT MR. HITCH.
NO ONE T' SAVE YOU NOW. BLOODY BLUEBAGS THINK YOU'RE SO MUCH BETTER THAN THE REST O' US.
BUT YOU'RE JUST A MAN, THORNTON.
A DEAD MAN!
AAHAA
HAKKA HAK HA
HA HA HA HA
NO!
YOU... I-I CAN'T BELIEVE...
BELIEVE, MR HITCH, 'CAUSE YOU'RE NEXT!
NO.

HA HAKKAHAHAA HAH HA HAKK
AAAAAAAAAKKK
D-DEAR GOD!
HAK HAH HAKKAHA
URKKK
YOU ARE.
I-I-I'M SO SORRY... I... I DIDN'T... I COULDN'T--
HAHAKKAHAK HAKK HA
HAA HAHH
≠HNNG≠ ENOUGH O' THAT.
NOW, ≠HUFF≠ FOR GOD'S SAKE, ≠HUFF≠ PULL ME UP!
NNGG

SPLSS
SO, HOW *DID* YOU END UP IN THE RIVER?
SOME KIND OF RESERVOIR, A CELLAR MAYBE, THE STORM MUST HAVE FILLED IT TO CAPACITY.
WHEN WE OPENED THE HATCH...
RIGHT, BUT HOW DID YOU COME TO BE OPENIN' THE HATCH IN THE FIRST PLACE? IF YOU DON'T MIND MY ASKIN'.
HOLMES MUST HAVE, *UM,* MISCALCULATED.
NOW, WHERE COULD THE CREATURE HAVE GONE?
SO, YOU WEREN'T LOOKING FOR ANYTHING PARTICULAR THEN?
IN THE TUNNELS?
EH? OH, I...I'M NOT SURE, TO BE HONEST.
IS THAT SOMETHING THERE?
AH, NO. ANOTHER SEWER PIPE. TOO SMALL...
FOR YOU? I RECKON YOU COULD'VE COME OUT THAT WAY.
WOULDN'T FANCY IT MYSELF MIND.
NO, NO, FOR THE BAT.
WAIT, THERE! AN OPENING! IT MUST BE THE PLACE.
WHY, SO THERE IS.

THIS LOOKS VERY PROMISING! THE ARCH THERE IS VERY LIKE ONES I SAW EARLIER.
AH, SO YOU THINK IT MIGHT BE CONNECTED THEN?
SKKRRKKK
SKWEEE
I THINK SO, YES. AH THAT'S IT, IT'S MOVING!
GREAT SCOTT! WHAT A CAVERN.
EVEN HOLMES WOULD BE IMPRESSED BY THIS, I THINK.
LOOK, A LIGHT!
WHAT? HE'S RIGHT!
SOMEONE'S THERE! INSIDE!
IT'S GONE OUT! THEY MUST HAVE HEARD US!

QUICK, MEN! LANTERNS!
GOOD LORD...
AN ACTUAL SMUGGLER'S CAVE!
MORE LIGHT, LADS, MORE LIGHT! DON'T GIVE THEM A SHADOW TO HIDE IN!
WE'LL SOON FLUSH 'EM OUT.

IT'S LIKE SOMETHING STRAIGHT OUT OF A BOY'S ADVENTURE NOVEL! UNBELIEVABLE.
THIS IS GOLD! WE MUST HAVE INTERRUPTED THEM UNPACKING IT.
AYE, MAYBE WE DID AT THAT.
NOTHING HERE, CAP'N. THEY MUST'VE FLED UP THE TUNNELS.
I *SAID* WE SHOULD'VE DYNAMITED THEM TUNNELS!
YOU...
THIS IS *YOUR* CAVE!
BRAVO, WATSON, YOU ARE CORRECT!
AND I'M VERY GLAD TO SEE YOU FOUND YOUR WAY HERE IN ONE PIECE.
VERY FLARE PISTOL
VERY FLARE PISTOL

THESE *GENTLEMEN* HAVE BEEN BUILDING THIS HOARD FOR MONTHS. YEARS, EVEN.
HOLMES! WHERE ARE YOU, COWARD?
"BUT WE WEREN'T THE FIRST TO FIND THIS PLACE.
"THAT HONOUR BELONGS TO POOR TOM CHRISTIAN"
HE STUMBLED ACROSS IT WHILE TRYING TO MAP THE TUNNELS.
ALL FOR A FEW PENNIES FROM THAT SO CALLED MEDIUM.
"TOM WAS ALREADY FLEEING BACK INTO THE LABYRINTH WHEN HE WAS ATTACKED.
"SLASHED AT FROM BEHIND WITH A LONGSHOREMAN'S HOOK."
YOU GAVE HIM UP FOR DEAD, BUT OLD TOM KEPT GOING.
BLEEDING TO DEATH, HE CLAWED HIS WAY THROUGH THOSE BLACK TUNNELS.
"UNTIL, EVENTUALLY, HE SURFACED IN SAINT MARY'S CHURCH.
"THE PRESS MISCONSTRUED HIS DEATH, BELIEVING INSTEAD THAT A MONSTER ROAMED THE STREETS"
IT MUST HAVE SEEMED, FOR A MOMENT AT LEAST, THAT LUCK WAS ON YOUR SIDE, CAPTAIN.
"BUT THERE WAS ANOTHER PROBLEM. SOME OF YOUR GOLD WAS ALREADY MISSING."
SOMEHOW, A CRATE DESTINED FOR THIS CAVE WAS MISLABELLED AND COLLECTED BY THE WILLIAM BROWN MUSEUM.

"SO, THE RETIRED CRACKSMAN REPRISED HIS CAREER.
"THE FIRST MATE'S TATTOOS MARK HIM CLEARLY. TWENTY YEARS IN NEW SOUTH WALES, UNLESS I'M MISTAKEN."
THE GOLD, TOO, ORIGINATES THERE. MINED WITHOUT THE COSTLY LICENCES REQUIRED BY LAW, NATURALLY.
PERHAPS ON YOUR VERY OWN PLOT OF LAND, EH?
"BREAKING INTO THE MUSEUM, YOU INTENDED TO RECOVER THE CRATES CONTENTS.
"BUT THE CURATOR HAD STAYED LATE, INTENT ON UNPACKING EVERYTHING THAT NIGHT."
KREE
HE WOULD KNOW THAT THE MATILDA BRIGGS WAS SMUGGLING GOLD INTO BRITAIN.
HE HAD TO BE SILENCED.
"IN DESPERATION, YOU ATTACKED HIM WITH WHATEVER WAS TO HAND.
"BROKE HIS NECK WITH HIS OWN PRISEBAR."
NOW YOU HAD ANOTHER BODY TO DISPOSE OF.
BUT SPRING HEELED JACK WAS BLAMED FOR CHRISTIAN'S MURDER. WHY NOT THE CURATOR'S, TOO?
"OLD TOM'S LACERATIONS WERE INFLICTED BLINDLY, IN DESPERATION. THEIR CLAW-LIKE APPEARANCE ENTIRELY ACCIDENTAL.
"THE CURATOR'S WOUNDS, HOWEVER, YOU INCISED WITH COLD DELIBERATION."
HEY! I'VE GOT 'IM! HE'S 'ERE!
HAWKINS, GET OVER THERE! FETCH HIM OUT!

I'LL GET THE TRICKSY BEGGAR!
YAAAAG
OOOOPH
CHAKACHAKACHAKKACHAKACHAKK
FWWPPP
YYYAAAAAAAAAA
AHA!
UFF
YAAA
IT AINT 'IM CAP'N! IT AIN'T THE DETECTIVE!

KKKKRRKREEEEK
GET ME DOWN! HELP! HELP ME!
IT'S SPRING HEELED BLOODY JACK!
HHHAAA
SSSCRREEEEEEE
AAGHH!
KLKK

GOOD LORD, A GIANT BAT!
"HOW EXTRAORDINARY!"
COME, MAN, SHALL WE MAKE THIS A FAIR FIGHT?
?
AYE, LET'S HAVE IT!
WHFFFFF
IT'S HARDLY *FAIR*...
GHAGH
...IF YOU HAVE A *WEAPON!* NOW IS IT?
UNGH
FLAMIN' BYE-BLOWS, I'LL CAP THE LOT O' YER!
MMNNn
MIND YOUR FOOTIN' THERE, MR HOLMES!
KRKKK
'VVV 'VWWPPP
AH! THE ROPE!

VVVVWWWWWPPPPAAAAAA
WUKK
MMM
GUHH
CRNCH CRNCH CRNCH
HUFF HUFF
SKIKK
NNG
?
THEY DO SAY A CAPTAIN ALWAYS GOES DOWN WITH HIS SHIP.
LUCKILY I CHANCED UPON THIS FLARE PISTOL...
BLAMM
"...ALLOW ME TO SIGNAL YOUR DISTRESS."
BA BOOM

...AT LEAST THE FELLOW COULD SWIM! MANY SEAMEN STILL CAN'T I UNDERSTAND. SOME OLD SUPERSTITION ABOUT WHATEVER FALLS IN "BELONGING TO THE SEA".
YOU KNOW THE REST, OF COURSE. THAT GRAVEDIGGER FELLOW LED YOUR OFFICERS THROUGH THE TUNNELS, FOLLOWING THE CHALK TRAIL FROM THE CRYPT IN THE CEMETERY.
HAPPILY, I WAS ABLE TO STAUNCH YOUNG JAMES'S KNIFE-WOUND, WHICH SHOULD HEAL IN NO TIME AT ALL.
BRAVE LAD THAT. NEARLY AS BRAVE AS HOLMES HERE! YOU SHOULD HAVE SEEN HIM ON THAT ROPE!
GREAT NORTH WESTERN HOTEL, THE FOLLOWING AFTERNOON.
AH WATSON, YOU EXAGGERATE.
STILL, I GIVE THANKS THAT YOU'RE HERE TO DO SO! AGAIN, MY APOLOGIES FOR THAT FOOLISHNESS WITH THE TRAP DOOR--
THINK NOTHING OF IT.
WELL, IT'S NO EXAGGERATION T' SAY Y'S DID A GRAND JOB.
ALONG WITH TAGGART AN' THE OTHERS PICKED UP IN THE CAVE, THE LADS'VE ROUNDED UP A FAIR CHUNK O' THE MATLIDA BRIGGS CREW.
I SHOULDN'T THINK MANY OTHERS KNEW WHAT WAS GOING ON. TAGGART AND JENKS WERE CLEVER ENOUGH NOT TO RISK THE WHOLE CREW BEING INVOLVED.
THE MEN WERE PAID HANDSOMELY, SO THEY ASKED NO QUESTIONS.

TRUE ENOUGH. STILL, BEST T' GIVE 'EM A SQUEEZE JUST IN CASE, EH?
NOT THAT I COULD ASK F' MUCH MORE.
A FORTUNE IN UNREFINED, UNLICENSED GOLD AN' Y'VE DELIVERED US THE MASTERMINDS T' BOOT.
COME NOW THORNTON, YOU WEREN'T EXACTLY STANDING IDLY BY, WERE YOU?
TELL US MORE ABOUT THIS BUSINESS AT THE MENAGERIE.
AH, NOT MUCH T' TELL REALLY, DOCTOR.
BIT O' SCUM BY THE NAME OF DRUMMOND GOT HIMSELF KILLED, BUT THERE'S PLENTY OUT THERE WAITIN' T' TAKE HIS PLACE.
Y' HEARD ABOUT THAT PANTHER? T'WAS HIS LOT SET IT LOOSE. Y'R BIG BAT TOO, AS IT TURNS OUT.
THEY'D BEEN HARASSING THE OWNER--A DECENT ENOUGH FELLA--AN' STEALING FROM HIM, LIKE.
MUST'VE SLIPPED OR SOMETHING. HITCHCOCK AN' MYSELF FOUND WHAT WAS LEFT OF HIM IN THE HYENA PIT.
INDEED. AND THE BAT?
THEY NETTED IT THIS MORNING. HARMLESS SUMATRAN FISH-EATER, APPARENTLY. BIG BUGGER THOUGH, EH?
HITCHCOCK'S GOING T' CALL HIM *JACK!*
WHMPP
GOOD LORD! WE'D BETTER GET GOING, HOLMES.

DOCTOR, IT'S BEEN A PLEASURE.
OH, AN' NEXT TIME THAT ONE'S OPENING UP SOME SECRET CHAMBER, YOU MAKE SURE Y'R HANGING ON T' SOMETHING, EH?
HA! I WILL INDEED. TAKE CARE, INSPECTOR.
HOLMES.
THORNTON.
GO N-EIRÍ AN T-ÁDH LEAT.
GURAB AMHLAIDH DUIT.
COME ALONG, WATSON. ENOUGH OF LIVERPOOL WITH ITS DEMONS AND LABYRINTHS AND WILD BEASTS, EH?
BACK TO OUR OWN FOG DRENCHED CITY, TO BAKER STREET, A FAMILIAR ARM-CHAIR, A ROARING FIRE AND TO ONE OF MRS. HUDSON'S EXCELLENT SUPPERS.
IF WE'RE LUCKY, THERE MAY EVEN BE A CASE WAITING.
THE END

Character Sketches
by Aaron Campbell
Sherlock Holmes

Character Sketches
by Aaron Campbell

Dr. John Watson

Year One Issue 1 Cover
by Francesco Francavilla

Year One Issue 1 Cover
by Aaron Campbell

Year One Issue 1 Cover
by Daniel Indro

Year One Issue 2 Cover
by Francesco Francavilla

Year One Issue 2 Cover
by Aaron Campbell

Year One Issue 2 Cover
by Daniel Indro

Year One Issue 3 Cover
by Francesco Francavilla

Year One Issue 3 Cover
by Aaron Campbell

Year One Issue 3 Cover
by Daniel Indro

Year One Issue 4 Cover
by Francesco Francavilla

Year One Issue 4 Cover
by Aaron Cambell

Year One Issue 4 Cover
by Daniel Indro

Year One Issue 5 Cover
by Francesco Francavilla

Year One Issue 5 Cover
by Aaron Campbell

Year One Issue 5 Cover
by Daniel Indro

Year One Issue 6 Cover
by Francesco Francavilla

Year One Issue 3 Cover
by Daniel Indro

Year One Issue 4 Cover
by Francesco Francavilla

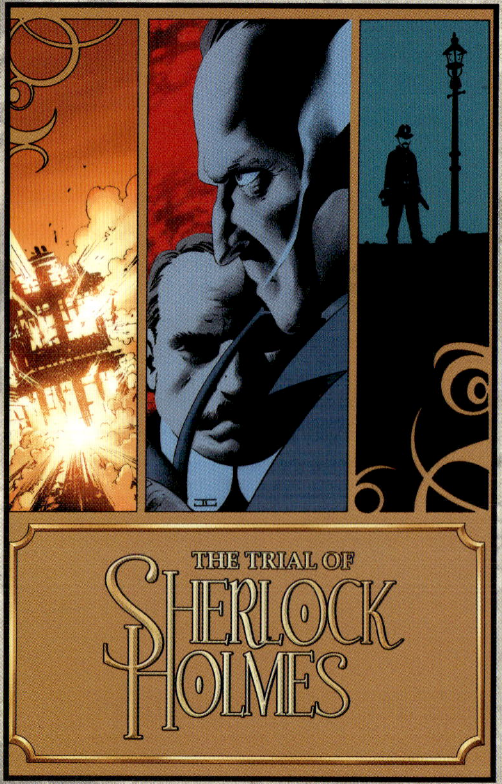

The Trial of Sherlock Holmes
Issue 1 Cover by John Cassaday

The Trial of Sherlock Holmes
Issue 2 Cover by John Cassaday

The Trial of Sherlock Holmes
Issue 3 Cover by John Cassaday

The Trial of Sherlock Holmes
Issue 4 Cover by John Cassaday

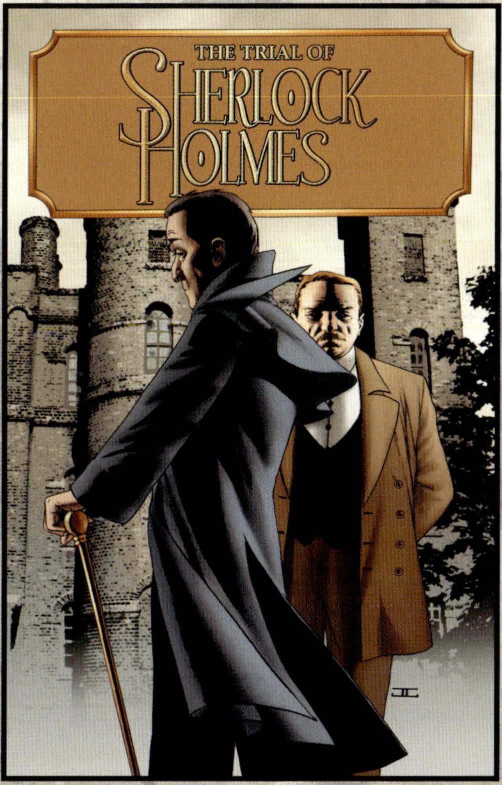

The Trial of Sherlock Holmes
Issue 5 Cover by John Cassaday

Liverpool Demon Issue 1 Cover
by Francesco Francavilla

Liverpool Demon Issue 2 Cover
by Francesco Francavilla

Liverpool Demon Issue 3 Cover
by Francesco Francavilla

Liverpool Demon Issue 4 Cover
by Francesco Francavilla

Liverpool Demon Issue 5 Cover
by Francesco Francavilla

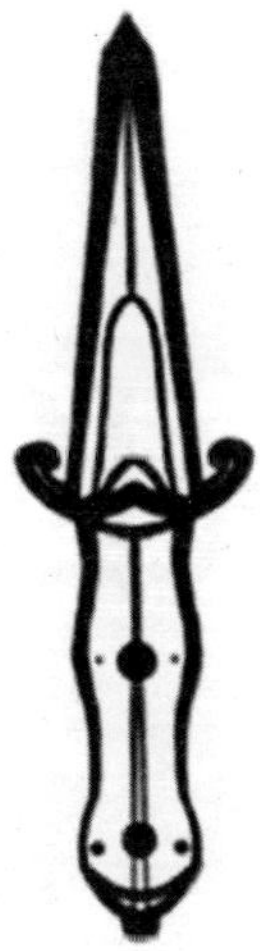

LOOK OUT FOR

SILKSINGER

COMING SOON . . .